THE IRON WORDS

Michael Fridgen

ISBN: 0615992692
ISBN 13: 9780615992693
Library of Congress Control Number: 2014905601
Dreamily Books, Rochester, MN

For Maria and Martha

Also by Michael Fridgen: *Ruth3:5*

Finalist for the 2013 Minnesota Book Award

In an utterly changed Philadelphia of the future, extreme religion has transformed the urban streets into God's chosen city and programmed its denizens to be fervent disciples. That is, except for Ruth3:5, a twelve-year-old girl who dares to pose a simple question that may forever bar her from the seemingly promised land. *Ruth3:5*, Michael Fridgen's penetrating, action-packed dystopian thriller, charts the journey of freethinkers in a postapocalyptic world, where purity of thought can exact the highest possible cost. Casting a cold eye on the perilous fallout of religious extremism, this page-turning philosophical work of fiction envisions a future where a doctrine that promises to save may very well be the agent of mental imprisonment.

Ruth3:5 is a devout young citizen of Philadelphia, who eagerly awaits the next allotment of scripture from her iPraise and the coming of ChristBirth, when she can wear her new green dress to praise the birth of Jesus. However, circumstances soon conspire to banish Ruth from the only home she knows. What her elders have made perfectly clear, however, is that those who dissent will feel the full force of GovernChurch and may end up in the grim and godless Magdelene House. During Biblecation class, Ruth questions the sacred text, therefore thrusting her fate into the hands of the fierce Captain Jeremiah48:10. His aim is to apprehend Ezra2:41, a mysterious woman working against the GovernChurch. Along with Ruth's young friend Two Samuel1:26, Ezra is consumed with saving them all from dogmatic oppression and the bizarre rituals that await Ruth and Sam when they reach sexual maturity. She soon entangles them in a perilous cat-and-mouse game, from which only those with the most resolute of minds can emerge. A contemporary spin on *Brave New World*, it explores the eerie implications of religious fundamentalism, while engaging readers in a fast-paced tale of suspense and danger sure to make the heart race and the mind reel.

Available at Amazon.com and other retail outlets on paper and Kindle.

Prologue

"Riley Hunter, please stand," said Judge Janet Peterson as she glanced over her varnished bench to the table where Riley and his attorney sat. The attorney showed no reaction as Riley, staring straight at the judge, stood calmly. Riley was ready for what was about to happen.

"Mr. Hunter," continued Judge Peterson, "two weeks ago you were found guilty by a federal jury of your peers, and I am now ready to impose a sentence. Let me remind the court of the crime that you are guilty of perpetrating."

She took a sheet of paper from a stack before her, cleared her throat with a brief grumbling sound, and began, "Mr. Hunter, two years and one month ago, in September of 2012, you did indeed…"

As Judge Peterson reviewed his crime for the court, Riley forced his mind to wander; he could not hear about his crime again. Inside of himself, he was finished replaying the details of that night over and over again. Oddly, he was anxious for the sentence and was ready to begin serving his time at a federal prison. He craved a chance to be left alone in a cell, and he knew he needed to be punished for the terrible thing he did. The only way he could become whole again was to interrupt his life for the punishment he deserved.

Keeping his head seemingly in full attention toward the judge, his eyes glanced behind and off to the right of her to look through an enormous window that displayed a panorama of downtown Minneapolis. It was a pleasant October day, and from the twelfth floor of the federal courthouse, he could see clear sky and the distant horizon. Minneapolis city hall, with its green roof and huge stone clock tower, sat directly across the street from the window. The giant clock face was about the same height as the judge's bench. To the left of city hall, he saw the gaping hole and army of construction equipment that had recently torn down the Hubert H. Humphrey Metrodome and were beginning to build a new stadium for the Minnesota Vikings.

Riley wondered if he would be out of prison before the stadium opened, but after the morning conversation with his attorney, he knew that was a dream. The worst they were expecting was ten years; the best was three. He briefly thought about all the games he would miss and then dismissed those thoughts with an internal shrug. At this point, it would not be so bad if he never attended another sporting event again; Riley realized some months ago that athletics helped to pave the path that brought him here before Judge Peterson.

Riley was a hockey player. He was a very good hockey player with everything he needed for success in the game: a family of means, a large suburban Twin Cities high school, and the perfect body. In addition, he possessed the most important ingredient to climb to the best of his sport. Riley had parents who could taste his success and were hungry for more.

He was twenty now, and although he hadn't played hockey or worked out for several months, his body was young enough to have remained muscled and sleek. He hoped to be able to exercise a lot in prison; he also hoped he would not see another ice rink for a long time.

"So now we come to the sentencing," said the judge as Riley quickly diverted his full attention back to her. His leg muscles started to tense up in anticipation of the judge's final word for his life.

Judge Peterson sat straight on her large chair and rested her hands on top of the bench. She shuffled a stack of papers and occasionally glanced at it. Next to her right hand lay the gavel she had used earlier to call the court to order. She was around fifty years old, and her long black hair blended into her robe. Riley's own hair was strikingly blond, thick, and wavy. He was expecting that he would probably want it shaved off soon.

"In your favor, Mr. Hunter," continued Judge Janet Peterson, "I have considered the fact that you turned yourself in. I am fully aware that you would have quite easily gotten away with the whole matter had you not confessed. I do respect this, and I think it shows a positive character that should be rewarded. I also suspect, because you turned yourself in, that you are craving the chance to do your time in exchange for some sort of resolution."

She paused and took the opportunity to look at the victim's family, who was sitting behind the prosecuting attorney's table.

"Still"—she looked back and continued addressing Riley— "Mr. Hunter, this court may be able to provide a means for you to be punished, but we cannot guarantee forgiveness for what you did. Things were taken away that can never be restored, and I must consider the victim in this matter.

"I will admit to the court that this has been a difficult sentence to decide. I am quite torn between your ability to repent and live a somewhat normal life with the inability of the victim to do so. Using the sentencing guidelines and conversations with the prosecution and defense, it was determined earlier that the minimum amount I should consider is three years and the maximum ten. Keeping in mind that the Federal Bureau of Prisons does not allow parole of any kind, I've decided to split the difference, with some consideration for the time you have already spent in the process.

"Therefore, it is the decision of this court that you be sentenced to six years in federal prison. The court encourages the Federal Bureau of Prisons to place you in its facility at Rochester, Minnesota, so that you can be close to your family. That is all I have to say on the matter. This court is now adjourned."

She made one soft tap of the gavel. Riley was shocked, not by the sentence, but by how quiet the courtroom remained. He imagined this moment would be much more like a courtroom scene in a movie, with screams and gasps. But here, there were only the sounds of shuffling papers and attorneys getting to their feet. His mind quickly performed simple addition. He would be twenty-six when released. *I'll be older than Jens was,* he thought.

Riley turned quickly to look behind the prosecutor's table. He had not had a chance to see the victim's family when he entered the courtroom earlier. There they sat, not moving or making a sound. His eyes moved ever so slowly to the floor, and finally, a voice broke the deafening silence as he felt someone pull on his arm.

Riley's mother, who was sitting directly behind him, reached over a railing that separated them and grabbed his left arm. He was wearing a very nice-fitting dark-blue suit that his parents purchased for this occasion from the Macy's in downtown Minneapolis. She clenched the fabric tightly, because she was not able to get her hand around Riley's entire bicep.

"Why did you do it?" she asked with an intense desire, almost begging to understand. "Why did you turn yourself in? You could have gotten away with it!"

Riley pushed her hand away from him and looked at his father, who was sitting still on a chair next to her. He then turned his face away from them and to his attorney.

"Let's get out of here," he said. "I'm ready to go."

Simply put, his parents made him sick. He was not surprised that his mother still did not understand him. She wasn't the least bit sorry for what he'd done. She was only sorry that his hockey career was over, and that her future as the world's best hockey mom ever was finished, too. He would not give her the satisfaction of acknowledgment.

As he followed his attorney past the judge's bench, he took a deep breath and felt strangely free. Now he knew his fate. Going to prison would be difficult, but he knew he could do it if he focused on the one person who'd inspired him to confess. As he walked out of the court, he was fully aware of the person whom he could not bear to disappoint. It was the thought of this man that gave him strength to follow his attorney and accept his punishment: Jens Jaenisch.

ONE

Riley was early for his appointment and sat on the concrete steps outside the old pillared building that contained the Sociology Department. It was one of the first real spring days, and the University of Minnesota students took full advantage. As he looked across the mall, which was framed by more historic-looking structures, Riley observed a sea of young adults in shorts and T-shirts. Somewhere else, this fifty-three-degree day might be considered cold, but after the long Minnesota winter, it might as well be tropical.

Riley was no exception and wore a pair of brown cargo shorts and a baggy white T-shirt with "UMN Athletic Orientation Week" written across the chest; a picture of Goldy Gopher opening a locker was under the words. After a semester and a half, the other, older white T-shirts across the mall were a variety of pinks and grays after being washed with reds and blacks. Some students did this out of the necessity to save money, others because they simply didn't care. Riley's white T-shirt, however, remained very white, because he had the luxury of being a top recruit for a division 1 hockey team and used the Athletic Department's laundry service.

That morning, as he was throwing on his clothes, he was tempted to wear a gray, much smaller T-shirt that he had from

Hastings High School. He liked the way it showed off his arms and chest. But earlier in the fall, a hockey teammate commented that the tight-fitting shirt made him look gay, so Riley took it out of his T-shirt rotation. Perhaps when it was just a bit warmer, he could take off his baggy athletic T-shirt and show off for the girls milling around the mall.

Suddenly, as he thought about girls, T-shirts, and showing off, he saw Abby and a group of her friends walk down the steps in front of Northrup Auditorium and cross the grassy space between the sidewalks that defined the mall. They were wearing identical green, very tight T-shirts that said something about St. Patrick's Day 2013. Riley couldn't help but stare at Abby. He didn't need to imagine what was underneath St. Patrick's; he knew from experience. As the group passed in front of the building where he sat, Abby caught him staring and blew a kiss as she continued to talk and laugh with the others. Riley just nodded and kept looking.

"You can look and touch," said a deep voice behind him, "but don't make the mistake of buying anything."

Riley turned his head, and when he saw who had just exited the building, he stood immediately and gave his full attention.

"You know that a lot of girls here are going for their MRS degree," continued the head hockey coach as he crossed to Riley. "But see, that there girl is going for her PAW degree: professional athlete's wife. I've seen it time and time again. I'm willing to bet she's doing the same thing to a Gopher football player that she's doing to you. Whichever one of you has a better season is who she's going to stick with."

Riley was shocked to see the coach in this part of campus. He was tall, muscular, and about forty-five years old. He wore tan dress pants and a maroon polo shirt with "UMN Athletics" embroidered on the left chest. He was a typical coach, and Riley had the typical love/hate relationship with him.

"Sit and listen," commanded the coach. He gestured to a concrete ledge at the top of stairs.

Riley knew better than to say anything and sat quickly. Before him stood the man who had the power to control his destiny. Riley had been playing this game, both on and off the ice, since he was in kindergarten. This might be a different coach, but the same tactics were required for Riley to get what he wanted.

"It's no coincidence that I'm here," continued the coach. "I know you have an appointment with your soc. professor, and I wanted to catch her and soften her up for you."

Riley nodded and noticed that the coach's voice had become even more intense than normal. This situation must be more important to the hockey team than he thought. He had been a good student at Hastings High School, but that had been vastly different, because his charm, looks, and popularity had got him through. No teacher in Hastings would dare take on the whole community by failing Riley. Hastings was a small river town twenty miles southeast of St. Paul, and Riley Hunter continued to be a legend there.

"So here's the deal," said the coach. "We've been able to take care of your other classes, so don't worry about those. Your grades are set. But since those faggots at Penn State messed up, all these student-services people think they can tell me how to manage my team. These women soc. profs are the worst to work with. Why did you take this class, anyway?"

Riley didn't know if this question was rhetorical or required an answer, but in these situations, he knew it was best to keep his mouth shut.

The coach stared directly into Riley's eyes and continued in an even more intense timbre, "You can't get on academic probation. You hear me? You can't. We're putting a lot of money and time behind you. Now that your buddy Fredrichs messed up, you are our only top recruit this year. I wasted a lot of money on Fredrichs, and I'm not about to do the same on you."

Even though his face did not show it, Riley's stomach tightened when the coach mentioned the name of his best friend and teammate from high school. Jacob Fredrichs would never play hockey again. Riley was angry with the coach for using Jacob's unfortunate situation to motivate him, especially since the coach knew how close they were.

"Now, this soc. prof you've got is not just a woman, but her fag-loving brother is a damn U of M regent," continued the coach, still intense, but much softer. "So, here's what you're gonna do. You're gonna march in there and do whatever project she throws at you. I talked her into letting you do some extra credit to pull up your lousy grade. Now, I don't give a shit what she wants you to do. If she wants you to dress up as goddamn Susan B. Anthony and parade around campus getting votes for women, you'll do it! Do you hear me? From this moment on, your whole life is hitting the gym, hitting the ice, and working on this project."

The coach did not wait for Riley to react. He turned to walk down the steps. Riley was a mix of emotion. He was disappointed in his grades, upset for Jacob, frustrated at the pressure for hockey success, and apprehensive about seeing the sociology professor. As the coach turned to walk past the ledge where Riley still sat, he stopped and looked up.

"One more thing," added the coach as Riley turned to look down. "You can still get with your PAW when you need some release, but remember what I said about her."

TWO

"Well, that was fun," said Professor Weber to herself as she set down her pen and watched the hockey coach leave her office. She shook her head and sighed when she heard his footsteps far down the hall.

Dr. Jade Weber was the kind of professor whom students either loved or hated. Those who were fascinated by the world loved her; those who spent little time thinking about such things hated her. Jade genuinely loved people and was interested in their relationships and lives. Sociology was the perfect field for her to study and teach. She never thought about her job as being work, because she loved it so much.

Jade was almost fifty years old and looked every bit the middle-aged college professor. Her gray hair fell on her shoulders and over the blue cardigan she usually wore in her office because it was always cold, even in the summer. Her family was well connected from the days when her father was a leader in Minnesota's thriving union movement of the seventies. Because her brother was a prominent Democrat in the Minnesota Senate and a university regent, people assumed she was wealthy. However, this was not true. Her husband, a St. Paul cop, and their three kids lived in a modest house in St. Paul perched on the banks high above the

Mississippi. Only one kid was left at home, and Jade constantly badgered her husband about selling the house and moving into an apartment in downtown Minneapolis. She had never lived downtown and wanted to experience it.

She checked her watch. He was late.

She was sitting behind her desk in the small office, facing the open door. A large bookcase with hundreds of books filled the wall behind her. On the wall to her left, there was a small window that overlooked a narrow sidewalk between her building and the next. Jade sighed and turned back to her computer to continue reading an online article. She took a moment to realize that Mr. Hunter was probably late because the hockey coach caught him in the hall to tell him all sorts of horrible things about women sociology professors.

She had a project in mind for Mr. Hunter. Dr. Weber was not the kind to assign busywork or come up with research for the sake of research. If she was going to give this kid a chance at extra credit, she would not squander it by having him read articles and write a paper. However, she knew that he was a typical athlete and would probably need a lot of assistance with digging deep into a single subject. At the same time, she also knew that he would have a lot of time to devote to her project, since his season was over, and his other classes were taken care of.

Jade hated that Riley's classes had been fixed. There was nothing she could do about what other departments and professors did in the name of Goldy Gopher, but there was plenty she could do within her own world to ensure that even athletes had the opportunity to learn. This was not the first time she'd gone up against a coach, and it would not be the last. These things had gotten much easier since her brother was named a regent. However, it was frustrating for her that she had to use that connection. At the same time, she wasn't above doing what she could in the name of academic integrity.

Finally, Riley Hunter knocked at her open door. She looked up and immediately noticed that he dressed like a typical college boy. As a sociologist, it fascinated and frustrated her that none of the students wore clothes that fit. The boys wore clothes that were way too big, and the girls wore clothes that were way too small. She noticed his cargo shorts and flip-flops, making her feel even colder.

"You students are always rushing the summer," she said and gestured for him to enter and have a seat.

"Thanks for taking the time to meet," Riley said, remembering what the coach had just told him.

Jade sighed and replied, "Well, there is nothing that frustrates me more than a student who turns off because they know they are failing. Why waste the last half of the term?"

She often thought about how people's appearance predetermined the ease with which they could go through life. The kid before her was certainly blessed; he was one of the most stunningly handsome young men she had taught. While this blessing made it much easier for him to get into most doors, she wondered if it was ever a curse that kept people away because they felt inferior.

"Well, thanks, anyway," said Riley, attempting to seem appreciative while wondering if it was the appropriate response.

"I'm not going to get into the whole hockey thing and why your grades are failing, why you're getting this second chance. But I want you to know that I've thought a lot about this, and I didn't create this project lightly." She looked at him and saw that he was listening intently; she hoped it wasn't just an act but thought it probably was. Still, she knew it was not her role to be a judge but to give him a chance. Whether he took advantage of that chance was his business.

"Why did you take Sociology of the Aged and Growing Older in America?" she asked.

He hesitated for a minute, partly because he didn't have an answer, but mostly because he'd forgotten the name of the course.

"Um," he began, "I was just really interested in the subject. You know, there are a lot of old people, and I wanted to learn about them."

He knew this was a poor answer. He was capable of a much better lie; he sat up straighter to bring his A game. He was hoping his hockey instincts would kick in and give him energy to deal with her.

"You're going to have to be smoother than that if you are going to face sports reporters some day," Jade replied through a chuckle.

"Sorry, I'm just tired."

"Why is it that all you student athletes are so tired all the time?" she asked. "If I had a dime for every time one of you came in here and told me that…well, I'd be too rich for this job."

"I just—I'm not sure what to say."

"I sort of figured that," she said. "So why did you take it? And please tell me the truth. Don't tell me what you think I want to hear."

"Okay," he answered. "I didn't really choose your class. My adviser picked my schedule and registered me."

"This wasn't your departmental academic adviser, was it?" she asked, already knowing the answer.

"No," he replied, "the adviser in athletics who takes care of these things."

"Right." She nodded.

Riley slumped back down in his chair, finally realizing that Dr. Weber had been around the university long enough to know how things worked.

"I have a project for you," she began. "It might be a bit difficult, but I'm hoping you will approach this with the same energy you use to approach hockey. I assume you have a car?"

"Yes," he answered. She made the assumption because most of the top athletes had mysterious access to nice cars.

"I have a neighbor in St. Paul," she said. "Are you from the area? Do you know your way around?"

"I'm from Hastings. Yeah, I know my way around."

"Fine," she said. "I live on the west side of St. Paul, not too far from the river. I have a next-door neighbor whom I'd like you to interview."

"Okay." He desperately tried to hide his frustration for the project.

"He's a bit shy…well, really shy," she said. "He was a professor here at the U of M, but he retired in 1994."

"That's the year I was born," said Riley quickly.

"Exactly, so he's up there in years, which is why he makes a good subject for this course. I know he has a story; I know parts of that story, but not too much. I'd like you to get more."

"Should I just show up at his house? How does this work?" Riley asked.

"Okay, well, here is what I've done," Dr. Weber explained. "As I said, he's shy and not willing to be too social. However, he needs some help around the house. I asked him this past weekend if I could provide someone to help him out. He was reluctant, but I talked him into it, because I think he realizes that he can't take care of things alone."

"His wife is dead or something?"

"I'm not sure exactly what happened. I just know that he's had a long life, and I suspect there is something he has to say about it. Sorry, let me rephrase that. I suspect there is something he wants to say about it."

"So I go over there and help him out and talk to him. How many words do you want?"

"What do you mean?" she replied. "How many words should you talk to him for?"

"No, how many words should I write in my report about him?"

Jade laughed at the misunderstanding and then sighed again in frustration. She found it sad that this was the first question he had about the assignment. "I'm not that kind of teacher. I don't care how many words you write. I don't even care if you write anything at all. Just help him out and find out about his life. Before the end of the term, you can come in here and tell me what you've learned. I'll give you a grade for that."

Even though he liked not having to write anything, Riley was not too excited about this project. First, it required him to leave his dorm and the campus; second, it probably would require a bunch of manual labor on a house that hadn't been cared for. Riley looked at Dr. Weber and realized that she was serious about the project. He also remembered the pressure that the coach had just put on him. He didn't really think he had a choice.

"Okay," he replied. "I can do this."

"Don't rush it," she said. "You might have to help him out several times this spring. Remember, this is a four-credit course. You should spend at least eight hours a week, of your own time, on this project."

"Got it," Riley said.

Jade grabbed a small scrap of paper from a pile on her desk and took her pen.

"Here is his address," she said. "He is always home, so you don't need to call. Just stop by. His name is Jens Jaenisch."

THREE

"Hi, Mom," Riley said into his iPhone. When the ringtone reverberated off the concrete walls of his private dorm room, he noticed it was his mother calling and that it was 10:17 p.m. He was surprised she would call at this time; it was quite late for her.

"Where are you?" she asked.

He was annoyed that she didn't even greet him. "In my room."

"Are you alone?"

"Yep," he said. He took a deep breath, knowing that she was not in a good mood.

Riley was often alone in his room at night. Many of his teammates, and other students, were surprised to learn that he did not like to party. It was almost shocking that a student athlete with such great looks and social status did not party like the rock star he was. Riley felt that alcohol was poison, and at a young age he became determined not to damage his body, his most prized possession. Of course, he was sexually active, and it could be argued that having sex might lead to a disease that could destroy his health, but he was always vigilant on that account. It was not a surprise to him, or his mother, that he was ready to go to bed at 10:17 p.m. on a Wednesday night.

"So," she continued, "I got a call from your coach tonight."

Riley, already agitated, became a bit more anxious. "Yeah?"

"Riley, you'd better be happy it was me he talked to and not Dad. You know how busy we are. We don't have time to deal with this."

Riley raised his right eyebrow. They had all the time in the world to enjoy the benefits when he did something good. It was just these times when they were suddenly so busy.

"Are you listening to me?" she asked in a raised voice.

"Yes, Mom," he replied as he attempted to match her vocal strength. "I'm listening!"

"You have one job. One job!" she stated sternly. "You are to be a student athlete. That's it! He told me your grades are failing, and he can't take the pressure you're putting on him. Do you know how much money is riding on this?"

Riley sighed. "Yes, Mom, of course I know about my scholarship and all that crap—"

"It's so much more than that, Riley!" she interrupted. "Oh my God, he was so mad! There are tickets to sell and donors to please. People lose their jobs if the team doesn't do well, Riley! Get your act together. A whole staff of people and millions of donations could be gone because of you."

"I know, I know! I've always known about all that stuff. Nobody lets me forget it!"

He knew what she would say next, because it was what she always said next.

"And," she continued, "don't forget all the time and money your dad and I put into this. All the camps, the equipment, the traveling teams, the overnight weekends all winter, not to mention the ice we put outside our house. When I think about the money we gave—"

"Yes, Mom, I know. But you have to admit that you did a lot of that for yourselves, too. I know that those overnight weekends were just an excuse to let a bunch of boys babysit themselves in a hotel pool while you parents went drinking all night."

"I'm going to pretend you didn't just say that," she interjected. "You don't have any idea what you're talking about."

Riley knew that he did have an idea and that he was correct. However, now that he had pushed her most sensitive button, he realized that the only way to end this conversation was to sound calm and apologetic; it was how he often proved to her that he had listened. He was tired, and he would give in so that she would leave him alone.

"Mom," he said in a much calmer and resigned voice, "I really do know. This is the first time I've really messed up in college; it's just so much harder. But I'm going to get through it. I know what I have to do and who can help me."

"Good. Then is this all going to be okay?" she asked in a calmer voice as well.

"Yes," he answered quietly.

There were a few awkward moments of silence as his mother tried to figure out whether she needed more of a verbal commitment from him.

"You were such a good student at Hastings," she said. "Is this all about Jake?"

There it was again, the name of his buddy, followed by a horrible cramp in his stomach and the sinking feeling of his spirit. He did not respond to her when she asked about Jacob. He wondered how long it would take for people to stop bringing up Jake's name all the time.

"Do you need to see that athletic doctor about it again?" she asked. "You told me that it helped the last time."

"I'm fine." He tried not to sound annoyed. "Everything is fine, and I'm on top of it."

"Okay, then," she said, "get some rest."

She hung up her end of the phone, and Riley tapped the red button on his iPhone with his thumb. He set the phone on his desk and turned to stare at his dorm-quality single bed with fresh sheets. On top of the coach, Dr. Weber, sociology, and the old guy he needed to meet, now his mother had his mind reeling about Jake and the athletic department physician. He would never get the sleep he wanted and needed.

Riley's bare feet crossed the small room to a cabinet that was bolted to the wall next to a small sink. He was already dressed for bed, wearing oversize boxer shorts and a blue T-shirt. He opened the cabinet door, looked at the small shelf that was attached at the top and pushed aside a bunch of miscellaneous stuff to find a prescription bottle in the back. As he retrieved the bottle, he knocked a small trophy off the shelf. His reflexes were quick; he grabbed the trophy in midair and placed it back on the shelf. He took a moment to glance at the fake-gold hockey stick, four inches high, attached to a solid wood base. The inscription read "Hastings Hockey MVP 2011." It was the only year he'd won; Jake received all the others.

When Riley moved into his dorm that August, he had a difficult time adjusting to the noise of the building, even though he had his own room. His lack of sleep was beginning to show up on the ice, and the coach sent him to the Athletic Department physician. Riley received a prescription for twenty pills of a drug called Klonopin. The doctor informed him that Klonopin worked extremely well but could be addictive if not taken properly. Riley, already obsessed with protecting his body, had only ever taken four of the pills. He consumed one pill the night the doctor gave him the bottle, and three pills for the first three nights after Jake's accident. They did indeed work well.

Thinking he would take a fifth pill because he was so agitated, Riley began to unscrew the cap when suddenly there was a knock at his door. He quickly set the bottle with its thirteen pills back in place on the shelf, closed the cabinet door, and crossed in front of the sink. He wasn't expecting any visitors, but judging by the way the day had gone, it could be anyone from his dad to the coach to Dr. Weber's old guy. He looked through the peephole and smiled for probably the first time that whole day.

"Of all the nights," he said as he opened the door to Abby, "I need you tonight the most."

"Good," she said in her tight jeans and pink U of M T-shirt.

There was nothing more to be said. Riley put his right arm around her waist and scooped her into the room, closing the door with his left foot in one graceful move.

She laughed and threw her arms around his neck. There was no need to tell him that his hockey coach had sent her. There was also no need for Klonopin to help him relax.

FOUR

Even though Dr. Weber told him to just stop by, it still felt weird for Riley to show up at the old guy's house without calling. Riley was worried he might be sleeping, eating, or dead; he had not learned enough in Sociology of the Aged and Growing Older in America to know how destructive it was to always associate the elderly with death.

Riley did not have a lot of experience with older people. His mother was from an affluent Hastings family, and her parents moved to Arizona to escape the Minnesota weather. They came up north sporadically and had seen a few hockey games. However, the only thing Riley knew about them is that they missed the way Hastings was in the fifties because that's all they ever talked about. His father was also from Hastings and equally affluent, but his parents had died in a car accident on the now-replaced Hastings bridge over the Mississippi when Riley was only six years old.

The car clock indicated that it was 2:27 p.m. He turned left onto the street told to him by Professor Weber. A few seconds later, he passed what he assumed was the Weber house because of the off-duty police car sitting in the driveway. A row of neglected shrubs separated that property from the one next door, presumably belonging to Jens Jaenisch. It was a middle-class St. Paul neighborhood. The modest homes had incredible views of the river that appeared beneath a steep bank. The residents could see Minnehaha Park across the river on the Minneapolis side.

Riley turned into the driveway that was placed on the side of the house; the driveway lead to a one-stall detached garage that sat back and to the right of a side porch. The house was small, Tudor style, with beige stucco and dark-brown wood trim. The stucco was in good shape and had perhaps been recently renovated, but the wood trim was shedding flakes of paint. It looked like someone had grated chocolate all over the side porch. He pulled the car up to the closed garage door, also covered with grated chocolate, and turned off the ignition.

Let's get this over with, he thought to himself as he took the key and opened the car door. He could almost feel his parents, the coach, and Professor Weber physically push him toward the side porch, although for different reasons. He stepped up the two concrete steps to the side porch and rang the doorbell, hoping Jens wasn't one of those cranky Minnesotans who preferred that you use the front door.

"Hello?" said a voice as the wood door on the other side of a screen door opened. Riley was surprised at how fast the door opened; he had expected to have to wait a bit longer or even to ring the bell one or two more times.

"Hi," said Riley. "I don't know if you know who I am. Dr. Weber sent me?" Like many his age, Riley turned every statement into a question when he was nervous.

"Oh"—the man completely opened the door—"she told me someone might stop by."

Jens was five foot ten inches tall, had a full head of white hair, and wore glasses with thick black frames. Most he encountered made the incorrect assumption that the glasses were so old that they were back in style. They would be surprised to learn that Jens took pride in his appearance and fully understood that his brand-new glasses had retro appeal.

He was wearing blue jeans with a maroon-and-gold U of M sweat shirt. He was thin. The only difference in his attire from a typical college student's wardrobe was that he wore tennis shoes, while most students slapped around in flip-flops.

"Come on in." He opened the screen door.

"Is this time okay?" asked Riley, hoping to be told no so that he could go back to campus.

"Yes," Jens responded. "I guess I don't get out much, so it's as good as any other time."

Riley entered the house and let the screen door slam behind him; the door did not have the modern mechanism that allowed it to close slowly.

The man let the wood door remain open and extended a hand to Riley. "My name is Jens."

"I'm Riley. Riley Hunter."

"Have a seat," Jens said. He motioned to a small table with two chairs near the door. The side porch opened into the kitchen. The pride Jens took in his appearance did not transfer to his kitchen, which was stuck in 1985. Riley sat down in the chair closer to the door. Jens crossed the kitchen, opened the refrigerator door, and grabbed a bottle of water. He crossed back and set the bottle on the table in front of Riley then immediately sat down in the other chair.

"So," said Jens, "Professor Weber told me that you were looking for some community service, but I've been around the block enough times to know that there must be more to the story."

Riley was surprised he called her Professor Weber and not Jade, but then he remembered that Jens was a former professor.

Perhaps there was some code that dictated professors address each other in this manner for life.

"Well, ah," responded Riley, "I need some extra credit."

"You must be an athlete," said Jens without a hint of a question.

"Yeah, hockey," answered Riley.

"I came to the university in 1954 and saw many changes, but we've always treated the athletes with the same reverence," Jens said. "Don't think I hold that against you; it's not your fault. It's just society."

Riley wasn't quite sure if that statement was positive or negative, but he now knew that Jens was quick enough to know exactly why he was there.

"What did you teach?" asked Riley.

"German literature," responded Jens. "Boring, really."

Riley showed a small smile, and Jens reciprocated.

"Anyway," continued Jens, "I have some things that need to be done around here, and I'm afraid I'm getting too old to do them. I'll be eighty-eight next month."

"No problem."

"Can you come back tomorrow?" He really did not want to seem like a demanding old man, but there was one thing he needed badly enough to be blunt.

Like most his age, Riley pretended to be uncertain about his schedule, in case something better turned up. "Um, I think I can come in the afternoon."

"Good," said Jens as he stood up, pushed in his chair, and crossed the kitchen again. He opened a drawer next to the sink, took a twenty-dollar bill off a stack that was in the drawer, and closed it with some struggle, as it lacked modern lubricated tracks.

"I need you to bring me something from Target." He put the money next to the unopened bottle of water on the table. "I need a clear shower curtain."

"No problem," said Riley again. He decided to take the opportunity to make a quick exit; he took the money and stuffed it in his pocket. He also took the bottle of water, because he didn't want to be rude and leave it. He pushed in his chair and walked toward the side porch door.

"Okay then," said Jens, "I'll see you tomorrow, and don't forget that it has to be a clear shower curtain. Do you know what I'm talking about? One of those plastic shower liners in the bathroom aisle. It must be clear."

"Yep," said Riley, "I understand." He thought the request was a bit odd, but he wanted to get out of the awkward situation and back to campus. He hoped that this kind of errand was the only sort of thing the old man would ask of him; it would be so much easier than scraping and painting the brown trim.

Jens opened the screen door, and Riley went out. As he crossed the concrete porch and descended the steps, he looked across the backyard and over a few short trees and caught a glimpse of the river way below the embankment.

"It's a nice view from up here."

"That's why I bought this place when I retired in '94," replied Jens. "I grew up on a river, and I miss it. I've always liked to watch water flowing freely."

"I was born that year, in 1994."

Years ago, Jens had become accustomed to meeting students who were born after the time he started working at the university. Then he encountered students whose parents he could have taught. However, this was the first time he met a student who was born after he retired.

"I grew up close to the Mississippi," said Riley. "Which river are you from? Mississippi, St. Croix, Minnesota?"

"No, the Rhine," answered Jens. "I was born in Germany."

"You speak English without an accent," remarked Riley.

"I've been here a long time, since 1954, and worked hard on the language," replied Jens. "I'm proud to speak English. The river is the only thing I miss about Germany."

FIVE

66 **T**here goes one *gutaussehend* kid," said Jens to himself as he watched the handsome young man back his car out of the driveway. Even after all these years, Jens still caught himself thinking half in German, half in English; he didn't like it. It had been easier to change his accent than it had been to change his thinking.

After forty years of teaching at the University of Minnesota, Jens was well aware of the special privileges and outright benefits that were given to athletes of certain sports. However, unlike most other professors, Jens didn't blame anyone and especially never held it against the student athletes. He learned at a young age that humans create systems that are quite flawed; he didn't believe that anyone who took advantage of those systems was acting poorly. In fact, he found it rather stupid if a student did not take full advantage of a special privilege. He also knew from experience that systems can change quickly; students should take advantage while they could, because tomorrow they might be on the bottom.

As he stepped back inside the kitchen and closed the screen door, he looked across the neglected hedge to see the Weber home. *How much does she know?* he wondered as he closed the wooden door and crossed the kitchen to enter the living room.

Even though Jade told him she had a student who was looking for community service, he was intuitive enough to know that her intentions might not have been fully revealed. The Webers were already living in their house when Jens moved next door in 1994. They had two kids at the time, and a third was on the way. Jens was not unfriendly but was also not entirely neighborly. He liked to keep to himself and was a bit ashamed to admit that he didn't even know the names of the Weber kids. However, Dr. Jade Weber was a fellow professor, and even though she was in a different department, they knew each other well enough.

"What is she using this kid to get?" he asked out loud as he sat in his comfortable recliner.

He grabbed the remote from a small table next to him and turned on the television. Jens was near ninety, but there would be no Weather Channel or yesteryear Lawrence Welk crap; he preferred *The Amazing Race* and *The Big Bang Theory*.

SIX

"Okay, look here," said the Target employee in her standard khaki pants and red shirt. "This one is white, and this one is clear."

"Oh, so there is a difference," responded Riley, noticing the contrast between the two shower liners that the employee held in front of him.

Riley had just been at Jens's house. He'd barely got out of the car when Jens met him on the side porch and immediately asked to see the shower curtain; he noticed that it was white and not clear. Riley started to protest that there wasn't a difference between white and clear because white was the absence of color, then he remembered his mom, the coach and Professor Weber's pressure to pass sociology. He apologized, took the liner from Jens, and started back to the nearest Target on University Avenue in St. Paul.

During the drive, Riley spent a few miles thinking about Jens's obsession with the clear shower liner; he hoped it wasn't needed for some perverted activity. If he had attended Dr. Weber's class more often, he would have learned to question his reaction. When someone young has an unusual request, people attribute it to creativity. But when an old man has an unusual request, people often assume he's a dirty old man.

Jens had not asked about the twenty-dollar bill, and Riley was glad about that. The truth was, Riley hadn't even purchased the shower curtain in the first place. The night before, when Abby came over to his dorm, he'd given her the cash and asked her to get the curtain. She returned forty-five minutes later and apparently didn't know the difference between white and clear either, or perhaps he just told her the wrong thing, or maybe she didn't care. In any case, he forgot about the money.

"How much is that?" he asked the Target employee.

"Which one you want?" she said.

"Clear!" he replied sharply.

She bent down to read the price posted on the shelf. "Two twenty-four."

"That's it?" he remarked as he took the clear liner from her hand and started toward the front of the store.

The Target employee wanted to make a sarcastic "you're welcome" comment in response to his lack of gratitude, but she quickly decided to forgive him, because he was so handsome. She appreciated him more as she watched him walk away and then went back to whatever she was doing when he'd interrupted her to ask for the shower curtain.

Even though the store was on a street called University Avenue, it was much closer to a group of small private colleges than to the University of Minnesota. On his way through the store, Riley noticed T-shirts of Hamline, Macalester, and Concordia; there was not a maroon and gold in these parts. He wondered what it would be like to play hockey for a much-smaller program. He could very much get used to less stress, but that would mean less fame and scholarship money, and fewer chances to be noticed by the NHL.

He passed through the housewares and was now walking in the grocery aisles. He was hungry; he was always hungry and wondered if Jens had anything to eat. He didn't know how long he would be working at the old house that day. As usual, he was anxious to get back to campus and the cafeteria.

"Riley?"

He stopped abruptly and turned to look into the aisle that contained snacks and soft drinks, or what the locals called pop. His heart skipped a beat, and he felt his whole spirit drain into his feet as if it were thick syrup. There was Jake's mom, Dot Fredrichs.

"Mrs. Fred?" He stood still.

"Riley"—she immediately left her cart and quickly walked to him—"how are you?"

She grabbed him and gave him a tight hug; for a brief moment, he remembered that she was his second, and probably better, mother. She was short, and he was surprised to see that she had stopped dyeing her hair. It was now short and gray instead of the usual short and red. As she pulled away, Riley saw how much older she looked than when Jake had graduated from high school just ten months before.

A lot had happened in those ten months. When he thought about this, Riley's spirit sank lower and seemed to be pushing through the floor of the pop aisle.

"How are you?" she asked again. "How is school?"

"Good, everything is good," he answered. "What are you doing up here?"

"Did you know that Jacob had another surgery yesterday?" asked Dot.

"Uh, no," he replied sheepishly.

Dot looked down at the floor, silent. She wanted to say something she had wanted to say to Riley for a long time, but she hesitated.

"I'm really sorry"—he noticed her hesitation—"I've been really busy with school."

"Of course you are," Dot responded genuinely. She raised her head and smiled. The two just looked at each other for a moment. "Jacob had surgery yesterday at Gillette to remove some scar tissue from his back. They're hoping it will get rid of the pain he's been having there."

"Oh," said Riley. "How did it go?"

"They said it went well, but we won't know if it will help the pain until he gets back home and stops taking pain meds."

"How long will he be in there?"

"Probably three more days," Dot said. "I'm just getting some snacks for the room."

Riley felt the shower liner and saw his excuse to leave. "I have to go. I'm doing some community service for a class, and this really old guy is waiting for me to help him."

Dot smiled briefly. She was sad that her Jacob was not running around the Twin Cities as he balanced school, hockey, and life. Instead, it was a good day if Jacob could manage to balance an inflatable ball the physical therapist would give him.

"Okay, well, I'll see you around," Riley said and started to walk away.

"Yes, Riley. Please take care."

He nodded and turned to walk down the aisle.

As she watched him leave, Mrs. Fredrichs realized that there was no time like the present; she mustered the courage to say what she needed to say. "Riley!" Dot said, louder than what was probably acceptable at Target.

Riley was startled. He turned to her.

Mrs. Fred quickly rushed to him. "Riley," she said urgently as she grabbed his hands in hers, "please come and see Jake. He really needs to see you. You guys have been best friends since kindergarten."

"I know," he said as he shook his head. "It's just hard to see him."

"He knows how stupid he was," she continued. "He knows that this whole thing is his fault. That one stupid night, and he ruined everything; I know that, too. He needs you to come to him and tell him how stupid he was. He needs that, so you two can be friends again. He's just paralyzed, Riley. He's not dead. In order for the two of you to move on, you have to get things out in the open. He needs you to blame him and forgive him."

Riley stared at her, but he could not deal with the words she spoke. Even though his spirit attempted to cement his feet in place, he desperately needed to get away from her. In fact, he needed to get away so badly that he lost any ambition to speak to her.

Riley nodded quickly and walked away. He didn't turn back to see her reaction to him leaving. Once again, he'd escaped without facing the truth of what Jacob had become.

Riley continued quickly up to the front of the store. He immediately located the shortest checkout line and got into it. There was no way he was going to take the chance of having to look at Mrs. Fred before he left that store. Then it hit him like a hockey puck to his helmet. *They think I'm avoiding Jake because I'm mad at how stupid he was?* He approached the checkout counter. *I'll have to go and see him and then keep pretending that I'm too angry with him to stay friends. It's the best way to keep my secret hidden.*

Before allowing his spirit to creep back, he wanted to protect himself from the feelings that it would bring. As he stood in line, he built a wall inside. Riley had felt many things over the past six months: guilt, loneliness, sadness, anger…However, this was the first time he felt sinister.

SEVEN

On the drive back to Jens's house, Riley made the decision to visit Jake in the hospital. Soon. Before Jake went back home. Not only was the hospital thirty minutes closer than Hastings, but also there was less chance of running into a family member or friend whom he would then have to talk to. Talking to people about Jake's accident was exhausting for Riley; he constantly had to monitor his reactions and remember the difference between what they thought was true and the truth only he knew.

It wasn't that he had completely forgotten about the Fredrichs family and what they meant to him. On the contrary, he missed Jake and his parents—whom Riley called Mr. and Mrs. Fred—very much. The Fredrichs household had been a special place for him, because it was so different from his own. Riley missed playing video games with Jake, giving Mr. Fred a hard time about not having a cell phone, and eating Mrs. Fred's homemade pizza after a late Friday hockey game.

Riley turned onto Jens's street and saw the Weber house with the usual off-duty squad car parked in the driveway next to a blue Ford Focus. Riley did not have much to share yet with Professor Weber about what he was learning from Jens. Really, the only thing he had to say was that Jens liked clear shower curtains and bottled water.

He turned into Jens's driveway, pulled up behind the garage, and turned off the car. Taking the plastic Target bag from the passenger seat, he opened the car door and made the journey to the side porch. He rang the bell. Once again, he was surprised at how fast Jens answered the door.

"Back already?" asked Jens as he opened the door.

"Yep," replied Riley. "It's really not that far."

"Sometimes I forget how fast you kids drive. I still move fairly well, but I don't drive much anymore. When your reactions get slower, you find that driving is one of those things that's just not appealing."

Riley walked through the door and handed the plastic bag to Jens. Jens pulled the curtain package out of the bag, smiled, and nodded approvingly.

"That's the one I need!" he said happily. He placed it on the kitchen table. Jens then walked to the fridge, grabbed a bottle of water, and handed it to Riley. Riley unscrewed the cap and started to drink.

"How much time do you have today?" asked Jens.

"Oh—uh," Riley tried to decide if he wanted to attempt to get out of there, or if he would put in his time. He figured that at some point, he would need to spend a bunch of time with Jens, and at least he had nothing else going on that day. Besides, he assumed the Ford Focus in the Weber driveway was the professor's car, and maybe she would see him spending time there.

"What was that?" asked Jens.

"Uh, I have a couple of hours."

"Good" Jens smiled. "I've got something for you to do."

Riley regretfully pictured himself scraping the peeling brown paint on the outside of the house.

"Come in here." Jens motioned for Riley to follow him into the living room.

Riley took his water with him and walked beside Jens to a small desk that sat against a wall. Behind them, in the middle of the room, sat a modern leather sofa with an enormous ottoman that could also be used as a coffee table. The room was immaculate. Across from the sofa loomed a giant LED television on a stand. Riley might just as well be in the home of a yuppie with his first job than in the living room of an eighty-eight-year-old. He wondered why the living room looked so modern when the kitchen had been stuck in time.

"Wow! Nice TV," Riley said.

"Thank you," replied Jens. "I watch a lot of it. Perhaps too much, but when you're my age and don't drive, the television is very helpful to experience the world."

Riley smiled and nodded. It was nice to hear good things said of television. After receiving warnings all the way through school about the perils of too much TV, Riley was pleased that Jens recognized the good things that television offered people.

Jens turned his attention to the desk. "So this is a project I want to do."

Riley noticed three leather boxes on the desk, each labeled DiscOrg.

"These boxes," continued Jens as he pushed a bar on the bottom of one and opened it, "can hold three hundred DVDs each. And in here…" Jens opened a door next to the desk and revealed a small closet. "In here are about a thousand DVDs, I think."

Riley looked in the closet; indeed, it was full of DVDs stacked neatly in their plastic containers on four or five shelves. The entire small closet, which was probably originally intended for coats, was full.

"I'd like you to take a DVD, get rid of the plastic case and place just the disc in a slot in the organizer," instructed Jens. "Then write down the title of the DVD and the number of the slot you put it in."

Immediately, Riley smiled; he was actually looking forward to snooping through the movie collection. It seemed odd that someone so old would have amassed such a modern collection. Attempting to be enthusiastic and helpful, he asked, "Do you want me to alphabetize them?"

"Oh, they are already alphabetized," said Jens. "I could never live with an unorganized closet. It's just that I get sore and weak every now and then, and these organizers will be much easier to get at. You can't imagine what a problem it is when I want to watch something that is in the back of the closet; I have to lift the stacks out. Plus, I don't need the cases, so I will get some extra closet space. Got it?"

"Yep," replied Riley. "Got it."

"I'm going to hang the shower curtain," said Jens. "Help yourself to any food you can find. The grocery delivery came this morning, and there are some chips in the cupboard above the toaster."

Jens returned to the kitchen, picked up the shower curtain, and crossed back through the living room to a hall that began aside the television. Riley heard the bathroom light click on and went to the kitchen. He found a bag of Doritos in a cupboard next to the fridge and brought it with him back into the living room. He put the Doritos on the desk and took the first DVD from the closet, a film called *1492*.

They each worked separately for nearly twenty minutes. Riley began to amass a large collection of plastic DVD cases on the floor next to him, but the discs themselves looked good and more efficient in the leather boxes. He wondered how Jens would get rid of all the cases.

Riley had just finished storing a movie he'd never heard of, *Citizen Kane,* when there was a loud thud from the bathroom. Riley stopped what he was doing and heard Jens grunt. He walked down the hall to the only room with a light on; he had never seen this part of the house before.

"Jens? Are you okay?"

"Oh," responded an older-sounding voice than Jens normally used, "yes."

Riley stepped into the bathroom, which was as dated as the kitchen. A small sink and vanity sat to the right of the door. Jens was sitting on the closed toilet seat. A bathtub that doubled as a shower was opposite the toilet. One end of the shower curtain rod rested diagonally on the base of the bathtub.

"It's not a big deal," said Jens when Riley walked in. "Everything is fine."

"You need some help?" asked Riley.

"No!" responded Jens quickly. "I'm fine."

"You sure?"

"Yes, I have this condition called Guillain-Barre syndrome, and sometimes I just get dizzy and have to sit down. Every once in a while my muscles get weak, and I have trouble getting air, but I will be fine. I will fix the shower rod later."

Riley, wanting to help someone who obviously needed it, took a few steps toward the shower rod.

"No!" stated Jens, "I can handle it."

Riley didn't know if he should be persistent but decided to be polite instead.

"Okay, I'll just go back to the DVDs," said Riley.

Riley turned toward the door, took a few steps, then stopped. "Hey!" said Riley in an astonished voice. He looked at the shower curtain, which was still attached with rings to the fallen tension rod. "You have a plain brown shower curtain?"

"Yes, now go away." Jens tried to stand then immediately realized the Guillain-Barre would keep him seated. Jens hoped that Riley's curiosity would subside.

Riley walked over to the curtain and saw a very yellowed and crinkly old liner in the trash next to the sink. The liner had been clear at one point, but must have been quite old, because it looked anything but clear now.

"I bought you that clear thing. What is this?" asked Riley again. He was not intentionally angry or even frustrated with the task Jens asked of him, but he was now genuinely curious.

Jens, still sitting on the toilet lid, took a deep breath and winced when he noticed that Riley's curiosity was not abating. "Just leave that there. I need the clear one to protect the other side from water."

"Why does it matter if it's clear or white? What…" Riley lifted up the tension rod. Sliding over the plastic rod, on a single row of circular hooks, hung two shower curtains. The brown outside curtain was made of cloth, and indeed, the new clear plastic liner hung toward the tub. It served as a way to protect the brown fabric from the water of the shower.

But then, Riley noticed something very strange. On the backside of the brown cloth, photographs of people were fixed with safety pins. There were probably twenty photos of various groups of people pinned in neat rows. If not for the clear curtain, these photos would surely be ruined by shower water. Riley, thinking it odd that Jens looked at people while in the shower, now wondered if Jens was indeed up to something perverted.

"What are these photos?"

Jens sat still as Riley inspected them. They were old photos, mostly in black and white, with a few in color. The people depicted in the photographs were generally well dressed and looked happy. Riley, not wanting to seem rude by staring, began the process of placing the tension rod, and thus the two curtains, back into place. He could sense that Jens was uncomfortable.

Jens sat in silence for a few moments. He wondered if it was time to give Dr. Jade Weber the information she obviously wanted. In those few moments, he attempted to discern if he could trust both Jade and Riley.

Then, a thought came that was more important than worrying about their discretion. A simple question formed in his mind. *Is it time for me to have some peace that doesn't come from the escapism of Hollywood?* He took another deep breath and sighed.

"All right," said Jens abruptly. He had made up his mind. "I'm going to tell you about these photos. But that's it. I don't want to answer any questions. And especially, I don't need any judgment from you."

"Okay," answered Riley, still working on the rod. He really wanted to tell Jens that he didn't need an explanation, but he was curious, and perhaps he would get a good story to tell Abby. It also crossed his mind that these photos might be a story Professor Weber would want to hear. If he could just gather some information about Jens's life, he might get a passing grade. Riley paused from working on the rod and turned to Jens.

"You remember I'm from Germany, right?" asked Jens.

"Yep," answered Riley. "The river...Rhine, right?"

Without acknowledging the young man's question, Jens blurted out, "Well, I was in what you Americans call a concentration camp during the war."

The Iron Words

There was silence in the room; Riley had no idea how to respond. He eagerly turned and finished fixing the shower rod. He desperately tried to think of something to say, but it was difficult to respond when he didn't know how willing Jens was to talk about it.

"So," continued Jens after those awkward moments, "when I first came to the United States, I had a small old apartment in Minneapolis with just a bathtub, no shower. I bought this house in 1994, because I wanted to see the river, and this house had a shower that I was most eager to use. After forty years of baths, I'm sure you can see why. But there was a problem. When I tried using it, I was reminded of the showers in the gas chambers the Nazis used to kill people in the camps. I had avoided them in Germany, but now I had severe panic attacks and could not use the shower. Oh, I'd get undressed and stand in the tub, but I just couldn't turn on the water, because I was so scared. It got very bad, but I knew I had to get over it to fully live in this house. So I came up with the idea of putting photos of survivors in the shower. Now, I look at the photos and I can turn the knob because I'm reminded that it is just water coming out of the pipes."

Riley remained silent. A few more awkward moments passed. Then, Jens said bluntly, "You should just go. I'm not comfortable with you being here."

EIGHT

Later that evening, Jens sat at the desk next to the messy pile of plastic cases and contemplated whether to start organizing the DVDs again. However, his mind was preoccupied, and he slumped back in the chair with a heavy sigh. *Well, he can just think I am a Holocaust survivor and leave it at that.*

He knew that Jade would respect his privacy. He figured that Riley might tell the story of the shower curtain from time to time, but there was nothing that could be done about that.

NINE

Riley answered his phone when he noticed that the call was coming from a University of Minnesota number.

"Riley? This is Dr. Weber calling," said the voice. "I just got your e-mail and thought it would be easier to discuss over the phone."

Earlier, after Jens asked him to leave without finishing the DVD project, Riley drove straight back to campus and wrote a message to Dr. Weber. Riley, like most of the students, hated that e-mail was still the preferred method of communication with professors instead of the more efficient text message. However, he was anxious to get some help with Jens.

"First of all," began Professor Weber, "thank you for letting me know what happened this afternoon. Don't ever be afraid to ask for advice or guidance with your project. Now, as for Mr. Jaenisch, do you think he meant it when he told you not to come back? Maybe he was just uncomfortable that he told you such an intimate detail about his life."

"I don't know," answered Riley. "It was weird, and it happened fast. I didn't know how to respond, so I just didn't say anything."

"That's all right," she said. "You're young, and one thing college is good at is giving young people a chance to practice being an adult."

"Did you know he was in a concentration camp?" Riley asked. "Did anyone know?"

"I didn't know for sure, and I don't think anyone else did either," she answered. "He taught in the College of Liberal Arts here for a very long time, and I never heard anyone say anything or have a rumor about it. I certainly never heard that he would speak about the Holocaust in his classes."

"You said you didn't know for sure. So you suspected it?"

"Well," she said, "you don't live next to someone over twenty years without learning a few things about him."

Jade felt a little embarrassed but kept that emotion to herself. She realized that it wasn't completely ethical to have used Riley to learn about her neighbor due to a mere suspicion, but now that she knew her guess was correct, perhaps she could use this information to make both their lives more meaningful. She chose to think of it as undergraduate directed research, rather than using a freshman to spy on a neighbor. Besides, she chose Riley because he was an athlete and probably didn't know too much about academic integrity and institutional research boards; there was little chance he would file a complaint. Another student might have hung up the phone and contacted her department. "So, Riley," she asked, "what do you want to do with this information?"

"Well, I think I'm done with the whole thing. He asked me not to come back. So, that's it, I guess."

"Was he angry?"

"No, I don't think so," he said as he sighed. "He sounded more disappointed, in a way."

Jade took a moment to think and then began, "Okay, I know him well enough to know that he is a fairly calm person and a rational thinker. He probably just needs some time to deal with the shock that someone else knows about his past."

"But it's not like he did anything wrong," interjected Riley. "What is he so ashamed of?"

"We can't know what he is thinking," Dr. Weber responded. "Riley, he was forced to experience something that we cannot possibly relate to. World War Two was a very long time ago, and he may have lived with this secret that whole time."

"So…what should I do?"

"I thought about that before I called you," she said. "I think you should make a gesture to let him know that you are willing to talk, if he wants to. You should also let him know that you are willing to finish any project he has for you without talking about the Holocaust, if he doesn't want to talk about it."

"Should I just stop by sometime?"

"Hmmm, well," she thought out-loud, "Passover is coming up. Why don't you bring him a card? That could be a way of letting him know that you are there for him without expecting him to answer a question from you."

"What's Passover?" Riley asked.

Jade was stunned at his ignorance, but she reminded herself how young and inexperienced all the freshmen were. The new students coming to the university knew what they needed to know about math and reading, but they knew absolutely nothing about how people live around the world.

"It's a Jewish holiday," she said. "Did you grow up in a religion?"

"My parents are Lutheran," he answered. "But we are not a religious family."

"Okay, do you know who Moses is?" Jade asked.

"Yes," Riley replied, "he led the slaves out of Egypt. We watched *The Ten Commandments* in some class in high school."

"So, when Moses—" she stopped midsentence and decided it wasn't worth her time. "It's just a Jewish holiday."

This was the first time that Riley thought about Jens being Jewish. Since that afternoon, he had been picturing Jens and the others from the shower curtain in horrible Holocaust situations. Thinking about Jens having a whole culture and faith in addition to being a survivor required Riley to adjust the label he had placed on him.

"Do they have cards for that?"

"Yes, they have cards for everything," she said. "Just go to Target and look for them by the Easter cards."

TEN

"What the hell is Passover, anyway?" asked Abby to her friend as they stood in the card aisle at Target.

"Don't be a hater, Abby," her friend replied. "Respect the faith." As she said this, she pumped her fist in the air to mimic a gesture of religious empowerment. They both laughed.

"Shut up," responded Abby. "If I have to go to Target every time the old geezer needs something from Riley—"

Her friend laughed. "You're at Target for condoms every day anyway."

"Shut up, bitch," said Abby. She gave her friend a light shove and joined in the laughter.

"Well, you know," added her friend, "the best way to a man's heart isn't his stomach."

"What is it, then?" asked Abby.

"It's doing enough of his shit that he can't live without you."

"Argh, I know!" growled Abby as she finally found the two Passover cards that were on the rack next to the hundreds of Easter choices.

ELEVEN

"Jake is in that room right there," replied the nurse as she pointed to an open door very near the nursing station.

"Thanks," Riley responded and walked the few steps to the doorway. He stood still and peered in. At first glance, it looked like the typical hospital room he was expecting. He noticed the standard equipment and monitors attached to various walls. A television was bolted opposite the bed.

On the other side of a blue curtain that was pulled about four feet out from the wall, he saw Jake propped up in an inclined bed. First, Riley was relieved to see that Jake was partly sitting up and didn't look too sick. Second, he was relieved to see that there was nobody else in the room, especially Mrs. Fred. Riley conjured inner strength, as he would to make an impossible hockey goal, and stepped into the room.

"Hey, man!" Riley feigned enthusiasm as he walked over to the bed.

"Riley!" replied Jake in a very surprised voice. "Hey man!"

Riley moved to do a fist bump with Jake. Then he remembered Jake's condition and lightly tapped him on the shoulder instead. Jake was so glad to see his best friend that he didn't notice the attempted fist bump.

Jake did not have the clean Nordic look of Riley. He was more solid in his build, with thick dark hair and a scruffy face. While Riley was stealth on ice, Jake was brute force and aggression. This was most evident when Riley smiled with all his natural teeth, while Jake's mouth was a mix of implants and metal. However, as rough as Jake appeared on the outside and on the ice, his parents had raised him to have a heart of gold. Jake was a true gentle giant.

Now that he was fully in the room, Riley noticed a rolling tray with snacks on it. A few chairs were scattered around, mostly near the bed. On the wall opposite the door was a small window with a brown granite ledge below it.

"How are you doing?" asked Riley.

"Pretty good now," responded Jake. "I'm on a lot of dope in here. We'll see what it's like when I get home and have a chance to sober up. Hopefully, the pain will be much better in my back."

Riley nodded his head and stood in silence. After a few awkward moments passed, Jake motioned to a chair that was next to his bed. "Have a seat, man," he said. "Or you got to run to some chick that's waiting to jump your bones back on campus?"

Riley shrugged and grabbed a chair that was near where he was standing. He pulled the chair closer to the bed and sat down.

"Anyone else here?" Riley asked.

"Nope," replied Jake. "My dad is at work and my mom went over to my sister's for lunch."

Riley was about to tell him that he wasn't heading back to Abby on campus but was going to deliver a Jewish card to some old Holocaust survivor. Then he decided that complaining about his trivial academic problems might be upsetting to Jake, who would probably love to trade places with him.

"I saw your mom at Target," said Riley instead. "She said you had surgery for pain in your back?"

"Yeah," replied Jake, "it's kind of funny; I can't feel anything in my legs and very little in my arms, but the pain in my back I can sure feel."

Riley smiled a little at Jake's attempt to use humor to make the truth seem less depressing. Jake turned his head and took a drink through a long plastic straw that reached from a water pitcher on the tray. It just about killed Riley to see Jake have to drink this way.

Again, there was a long awkward silence as they both tried to think of something to talk about. Riley quickly realized that all their common interests were off the table; hockey, girls, and school were things that Jake could no longer do. Riley didn't know if watching a hockey game on television would be fun or frustrating for Jake, and he thought it was too soon to find out.

Jake, on the other hand, decided to shoot his own puck and say the things that his mom had been suggesting for the past couple of months. It would be difficult, but he decided to just jump right in. "You hate me," he said. "Don't you?"

"What? What the hell are you talking about? I don't hate you."

"Yes, you do. I ruined everything," said Jake desperately. "We were going to be teammates and all the things we talked about since kindergarten. And I ruined them in one stupid night."

Riley didn't know what to say. The fact that Jake felt this way was killing him inside; he wanted so badly to run. Scraping Jens's peeling house would be better; even working out with the coach yelling in his ear would be better.

"You don't have to say anything, Ri," said Jake. "My mom thought I should say that, so I can move on. It's been burning me up that I ruined everything. I guess the fact that I hurt my friendship with you is worse than the fact that I can't walk or do much of anything else."

"It's just one of those things, man," replied Riley, still stunned. "You didn't know it was going to happen."

"All I had was two beers." Jake was on the verge of tears. "I just can't believe this happened from two beers. I've been a lot drunker before, and nothing happened. I am the stupidest idiot alive."

Riley swallowed hard. The events of that October night were things he did not want to talk about. Ever. He didn't even want to think about them. "You can't beat yourself up. It happened. That's it."

"Two beers and a metal fence," said Jake, "and now I can't piss on my own."

Riley could not hear this. His stomach grew tight and queasy.

"Nothing works down there, Riley," added Jake. "Nothing."

Riley knew what he meant. Over the past months, he had often wondered whether Jake would be able to be sexually active again. Now he knew the answer. The nausea got worse. "So," began Riley awkwardly, "what do you think you will do next?" He didn't know if it was okay to ask this, but it was a better alternative than talking about the accident. Riley was grasping at straws, desperate to find a way to move on.

"Well," responded Jake, "in the short term, we're working on a lawsuit."

"Over what?" asked Riley.

"I'm not really sure, because my parents don't tell me all the details," answered Jake. "But there were some weird things in the toxicology report from the night of the accident. My parents seem to think that something the doctor gave me might have had some-thing to do with why I was so drunk on two beers."

Jake's words were paralyzing for Riley to hear. He sat motion-less, unable to breathe. He was shaking slightly. Then, as he realized

Jake noticed his silence, Riley's survival instincts kicked in. "Which doctor?" asked Riley.

"The Athletic Department guy," replied Jake. "Whatever his name is."

"Oh yeah, I know him." Riley checked his phone to find out the time. He could no longer handle being in that room, and he especially could not handle any conversation about doctors and medication. Even if it was abrupt and rude, Riley needed to leave immediately, without hearing anymore about the lawsuit and the Athletic Department's physician.

"Hey, man," Riley said quickly, "I have to go. I'm working on a project for my soc. class, and I have to be somewhere."

"No problem, Ri. I'm glad you came by."

"Me, too," said Riley. He wanted to make a joke by telling Jake not to go too crazy over the nurses, but he remembered Jake's condition and stayed quiet. He turned to leave.

"Riley," said Jake with more energy than usual, "please come and see me at home."

Riley stopped and turned back to look at him in the bed.

"We don't have to talk about hockey, or the accident," continued Jake. "We can just hang out."

"Yeah, I will," said Riley as he left the room. His face crumpled under the weight of a million feelings as he walked down the hall.

TWELVE

Riley was extremely relieved on the drive from the hospital to Jens's house. He was just glad that the visit with Jake was over; he didn't know if or when he would pay a visit to Jake's house, but he would not think about that until he absolutely had to. Of course, some of the things they had spoken about were troubling to Riley, but he was able to push them off.

Riley opened the car window and let in the spring breeze. It was, perhaps, a little too cold for his T-shirt and shorts, but he was glad to feel something to bring his mind back to normalcy. He turned into the neighborhood high on the bluff overlooking the Mississippi.

He wondered if Dr. Weber's husband ever worked. The squad car was in the driveway again as he pulled in next door. He had not called, but he knew that Jens would be home. Riley expected to deliver the card, exchange a short greeting, and be on his way back to campus.

He switched off the ignition and picked up the card that Abby purchased from the passenger seat. As he walked up the few concrete steps, he noticed that the inner door to the kitchen was already open, allowing the screen door to let in the pleasant April weather. Jens, like all other Minnesotans, knew that there could still be one more blast of winter. It was a good idea to capitalize on a nice spring day while it was available.

Riley stepped up to the screen door and rang the bell. After a brief moment Jens came into the kitchen from the living room and crossed to the door.

"Riley," said Jens with a surprised expression, "nice to see you."

Jens didn't really think it was nice to see the young man; in fact, he was both annoyed and scared that Riley had come back to the house. Jens still felt embarrassed that Riley had seen the shower pictures, and he knew he'd have to tread lightly in order to avoid talking more about it.

"I have something for you," said Riley from the other side of the screen door.

"In that case, come on in." He opened the door for Riley, who stepped into the kitchen. Jens was hoping he would not stay long and did not offer a bottle of water this time.

"How are you doing with your class?" asked Jens, knowing enough about athletics to not make the last word plural.

"I'm still working with Professor Weber," replied Riley. "How are you doing?"

"On a day like this"—he gestured at the blue sky—"I'm very fine."

"I wanted to give you this," said Riley. "Uh, Happy Passover."

He gave the envelope to Jens, who said without thinking, "Thank you, but I'm not Jewish."

Panic instantly filled Jens's upper chest as soon as his words left his lips. He realized that he'd made a crucial mistake and began to think of a way to rectify it. Inside, he was beating himself up for his lack of thought and filter.

But before Jens could speak, Riley said in a confused manner, "Oh…I thought that because you were in a—"

"Yes, that," interrupted Jens. "Ah, well, you see, I was Jewish back in Germany but left all that behind me when I moved to Minnesota."

"Oh," Riley said. "I guess I can understand that, after what happened to you."

"Well, faith just is not that important to me anymore," Jens said quickly. "But sit down and tell me more about yourself; I don't really know much about you."

Jens was calm once more, because he felt he did an adequate job of covering up for his slip and turning the focus back on Riley. The change of the conversation's focus might have been abrupt for some, but Jens knew that college students loved talking about themselves. "Thank you for the card anyway. It's nice to know that someone was thinking about me, even if I don't practice the faith anymore."

"No problem," said Riley as he sat down at the kitchen table.

Jens took the card and put it on the table between them. He did not open it up. "Where are you from?"

"Hastings," Riley said.

"That's not too far." remarked Jens.

"About twenty miles from here. It can take a while, though, depending on traffic. There really isn't a back way to get there because of the river."

"And which sport do you play? I can't remember if I asked you."

"Hockey."

"Hastings must have a good program if you were picked by the Gophers." Jens tried to sound impressed.

"Yeah," said Riley, "it's pretty intense. I like this time of year when the season is done, and I can concentrate on working out and skating without all the hockey stuff."

"Usually people who skate fall in love with the ice," said Jens. "Did that happen to you?"

"I like skating a lot," answered Riley. "But I don't get too many chances to just skate without working on something."

"I see," said Jens and then paused to think about it. "I suppose that's the price you have to pay for being so good at it. We all have to work, and even those who enjoy their jobs have to sacrifice something."

"If I can get in the NHL and not have school and everything else to worry about, things will be better."

Jens laughed inside at Riley's ignorance. He knew that the real world contained way more to worry about than the protected environment of the University of Minnesota. Jens also wondered what Riley thought about the other, nonathletic students on campus. He was curious what Riley observed about those that had to balance jobs, family, and multiple classes when he couldn't even manage one class, a private dorm, and laundry service.

"Tell me how you got this far with hockey."

Riley began to explain the long road that led from a four-year-old skating with a plastic support to a college freshman zigzagging around the Big Ten. His explanation was full of words that Jens did not understand, like pee-wee, traveling team, bantams, and various types of tournaments.

Jens attempted to show genuine interest, but his mind wandered as he looked into Riley's earnest, but not passionate, eyes. Riley was a young man with the financial resources and appearance to pursue anything he wanted. Jens knew that a liberal arts education was little use in the real world, so he wasn't concerned whether Riley actually learned from his courses. However, it bothered Jens that Riley was choosing to pursue something he wasn't entirely passionate about when he could have the world. This young man was letting others—probably his parents—dictate his path. Jens hated to see students waste their potential on other people's dreams.

Just then, Jens pulled the focus of his mind away from Riley and began to think about himself. There was a time when he allowed others to dictate his actions. He wondered if he was still allowing that within himself. It was quite sobering for him to admit that lying to Riley about being a German Jew was not being true to himself. Even now, at eighty-eight years old, he was giving his past permission to control his present. He had lied to Riley and wondered if he should tell the truth and take just a bit of his life back. Besides, he could still control his own story and need not tell Riley anything he didn't want to. But he would not lie, either.

"Riley"—Jens interrupted the young man midsentence—"I need to tell you something."

Riley, in the middle of a story about the state hockey tournament, had just begun to wonder whether Jens was paying attention. Now, as the old man spoke, Riley knew that his mind had been preoccupied the whole time. "Sure. What?"

"I'm going to trust you with something," said Jens. "I really don't want to talk about it ever again. I don't want to tell you about what it was like in the concentration camp, and I don't want you to feel bad for me."

"That's okay, Jens," said Riley. "It's no problem and you don't have to say anything."

"I'd like you to come over next week again and help me get rid of the DVD covers. I just do not want you to be awkward around me, and I feel bad that I wasn't honest with you."

Riley nodded. "I can do that."

"So," said Jens, "I told you that I was born German and Jewish. That's not true. I was born in Germany, but I was born into a Protestant family. I've never been Jewish."

It took a moment for Riley to digest the information. It is always hard for a young person to remove a label they have applied. "Then...I mean, I thought you were in a concentration camp."

"I was," answered Jens. "But you did not have to be Jewish to be in the camp."

THIRTEEN

"What in the hell?" said Riley when he was alone in the car and driving back to campus.

By the manner in which Jens said it, they both knew that the conversation was over. Jens did not offer any more information, and Riley was polite enough not to ask. They managed to spend a bit more time talking about the weather and the new light-rail line that was to pass through campus. Then, Riley left abruptly after he committed to returning the next week.

Riley did not think about Dr. Weber or sociology in the car. He was confused, frustrated, and above all, way too curious to remember this was part of an assignment.

As he took the exit from I-94 onto University Avenue, he tried to recall what he knew about the Holocaust and where he learned it. He'd seen *Schindler's List* in a high-school class; he had read a chapter about it and taken a test. He was sure he'd seen pieces of various documentaries on the History Channel discussing the subject as he flipped between channels. However, in his head, there was only a general picture of what happened; he didn't know many details.

He knew the headlines: the gas chambers, the piles of dead Jews, the crowded beds, the lack of food. The images now flickered through his mind in black and white. He searched the images for any clue about prisoners who weren't Jewish.

Suddenly, he saw a face that he remembered from *Schindler's List*. He couldn't recall the actor's name, but he was the same guy who played Lord Voldemort in the *Harry Potter* movies. Riley replayed a scene in his mind, still in black and white, as Voldemort sat in a tower at the concentration camp and shot Jewish people with a rifle. *What did they call those people?* He should have paid more attention to the movie. *Oh yeah, SS. The guy playing Voldemort was a SS officer.*

That train of thought led to a logical conclusion as he entered campus from the east on University Avenue. He heard Jens's voice. "You did not have to be Jewish to be in the camp."

"Could it be true?" he asked himself.

"You did not have to be Jewish to be in the camp," he heard again.

"But," he said out-loud, "there were only Jews and SS shooting them." His eyes widened. "Jens is a Nazi!"

FOURTEEN

"Hey," said Abby, "did you know that Carrie Underwood is going to be in *The Sound of Music* this Christmas?"

"What are you talking about?" replied Riley. "Shut up, I'm trying to be serious here."

"I am serious," said Abby, sitting on Riley's bed in shorts and a very tight pink sweater. "*The Sound of Music* has Nazis, right? And Carrie Underwood is going to be one of them."

Riley, having never seen *The Sound of Music*, was surprised to hear that there were Nazis in it; he'd always thought it was about nuns. But maybe Abby was just being stupid.

"Shut up and listen to me." He sat next to her and placed his hands on each side of her head. "I'm telling you, the old guy is a Nazi!"

"How do you know?" she asked. "Was he walking like this..."

She broke free of Riley's hands and stood up from the bed. Abby walked through the dorm room, kicking her legs straight out in front of her. She stopped in the middle of the room and held her left arm straight out.

"Hi, Hitler!" she yelled and laughed simultaneously. "I know they shouted something weird like that."

"Did you even put the correct arm in the air?" Riley asked.

"Not sure," she answered. "I'm not the Nazi here."

She threw herself on the bed and over Riley's lap, facing up.

"Hey," she said coyly, "you have blond hair and blue eyes. Maybe you're a Nazi! Do you want me to be your little Nazi slut?"

"What do blond hair and blue eyes have to do with anything?"

"You'd better stick to taking care of this gorgeous body," she laughed as she ran her hands over his hard chest and worked down to his abs. "Even I know more about the Nazis than you, and I slept through most of high school. But it's okay. Who cares when you can score?"

He noticed her double entendre but did not respond. "Would you be serious for a minute? Help me figure out what to do."

"What do you mean?" She sat up on his lap. "What can you do?"

"Well, don't I have to report him or something?"

"I don't know. Do people rat out old Nazis?"

"I'm not sure."

"Isn't he, like, a hundred years old?" she asked snidely.

"He's eighty-eight," said Riley. "But he sometimes acts a lot younger."

"So who cares?" she said. "It was a long time ago and he's basically in the grave anyway."

"I guess you're right." He sighed. "I can ask Dr. Weber about it, anyway."

"Then why are you bugging me? How do you know he's a Nazi? I thought you told me he had pictures of Jews in his shower so he wouldn't worry about being gassed."

"Yeah, he does," replied Riley. "He said he did that so he could remember that people survived and he'd be okay. I can't really figure out why he'd have pictures like that if he wasn't a Jewish prisoner afraid of getting killed."

"Hmmm," she said. "Tell me what he told you about the pictures again."

"Jens said he was okay in the shower, because he would see that people survived, and so would he."

"Do you think he could be really guilty about the people he killed?" she asked.

Riley, thinking that she might be on to something, attempted to piece together the puzzle in his head.

He threw Abby's legs to the side and stood by the bed. "Yes, he's probably haunted by the memories and came up with a way to remember the survivors and not think about all the people he killed. Maybe when he was in the shower, he would see the faces of people he gassed, and that made it hard for him to turn the knob. You know, like he had to turn the knob to get the gas going." Riley found it easy and even fun to play armchair psychologist.

Up until this point, Riley had been infatuated with the idea that Jens was a Nazi. Now, he started to think that Jens was a murderer. It was hard to grasp. Jens, who taught German literature and had an awesome DVD collection, was a cold-blooded killer.

"That's so weird," Abby said. "And a little creepy. No, a lot creepy."

"I don't know," said Riley. "Okay, yes, it is very creepy. A Nazi keeps photos of Jews in his shower, because he feels bad about killing their loved ones while he enjoys a house and shower in America?"

"Probably," she said. "Now, shut up with all this Nazi stuff, it's spoiling the moment."

"What moment is that?" He lowered his voice and stared at her intently.

Abby laughed. "Don't pull that face on me and then wonder what kind of moment I'm going for here."

"Well, I didn't think you came over here just to talk about Carrie Underwood in *The Sound of Music.*"

Riley took off his T-shirt in one swift move and threw it on the floor in front of the closet. Abby stretched out on the bed and her sweater rode up, exposing her flat, tan stomach. Riley pushed all thoughts of Jens and Nazis out of his mind and threw himself on top of her.

FIFTEEN

"Why can't these people learn to text?" asked Riley to himself when his phone rang.

The call was coming from Dr. Weber's office. It was morning and he assumed she must have just read the e-mail he'd sent in the middle of the night. He had already showered and dressed, but he had not gone to the cafeteria for breakfast. Like most students, he didn't care if the weather was actually going to be warm or not, he just dressed in shorts and a T-shirt with flip-flops.

He answered the phone.

"Hi, Riley," said the familiar female voice, "it's Dr. Weber calling. I just read your message."

"Yeah," he replied. "Pretty intense, right?"

"To say the least," she agreed. "Now that I think about it, my suspicion that he was in a concentration camp came more from associating him with a certain time and place. I guess I made a mistake by assuming he was Jewish; I don't know why I did. Looking back, I can't recall any signs of that faith. I mean, I can't say I saw him celebrating the Sabbath, or Hanukkah, or any of the other Jewish holy days."

"So, don't I have to report him or something?"

"Well, Riley, you're making a very serious accusation. Although it is rare, because the war was so long ago, I still read about former Nazi officers being discovered and tried for their crimes. Often they are found in South American countries, like Argentina, but it is not unheard of to discover a former Nazi in the United States."

Professor Weber knew much more about the Holocaust than Riley. She was not ready to make the leap to convict Jens, but she wasn't able to abandon all thoughts that he was a Nazi, either. She wanted, and now needed, more information.

"But," Riley said, "he's almost ninety years old. Why bother now?"

Jade loved this question, because it led to a crucial lesson she desired to impart during her class on aging in America. For the first time since she gave Riley this project, she felt that it might be doing some good, and he was going to learn at least one objective.

"Riley, you tell me. Does it matter that he's almost ninety?"

"Yes," he answered. "I think it does. He's not going to be around that much longer. Why ruin his life now?"

"But what about the other lives he might have ruined if it turns out to be true?"

"Yeah," he responded, "I know. But maybe he's had all these years to think about it; maybe that's worse than being in prison. Remember I told you about the shower curtain? Well, now I think he's had a really hard time facing what he did. I think the photos on the shower curtain prove that he cares..."

"All right," she interrupted. "I understand all of that, and it's natural for you to think like that. However, why don't we let young people get away with things if they prove that they are remorseful? Let's say a twenty-year-old rapes and kills a woman. Should we let him go free if he promises to look at a photograph of her every night?"

He didn't have an answer for that question; a few moments passed.

"Let me ask you this," she continued. "At what age should people be able to stop facing their crimes? Ninety? Eighty? Seventy?"

"Okay," he said reluctantly, "I get the point. If old people want to be treated equally, that means even when it might not go their way."

"Exactly." She was happy he understood. "We marginalize aging people when we think we can stop dealing with them because they may die soon."

"I got it," he said. "But what if it wasn't his fault? What if he was forced into it by some other Nazis? Jens is a nice guy who spends a lot of time watching movies and television. He takes care of his house—well, most of it—and you said he's been a good neighbor. Why should we get involved if he's not hurting anyone now?"

"Is that for you and me to decide?"

Riley paused for a few moments to consider his previous statement. "I guess not."

"We have a society, Riley. We have systems in place," she said. "If what you say is true, then he should be sent back to Germany to face his past."

"What if I'm wrong?" He tried to think of how he could have made a mistake. In his mind, it was so simple. There were only Jews and SS. If he wasn't one, then he had to be the other.

"That's what you need to find out," Dr. Weber said. "You said it yourself. You are not completely sure. This is a serious accusation and he deserves fairness. But so does society. You need to ask him."

Jade hoped that he would investigate. She was willing to bet that there was more to the story. She also knew that Riley's information about only Jews and SS being in the camps was completely incorrect. However, she wanted him to discover the truth.

"I have to go there and ask him if he's a Nazi?" said Riley bluntly.

"Yes, it is the only right and fair thing to do."

"Man, this sucks," replied Riley with a sigh.

"This is life, Riley. And yes, sometimes it sucks. Please don't tell anyone I used that word."

Riley laughed. "No problem. Your secret is safe with me."

Riley wasn't entirely opposed to the idea of going over to Jens's house to ask the question. Even though he was awkward and hesitant about it, he was curious and thought the story at least deserved an ending. Then, he thought, *what if I'm responsible for Jens being led away in handcuffs and sent back to Germany? What if I'm responsible for ruining yet another life? Can I handle more guilt?*

"Just send me a message when you can," Professor Weber said. "Also, if you get into any sort of situation that you feel you can't handle, please call the number I called you from and leave a message; I get my messages forwarded."

"Okay, thanks."

"Oh, and Riley," she added in a very sincere voice, "you're doing a good job. You've helped someone face his past, and you've learned one small thing about equality. The term will be over in three weeks, so keep up the work."

"Thanks," Riley responded and pressed the button to end the call.

On her end of the phone, Jade hung up and took a minute to think about how much Riley had surprised her. She had not expected him to follow though. Usually, student athletes at Riley's level had people who did these kinds of the things for them. But she knew it had actually been Riley going to Jens's house because her husband saw him from the window each time. Officer Weber was sure it was Riley because there wasn't another student who looked like him; there were few people on the planet who were as handsome as Riley. *I hope that hockey coach isn't putting a lot of pressure on him. Poor kid. Maybe I should tell him he's got an A and give him some slack.*

She looked out her window and saw students who, she was sure, were handling multiple classes and responsibilities. She decided not to give Riley any slack.

SIXTEEN

"But," said Jake to Mrs. Fred in their living room, "I didn't take any Klonopin **that day.** I didn't take those pills for probably two weeks before the accident. I don't understand why you are asking me."

"Well," replied Dot, "that's what the toxicology report said. You had a larger than normal amount of Klonopin in your system. It absolutely made the beer you had worse. If you had just had two beers in your system, you would have been fine. But the combination of Klonopin and alcohol made you hit that fence. You have to face the facts and tell us the truth, Jake. The toxicology report is not wrong."

His parents had brought him home from the hospital that morning, and he was glad to be back in his massage chair in front of the television. He was also glad that so far, his pain was under control.

Mr. and Mrs. Fred were taking the opportunity to be frank with him. They were asking direct questions about any medication abuse in his past. Ms. Bender, the attorney working on the case, was adamant that she would not continue with any lawsuit until Jake was completely honest about what he had and had not done.

"Mom, don't tell me about facing the facts until you do it yourself. You've been telling me for weeks to face the facts and talk to Riley. I did that and it was hard. You also have to face the fact that I was underage drinking and driving while intoxicated. Even if it was just the two beers, it was still my fault. I've faced that and now you have to."

"Jacob, I know all that. Don't you think it kills me that you did those things? But here is my point: regardless of the cause, you will need a lot of care and special technology. Probably for the rest of your life. We need to know if there was any negligence from anyone else that contributed to your accident. Not only do we want those people to be held accountable, but we need money from them. I know it's hard to think that way. We have to be realistic. Besides what you did that was wrong, there was Klonopin in your body and it may not entirely be your fault."

"How could that be?" Jake asked. "How could I have it in my blood? You have to believe me. Yes, I had a prescription for Klonopin that I got in the fall semester. But I know I hadn't taken any for a long time."

"Listen," Dot replied. "There is a possible explanation for this whole deal. Your attorney found an expert, a psychiatrist, who says that you can be addicted to Klonopin and not even know it. You were probably taking it every day—many times a day maybe—and didn't even know it."

Jake didn't know what he thought about that. He supposed it could be true, but he felt it so strange to think that he had been taking pills everyday and didn't remember opening the bottle or getting water; he didn't even remember getting new bottles.

"So," he questioned, "if this is all true, then who are we suing?"

"The University of Minnesota Athletic Department," she answered, "and especially their doctor who wrote you that prescription. We think he was giving you more than you thought."

"How could I do that without knowing?" asked Jake. "How could I even get a bottle from him and take it with me when I don't remember doing that? I remember everything else about fall term, up until the accident anyway. How could I not know that I was taking drugs?"

"That's exactly what our expert will find out," Dot responded. "Jacob, your father and I want to know if you are on board with this. You may have to answer some very hard questions about your behavior during the fall semester. If you don't want to, we will stop."

"No, don't stop," Jake said. "I've accepted that it was drinking that caused this, and I know it was illegal for me to drink. I've accepted that all of this is my own fault. I made a very stupid mistake. Even Riley blames me for this, I think. But if someone else had a part in this, even if it was a doctor who was trying to do his job, then I want to find out."

Mrs. Fred was extremely proud of her son at that moment. She loved that Jake was not looking for an excuse or scapegoat. He was looking to find the truth.

SEVENTEEN

"**O**h, good," Jens said to himself as he noticed Riley's car drive up to his garage, "now, I can get all that *Scheiße* out of the living room."

Jens was sitting at the small table in the kitchen. He was wearing jeans and a University of Minnesota sweat shirt that he got as a gift for giving money to some kind of scholarship fund. Despite the sparse attire of the students on campus, it was still way too early in the season for Jens to wear less than a sweat shirt.

He grabbed a bottle of water from the fridge just as the bell rang. "Hello, sir," said Jens as he opened the door, "come on in."

"Thanks," Riley said and pulled open the outside screen door.

Jens handed him the water. "So let's get these plastic cases out of my hair."

Jens was anxious to get right to work. Even though he didn't like the plastic cases taking space in his living room, it wasn't the main reason he wanted them gone. The pile of trash was a constant reminder that there were things he was not physically able to do. He didn't like to think of himself as being incapable, and the plastic cases on the floor would not let him forget that.

Riley followed him into the living room. "Do you have a place to throw them?"

"Yes, I have a huge plastic trash can that I never have enough garbage to fill. It might take a couple of weeks, but I'll get them all out. I think we could just put them in trash bags and move them to the garage. I can handle the weekly trash myself."

"Sounds good," responded Riley.

Riley immediately noticed the large pile of plastic cases sitting on the floor next to the desk. It was shocking to see the waste of plastic and space. He set the bottle of water on the desk. "Why don't you sit and hold the bag open? I'll sort of shovel in the cases with my hands."

"That sounds like a good plan," responded Jens.

He sat in the desk chair and pulled a plastic garbage bag from a box that he had placed on the desk two days earlier. He never could have done this project alone. It would have taken too much time and strength. Walking down the few concrete steps off the porch was bad enough normally; carrying a full plastic bag would make it near impossible.

Jens shook the bag to open it up. He spread the top of it apart and held it between his legs.

Riley threw a handful of cases into the bag. As he did this, he noticed Jens's hands gripping the sides of the bag. Even though Jens's attire and aura seemed to be much younger, his hands did reveal his true age. Wrinkled and liver-spotted, they shook slightly. Thoughts of Jens being a Nazi had been in the back of Riley's mind. But now, as he looked at Jens's hands, Riley began to wonder if these were the hands of a brutal killer. *Did these hands turn on the gas in the showers?*

It was amazing to them both how heavy the empty plastic cases were. The bag, with the cases' corners already sticking out here and there, was only about half-full when Jens knew he would hardly be able to get them into the trash bin on his own. "I think we'll have to stop there," Jens said. "It will take more bags than I thought, but I won't be able to lift them into the trash if there are any more cases in the bags."

"You sure you're okay to hold the bags open?" Riley saw that the trembling in Jens's hands seemed to be getting worse.

"Yes," replied Jens, "it's not a problem. My illness makes me weak sometimes, but it doesn't hurt."

"Are you a Nazi?" asked Riley bluntly. He had been waiting for a good time to ask, but none was presenting itself; he decided to just shoot the puck to end his own anticipation. He was willing to be rude to get the answer to the question prodding his mind.

"What?" asked Jens in an odd voice. He wasn't quite sure he heard Riley correctly.

"Are you a Na—I mean, were you a Nazi? An SS officer?" asked Riley again.

Jens was shocked. He wondered how this young man could be so inconsiderate to ask such a horrible question. He didn't expect anyone to be ignorant enough to ask a Holocaust survivor a question like this.

"What are you asking?" Jens said with a lot of energy. "Why would you say such a thing?" He stared straight into Riley's eyes.

"I, well, you said you were never Jewish," answered Riley. "And you found it hard to tell me that. So I just assumed that since you were in a concentration camp, you had to be one of the Nazis."

Jens dropped the sides of the bag he was holding. He slumped in the chair as the bag fell to the floor. Jens had thought that Riley might wonder about his status as a non-Jew in the concentration camp, but he never thought the assumption would be this. "Is that what you think? Do you think there were only Jews and Nazis in the camp?"

"Well, yeah," answered Riley. "I've seen movies and things about it."

The first thought that went through Jens's mind was how uneducated the American youth were about what happened in Europe during that horrible time. He hated that American students had a romantic view of everything, including death and despair.

However, it was the second thought racing through his brain that filled him with fear. *Is there a way for me to explain my time in the camp without telling the truth of who I was? How can I prove that I wasn't a Nazi if I'm not willing to share my whole story?*

"Just…just sit," said Jens and motioned, with his eyes closed, to the couch. "I need some time. Please, just sit."

Riley quickly and quietly set down a stack of DVD cases and went to the couch. He looked at Jens sitting in the chair with eyes squeezed shut. His breathing was deep, but not rapid. Riley was worried and kept his eyes on him; he would not hesitate to call 911 if he saw Jens deteriorate any further. Riley also began to contemplate whether he'd done the right thing. He wondered if Professor Weber and her cop husband were home, and if he should run and get them.

Jens retreated into his mind. His thoughts were quick and random. He began to speak and see images in his mind that he wanted to hide from the young man.

"Ich bin ein warmer Bruder."

A flash of pink.

The cold.

A face.

"Ich bin ein warmer Bruder."

Another face.

A triangle.

"Ich bin ein warmer Bruder."

A dead face, and another. And even more.

The sound of men singing *Stille Nacht*.

His *capo*.

"Ich bin ein warmer Bruder."

The time was long in his head, but was only a few moments in reality.

Riley heard him attempting to say something. He got up, walked over to Jens, and put his hand on Jens's shoulder, shaking him lightly. "Jens, do you need help? Are you saying something?"

Jens quickly came back to Minnesota and opened his eyes. The first thing he saw was Riley's handsome face and concerned eyes. For sixty-five years he'd kept his secret; for sixty-five years he was ashamed. "I want…"

"What do you want?" asked Riley. "Can I get you something? Some water? Should I see if Professor Weber is home?"

Riley saw that Jens was returning to normal and took his hand off his shoulder. He stood tall in front of the chair; Jens sat up a little and continued to stare straight at Riley. Usually, sharing an intense look like this would be awkward, or even creepy. But somehow, the two realized deep within that Jens needed this time and energy, and the realization made them both very human in that moment.

"I was a homosexual," said Jens.

"What?" asked Riley, not sure if he'd heard correctly.

"I was gay," said Jens, his voice stronger this time. Inside Jens, there was no catharsis, no instant relief as he'd seen on *Oprah*. He felt the same, but perhaps a little more relaxed.

"Okay," said Riley as he stepped back to the couch and sat down, "I'm confused. Are you okay?"

"Yes"—Jens took a deep breath—"I'm much better. I'll be fine. I just need you to know that I was—am…gay."

"So you're not a Nazi?"

"Absolutely not!" shouted Jens. "Someday, we might laugh at how ridiculous that accusation was, but not today. No, today we cry because your teachers have failed you."

Jens seemed perfectly normal now, and he sat straight in the chair. Riley still looked confused on the couch.

"Riley, listen closely," began Jens, "not everyone the Nazis threw into the camps was Jewish. Plenty of others shared that horrible fate."

Riley finally put the pieces of the puzzle in the correct order. "Like gay people?"

"Yes, like gay people, homosexuals."

Riley's exposure to modern gay issues was as dismal as his grasp of the Holocaust. In high school, he'd heard whispers about who in the school was gay, which teachers were lesbians, and so on, but he didn't know any gay people and did not spend too much time thinking about it. On the other side of the issue, he had, of course, been witness to many acts of verbal homophobia in the hockey rink. But again, since he didn't know any gay people personally, he didn't spend too much time thinking about this, either.

Riley slumped back on the couch. "So gays were put in concentration camps, too. Didn't know that."

"Now you do," said Jens. "Let's finish getting these in the trash." Jens felt the need to get back to a normal situation as soon as possible, and the cases on the floor were the perfect diversion. The two continued working, without speaking, for some time.

It was natural for someone as young as Riley to have all sorts of curiosities about knowing a gay person as old as Jens. His mind was full of questions about Germany, Nazis, and gay sex, but he realized that Jens did not want to talk further about the matter.

If Riley had to work with a gay person, he was glad it was Jens. Riley had seen the gay activists running around campus and was quite turned off by their rainbows, loudness, and partying. Even though he admired many of the gay men for taking good care of their bodies, he hated that they were always strutting around wearing clothes four sizes too small.

Riley once again noticed Jens's hands. They were still old but somehow seemed much more kind. Perhaps for the first time in his life, Riley was about to make a personal connection. Of course, he'd had friends like Jake, and now there was Abby. But he had never told anyone else how he felt about them before. "Jens, I'm glad you're not a Nazi, even if you are gay."

Jens looked up and smiled; he did not speak. Riley continued working.

That night, Jens slept well.

EIGHTEEN

"Hi, Coach," said Riley into his phone when he saw the caller ID.

"Hey, Riley," responded the low, gruff voice. "I'm calling to find out how your grade is coming along. How is that project coming?"

"I'm not sure yet, but I've been working on the project for Dr. Weber a lot."

"Good," he said. "I called her this morning, and she told me that you surprised her with how well you've been doing on it. I'm glad to hear it."

"Oh, thanks." Up to this point, he didn't have any concrete evidence that he was doing a good job, so it was nice to know that Dr. Weber was noticing his time spent with Jens.

"Well, I guess I don't have to worry about you on academic probation anymore," said the coach.

"Nope," Riley replied.

"I talked to the trainer, too," continued the coach. "He says your lifting is going good, and you've been getting plenty of ice time. But he thinks you're slacking on cardio."

"Yeah," Riley said, "I know."

"Well, it's not that big a deal to me," the coach said. "I think ice time is the most important, but it would be good if you could go for a run a couple times a week. It's nice enough outside. Just a few miles maybe three times a week."

"I can do that," Riley said.

"All right then," concluded the coach, "I'm counting on you. We've got some good new blood coming out of Eden Prairie next fall, but we're going to need you to beat those faggots up in Duluth. I know we play a lot of teams, but I hate that bastard coach they got up there. Let's send those faggots back up north to their frozen lake where they belong!"

The coach hung up abruptly, as usual. Riley groaned and turned off his phone.

NINETEEN

"They should give us permission to arrest people who check their phones at the dinner table," said Officer Weber to his wife.

"It's just the two of us," she replied.

"Why does that matter?" he asked.

She laughed. "I've seen you before. I've already heard all you have to say." She glanced back at her phone and looked through several e-mails from her university Gmail account.

He knew that it would not make a difference to protest; she loved her job and took great pride in the quick response she offered students. He also realized that with the exorbitant fee that the students paid to take her course, it was the least she could do to be there when they needed her.

When Jade noticed a message from Riley Hunter, she selected it immediately.

Prof Weber—he's not a nazi—i don't know if i can say anything about it right now but will get back to you when i can—Riley

TWENTY

"I was really surprised that you do texting," said Riley to Jens, who was in the passenger seat.

"Oh?" replied Jens. "Because I'm old?"

"No...yes," answered Riley. "Not even the professors on campus do it. It's really annoying always using e-mail."

"Texting is perfect for people like me," explained Jens. "I can take my time and read over the message. You know, as you get older, it's not that you can't do things, it's just that it takes more time to process mentally. With texting, I don't have to make on-the-spot decisions; I can take my time."

"Makes sense," said Riley.

Earlier that day, when he was eating breakfast in the cafeteria, Riley got a text:

Riley—This is Jens. I received your number from Dr. Weber. I have a rather large favor to ask. Can you drive me to the Mayo Clinic in Rochester? It's around 80 miles from my house. I will pay for fuel. Let me know and thank you.—Jens

Riley decided it was the least he could do after accusing Jens of being a Nazi. Through texts, Riley discovered that Jens needed a weekly ride to the Mayo Clinic to receive a special treatment for his condition. The clinic was about an hour and twenty minutes from St. Paul; it would require a lot of driving for Riley, but he was happy to spend time in the car where he normally didn't have to think about much.

"Thank you again for doing this," Jens said. "I know it's a lot to ask, but I didn't have anyone else."

"It's just once a week," replied Riley. "It's no problem, really. What kind of treatment are you having and how long will we be there each time?"

"Well," Jens said, "I have a form of Guillain-Barre syndrome that was discovered right before I met you. Anyone can develop it, and it usually runs its course in a month or so. However, because I'm eighty-eight, it has been taking a while, and it's getting worse. My doctor in St. Paul is worried that my breathing might be a problem if the syndrome starts to reach the muscles in my chest. There is a shot I can get at the Mayo Clinic that should help. I'm not sure how long we will need to be there each time. It's just one shot, but the Mayo Clinic is a big place, and I'm not sure how much hassle it is to get in and out."

"Are you doing okay at your house?"

"Well," explained Jens, "I'm usually fine. My feet and hands shake and are weak; sometimes I get numbness in my legs and arms. I just have to be careful, but so far I've been able to handle it."

"I guess driving is difficult."

"It is," Jens said. "Actually, I haven't driven in a while. There are a lot of transportation options in the metro area, so it's usually not a problem. But Rochester is far; thank you again for your time."

"I'm actually glad that I don't have to scrape the paint on your house," Riley said. "I've been dreading that since I first came there. I'd much rather be driving you every week."

"I'm just going to ignore that trim paint," Jens said with a chuckle. "I am almost ninety; hopefully I'll die before it gets too bad."

Riley didn't know if he should laugh or not. He wondered what Professor Weber would have to say about it.

"Putting off things you don't want to do is one of the biggest benefits to getting old," Jens continued. "You don't have to care about some of the things that you don't want to do."

They were leaving Inver Grove Heights, past the turn that Riley normally took to get to Hastings. It was noticeably less urban now as the highway continued southeast across seventy miles of prairie. Riley was glad he didn't have to cross this flat terrain in the middle of winter.

Jens sat and looked at the passing landscape. Even though he was ill, there was something nice about getting out of town and going for a drive; it had been a very long time since he'd been this far away from home. He looked over at Riley's strong hands as they grasped the wheel. His shiny hair was covered with a dirty baseball cap. To Jens, Riley began to represent a completely different species of human beings. This young man was from a time and place that was different, and in many ways much better, than Jens's own "good old days."

"So you didn't know that homosexuals were in the camps, did you?" Jens asked.

After much soul-searching over the past couple of days, Jens had grown more comfortable with the idea of talking to Riley about his past. At first, he thought this desire was strange, but he'd decided that it was human nature to want to impart knowledge to the young before your own time was up. Jens was eighty-eight and feeling weak; perhaps it was now or never.

"No, I never saw that in the movies or on TV. I really thought it was just Jews."

"Oh, no," Jens said. "The Nazis had many 'enemies': Jews, homosexuals, Jehovah's Witnesses, Gypsies, Catholic priests, those with mental disabilities, people with physical handicaps…it was a rather long list."

Riley had spent time considering how much he could ask Jens about that time in Germany. Naturally, he was very curious, but he didn't want to offend Jens. However, he was starting to gain confidence off the ice, probably for the first time in his life. "So is it okay to talk about the whole concentration camp thing?"

Jens was quite glad that Riley had asked; he now wanted to talk about it, but wasn't sure how to bring it up without sounding desperate or self-centered. Jens knew that once the conversation turned to the Holocaust, there would be little Riley could do to turn the topic back to modern Minnesota. "Yes," Jens said. "I would like to talk about it."

"So I can ask a question, then?"

"Of course," replied Jens, "you can ask anything. I will try to answer. If you ask something that I don't want to answer, or something that I don't think you are ready to hear, then I will tell you that."

"Fair enough."

Silence fell for a few moments. Jens assumed that Riley was attempting to figure out a way to ask a delicate question without offending him.

Riley broke the silence abruptly. "I get how they could tell if someone was Jewish or any of the other things you said the Nazis hated, but how did they know who was gay? It's not like there is a test or anything."

"That's a good question," answered Jens. "There are many ways you can know if someone is gay. You just have to be open to looking for the signs. The Nazis were good at looking, and they had many ways to catch the people they wanted."

I was sixteen years old once. I know you might find it hard to believe looking at me now, but I was. In 1941, I was sixteen and very much like all the other sixteen-year-olds of the time. I had dark hair and strong bones; my muscles were steady, and I went swimming all summer long. I remember being happy.

In 1941, I met another sixteen-year-old boy, Karl, and my life was changed forever.

We lived in Konigswinter, where I was born, outside the city of Bonn on the Rhine. It's in northwest Germany, not too far from the French border. Konigswinter was small at the time and very different from the big cities of Europe.

In Berlin, there were all sorts of places for gay people to congregate. I'll use the word gay as I'm talking to you, Riley, because homosexual seems wrong to say. When I think of the word homosexual now, it sounds like a medical label. You have to understand that back then, many, including myself, thought we did have a medical disorder. But I don't think like that now. So

Michael Fridgen

I like saying gay better than homosexual, and I'm glad America uses it.

Anyway, Berlin was thriving with gay people under the Weimar Republic. But in rural Germany, like Konigswinter, things were bad. The end of World War One marked the beginning of unbelievable hardship for the German people. You see, we were being punished by England and the rest of Europe for what we, as a country, tried to do during the First World War. That punishment was in the form of harsh economic sanctions that made it impossible for Germany to rebuild. Our German money became essentially worthless, and people worked very hard for very little.

My father was a bookkeeper for a merchant in our town; my mother made extra money taking care of an elderly woman named Josephine, who lived in the basement in our house. I did not have any brothers or sisters, because my parents didn't think they could afford them. I went to school and helped my mother at home. I was always a good reader, and school was easy for me. In the summer, I swam in the river. It didn't cost anything to do that.

I don't remember the first time I ever heard the word "Nazi." I don't remember learning who Hitler was; I'd just always known, I guess. I was born in 1925, you see, and I'd lived during the transition years from the Weimar Republic to the Third Reich. I recall hearing things and seeing faces and looks; I remember my parents stopping their discussions when I'd enter a room. But propelled by the bad economy, the Nazis moved forward. By the time I came of age in 1941, the Nazis were fully in place with Hitler as their führer, and Europe was once again at war.

We all knew something bad was happening to people who were Jewish, but nobody said anything. I know how hard the Nazis were on the Jewish people leading up to the war, but we weren't Jewish, and back then we paid little attention. Remember, we were barely scraping by ourselves.

Karl was the son of the man who owned the store where my father worked. One day, when I was sixteen, I stopped by the store to bring my father the lunch he'd forgotten. That was the first time I saw Karl. He was standing behind the cash register in black dress pants and a white shirt; he wore a blue apron with the name of the store stitched on it. His hair was brown—just like mine, well, before it turned white. His eyes were deep and a color between green and yellow.

When I walked in, Karl said, "Can I help you?"

Those were the first words he spoke to me. I told him that I was looking for Klaus Jaenisch and that I knew my way to his back office; I also said who I was.

There was no such thing as "love at first sight" for gay people, especially back then. I felt some kind of strong connection from the way he looked at me, but it took quite a long time for us to figure out what was going on.

Riley, despite the war and the conditions in Germany, 1941 and the beginning of 1942 was the happiest time of my life. I started hanging around the store more often; Karl and I talked a lot. We started doing things around town, especially going to the cinema. He was funny and smart, and he liked the same books that I did.

My parents were extremely happy that I'd become friends with the son of my father's boss. They were hoping that maybe I could get a job at the store, or that somehow our friendship would make it more possible for my father to get a raise.

Karl talked about his parents a lot. His mother went on frequent long trips to Paris to get things for the store. His father was a dedicated merchant who felt the need to stay quite connected to the business community in Konigswinter and Bonn. Karl thought they were distant and told me he liked my mother better than his own. I tried to get him to understand that they were important businesspeople and had obligations to fulfill.

We were great friends who hung out and talked a lot, nothing more, though from the beginning, I knew that I was sexually attracted to him. I had always known I was gay, but of course, I had no way to explain or think about it, except to feel that there was something wrong with me. It was 1941, and nobody outside of Berlin talked about such things. I was hoping that if I could avoid the war, I would marry a woman and go into bookkeeping. I hoped my feelings toward other men would just go away, but that never happened.

On New Year's Eve, the last day of 1941—in Germany we call that holiday Silvester—Karl had come to our house for dinner, because his parents were in Paris celebrating the new year with an important supplier of goods for their store. It was a very cold night, so my father suggested that Karl stay with us so that he would not have to walk home and start a fire in his own house. My father did not know how wealthy Karl was and that his family's home had a modern heating system that was far superior to our woodstove. But Karl humored him and stayed.

My parents had their own room, with their own tiny woodstove, upstairs. Since the elderly woman was downstairs, I was left to sleep in the main room. I had a small single mattress that we kept in the closet during the day and moved next to the big stove at night. My mother made a bed for Karl out of blankets and quilts four feet away from me, also in front of the stove. I felt bad that Karl was sacrificing his own real bed to sleep on our floor, but he assured me that he didn't mind.

As we were falling asleep, Karl spoke. He told me he wanted to ask me something, but he didn't want me to stop being his friend. I said okay.

He asked me, "Do you ever think about men the way that you are supposed to think about women?"

Well, I can tell you, my heart came right out of my body! I couldn't believe he was asking the very thing that I had spent so much time thinking about. I told him, "Yes, I think there is something wrong with me."

"I feel that same way," he said.

Karl and I were silent for a long time. I remember I was incredibly mixed up with emotion. I was so happy that he felt the same way as me, but I was sad that there was something wrong with him, too. Then, after some time had passed, I heard his

quilts rustle around, and he scooted himself over to my mattress. He sat next to
me.

My heart was beating so fast! All these
years later, I can still feel how I felt
at that moment. I also sat up, although
because of the mattress I was a little bit
higher than him. He reached out with his
right hand and placed it on my left shoulder. I took my own shaking right hand and
put it on his chest. We stayed like that
for some time, just gently touching each
other. It was dark, but in the glow of the
woodstove I saw him looking at me.

Then, Karl leaned in toward me, and I
took the cue to do the same. We kissed. It
was nothing long or romantic like we had
seen in the movies, but it was soft and
relaxing, and I felt at peace. Perhaps I've
never felt that much at peace ever again.

Over the next few months, we refrained
from talking about that night and went back
to our usual friendship. I often thought
about touching him again, or at least talking about it. But honestly, it was just
something we knew we could never talk about
or repeat. However, it grew increasingly
difficult as our sixteen-year-old bodies
wanted more, and our minds knew the other
wanted it, too.

Two months later, I was visiting my father at the store. I didn't know Karl was there, and as I walked down the back hall, we accidentally ran into each other. I greeted him and apologized for stepping on his foot. We looked at each other, and I can still see the way his eyes probed mine. Without thinking, I grabbed him quickly and embraced him with both arms. We kissed, but this time it was much longer; even now I remember exactly how it felt. This time, it was long and intense as we pulled each other as close as possible. This kiss *was* like in the movies.

I wanted it to last forever, but it didn't. His own father had seen it; we had not seen him in the darkness of the store-room. Karl never told me, and I wouldn't find out for another two months, but his father was a very loyal Nazi.

"You're embarrassed," Jens said as he looked at Riley who was still driving the car. "I've been talking too much."

"No," Riley replied, "I like hearing about it. Your life was so different from mine."

The truth was, Riley was a bit embarrassed at hearing about the gay kissing and touching, but he was genuinely fascinated that two people could fall in love during such a horrible time. The images he created in his mind of Jens and Karl were still in the same black-and-white footage he had seen on television. But now, Riley was now quite curious about what happened next, just as if he were watching a movie. He was dying to find out what had Karl's father done, and how that had led to Jens's imprisonment.

"We must be almost there," Jens said. "Let me find out where to go." He pulled out a few sheets of paper from his light jacket and searched through them for directions.

"Seriously, Jens," Riley said unexpectedly, "I don't mind hearing about Germany at all, if you don't mind talking about it." Although he was developing empathy for Jens, it was more the curiosity of the next chapter that made him say this.

"Thank you, Riley," said Jens. "I have not spoken of these things before. It feels good, and nobody could be more surprised at that than I am."

Each week, until the end of the term and beyond, Riley drove Jens to the Mayo Clinic and heard more of the story. He thought about Jens a lot; he thought about Jake almost as much. He didn't spend so much time thinking about himself and hockey anymore.

TWENTY ONE

"**H**ow many gay people do you know?" Riley asked Abby as they walked across the grassy mall in front of the oldest library on campus.

"Why?" she responded. "Are you thinking of becoming one?"

"I'm serious."

"You've been serious a lot lately."

"Yeah," Riley said, "I'm really into this project for my soc. class."

He had not told her that Jens was gay, and he didn't know if she knew the history of homosexuals in the Holocaust. Riley had not said anything to Professor Weber, either. Because of how the discussions with Jens progressed, Riley did not think that Jens was comfortable with other people knowing he was gay. Riley wondered if he should ask him whether it was all right to talk about it with other people, but he hadn't done that yet.

"I had a really good gay friend in high school," Abby said as they came to the concrete sidewalk running around the perimeter of the mall.

They stepped onto the sidewalk and turned toward Riley's dorm. Since it was very near the end of the term, there was a lot of action on campus. Students were not only busy studying for finals, but they were making plans for the summer.

"A guy or a girl?" asked Riley.

"He was a guy, Anthony," answered Abby. "It was like that show *Will and Grace* from the nineties. We were together a lot. He was a ton of fun."

"Do you still hang out with him?" asked Riley. "I've never heard you talk about him before."

"Nope. I'm not sure what happened," she answered. "After graduation, he went to Hamline and I came here. We sort of stopped hanging out this summer. Hamline isn't that far from here, but I guess we had kind of an argument."

Riley asked, "Over what?"

"You know about that gay marriage vote we had?" she said.

"Yeah," said Riley. "One of the guys on the Hastings hockey team had a gay uncle and told me about it. He wanted me to go out and vote for gay marriage."

"Did you?" Abby asked.

"No," replied Riley. "I wasn't eighteen when the vote happened. Were you?"

"I'd just turned eighteen but I didn't really get around to it," Abby said with a touch of remorse in her voice. "Anthony was really upset that I didn't vote. It's why we stopped hanging out, why we had an argument."

"Over a vote?" Riley asked.

"Anthony got really into working on it," Abby explained. "He was busy all summer knocking on doors and calling people. By the middle of June, it was all he could talk about. I wasn't against it or anything like that. I guess I just didn't care enough. I was tired of waiting around for him all the time, and I told him that he needed to get a real life instead of working on gay marriage. I mean, the guy wasn't even dating anyone, so why did he care about it? Anyway, he got angry with me and just stopped calling me."

"You should call him and apologize," Riley suggested without hesitation.

"It's all done now," she said. "He's probably doing great at Hamline and has a ton of gay friends."

"The vote was important to him," said Riley. "It doesn't matter why, it just matters that he cared a lot about it. At least acknowledge that and apologize to him."

Abby looked up at Riley, studied him for a second, then shrugged her shoulders and kept walking. She was surprised by Riley taking Anthony's side but didn't think it was worth getting into an argument.

"Well," she said, "if you're going to be gay, can you at least wait until next month? I just got a new pack of birth control pills today. I hope I didn't waste my money."

"Don't worry." He pulled her toward him. "We won't waste them. There's no danger of me turning gay anytime soon, especially with you around."

They laughed and flip-flopped their way across campus.

TWENTY TWO

After his father ran me out of the store that day, I didn't see or hear anything from Karl for two months. I was very sad but not afraid. There wasn't much I could do about things, anyway; there was no way I could talk to my parents about it. I was really quite ignorant about the true situation with the Third Reich. Of course, I'd overheard adults talking about Jewish people, sometimes with approval and sometimes with a taste of disgust. I'd heard about the boycott of Jewish stores and the vandalism. I'd even heard some of the rumors about the work camps being built across the country. These things had, of course, been happening for some time. But I was young and our town was small. When I heard these things, like any teenager even today, I didn't pay attention unless it had something to do with my family, my town, or me. Also, I didn't know anything about what was happening to gay people in Berlin or anywhere else in Germany.

I incorrectly assumed that Karl was okay. I thought his father was just disappointed and would dismiss the kiss he saw as a one-time mistake. I think a lot of us, probably all German citizens, were just waiting with our lives on hold until more stability would come. I was hoping that after a few more months, Karl would contact me, and everything would return to normal.

But then, one day that spring, everything changed, and my life was altered forever.

My father was at work and my mother sent me to the market with a list of supplies that the woman downstairs needed. When I returned, I entered the house to find my mother sitting at the small kitchen table across from a uniformed officer of the Gestapo. She looked at me with more fear than I'd ever seen. However, she was not crying.

"Jens," she said, "this man would like to ask you a few questions in town."

I asked her what it was all about. She said that she had no idea.

"We will not burden your mother with this. You will come with me," the Gestapo officer interrupted our conversation. He got up from the table and motioned for me to follow him.

I set the sacks of groceries right on the floor. I remember wondering if I should at least bring the sacks into the room and place them on the table, but all of us were taught to have great fear of the Gestapo. It was better that my mother deal with the groceries rather than me risking making some breach of protocol.

As I walked through the door behind the man, I heard my mother say, "Jens, be careful."

Those were the last words I ever heard her speak.

I followed the Gestapo officer down the street and around several corners. I was too shy to walk right next to him and, of course, I had no idea what the protocol would be in this situation. People started to stare at the two of us. They knew that this was not good, and I could almost see their minds attempting to figure out what I had done wrong.

Of course, I still thought this was all a mistake. I couldn't think of anything I had done that the Gestapo would be interested in. I was still ignorant at this point and had every intention of being back in my home having dinner with Mother and Father that evening. Had I not been so naïve, I might have tried to escape through an alley. In fact, I spent many nights over the next years imagining how I could have escaped the Gestapo and somehow made it out of Germany.

We came to one of the main streets in Konigswinter, where there was a restaurant that had a large banquet room in the back. I had been to a couple of weddings and other events with my parents in this room. However, now the Gestapo was using that room as their headquarters in our town. The long rows of tables had been moved to make a ring of tables around the perimeter. Several of the tables had people working at them, and others were empty.

As I followed the man through the room, I looked up and noticed the large chandelier that hung in the middle of the ceiling. I remembered staring at that chandelier when I got bored at those parties. Opposite the door we entered, there was still the large wooden platform that served as a stage.

We walked to a table in the corner and the officer told a man sitting behind it that he had Jens Jaenisch to see the captain. I cringed at the sound of my name, because it confirmed that they really wanted to talk to me. I guess I was still hoping that they had the wrong person.

The man at the table stood, turned, and stepped to a door that led to the kitchen. He disappeared for just a moment then returned and said that I should follow him.

Leaving the Gestapo officer who brought me, I followed the new officer to a small

office off the kitchen, evidently the former office for the chef of the banquet room.
A shelf holding cookbooks was fixed to the
wall and hung over the side of a wooden
desk where a man now sat. Instead of the
white jacket and chef's hat, though, this
man wore a uniform befitting his rank as a
captain. I was immediately frightened of
him, as he looked quite imposing. Remember,
I was still young to be going through all
this without my parents.

He told me to sit in the chair in front
of the desk, which I did. The other officer
closed the door as he left.

The captain asked what my name was and
where I lived; I told him.

"Do you know a Karl Schneider?" he asked.

I told him that Karl was the son of the
man who owned the store where my father
worked as a bookkeeper.

"How well do you know him?" he asked.

"We are friends. We go to the movies and
stuff like that," I said. "I met him at the
store. We both like the same kinds of books."

"Hmmm," replied the Captain in a very
snarky tone. He looked at me and raised an
eyebrow when I mentioned books. Something
inside of me told me not to talk about reading or learning in front of him.

"Have you seen Karl Schneider around
lately?" the captain asked.

I told him that I had not seen him.

"Do you know where Karl Schneider has been for the last two weeks?" he asked.

"I'm sorry, sir, no. I haven't seen him." I was so young and ignorant. The thought that this had something to do with the kiss had crossed my mind, but I was young and still hoped to leave that room and go home.

"Karl Schneider sent you a letter the day before yesterday."

"I'm sorry, again, sir," I replied. "I haven't received any letters in a while, especially not from Karl."

"Oh, I know that," said the captain quickly. "Nobody at your house has received any mail for over a week now. It's all sitting on a table out there." He gestured toward the kitchen and the ballroom beyond.

I thought it was strange that our mail was there, but I didn't react to the news.

"Karl Schneider's father is a great friend of the Third Reich," continued the captain. "However, his heart has been broken where it concerns his son. The Gestapo thought it was wise to monitor your family's mail, because we had reason to believe that Karl might try to contact you."

I remained silent. A growing sickness was forming in my stomach.

"Would you like to see the letter that Karl sent you?" asked the captain.

Something in that letter had caused the Gestapo to find me and question me. I was finally starting to get concerned, as I should have been all along. This was a much bigger deal than I'd thought.

I didn't know how to respond to the captain. Was it better just to tell him that I didn't want to see the letter? I considered the different possible answers, not knowing if there was a correct one or not. We had all heard enough about the Gestapo to know that questions could be tricks, and answers could be dangerous.

However, the captain already had the letter in front of him on his desk, and he did not give me the chance to answer his question. Regardless of whether I wanted to read it or not, he smoothed it out and turned it so that I could see it.

I only had one chance to read that letter, Riley, but I'm telling you, it burned itself on my mind, and I still know every word. Practically every night of my life for the last seventy-three years, I have repeated that letter as I fall asleep. Of course, the image in my mind is in the original German, but I remember it so well that sometimes I think about it in English.

Dear Jens,

I hope this letter finds you well, and I am very sorry that I have not seen you in a while. I write to you secretly, and I know you will destroy this letter when you are through with it. My mother has taken me to Berlin where a doctor who is friendly with the Reich can treat me. I have been offered the choice of being castrated or going to a work camp. I am very glad that I have chosen to be castrated, as I will finally be free of the disorder we both share. I want you to know that you mean a great much to me, and I believe that I love you. After my procedure, I will not be able to have the same affection for you. I hope you will not have to face the Gestapo, but if you do, I beg of you to choose castration so that you may also be free.

With affection,

Karl

The Gestapo captain saw that I'd finished reading the letter and rotated it back to face him. He sat back in his chair and grabbed a pen with his right hand; he tapped the pen randomly on the desk as he spoke. "So," he said to me without hesitation, "you are a filthy faggot!"

Of course, in German, we had many slang words for homosexuals. Some of those words are long gone and don't mean very much today, others are still around. I will use the word faggot because it is the closest translation to an English derogatory word for homosexuals. Regardless, you should think of it as a terrible word, because I certainly did when I heard it from the Gestapo captain.

Again he said to me, "You are a filthy faggot!"

I didn't know what to do. You have to remember that I was so young and had heard many people around town, including my parents, speak of Nazis with great fear. I also heard people say horrible things about homosexuals. Nothing in my short life—not my parents, school, or church—prepared me for what I should do in that moment. I just sat there.

"You will agree with me!" he yelled. "You are a filthy faggot!"

"Yes," I said.

"No, repeat it!" he yelled again.

"Yes!" I said much louder.

"No, faggot!" he screamed at me. "Repeat the whole thing, you filthy pig!"

"Oh," I said as I finally understood. "Yes, I am a filthy faggot."

It actually didn't bother me that much to say it, because I really didn't feel like I was one. I was willing to say anything to get back home to my mother and father.

"That's what I thought," the Gestapo captain said calmly.

The captain grabbed a form from a stack of papers that was sitting on the left side of the desk. He began to fill out the form as we continued to talk.

"Do you know what Paragraph 175 is, faggot?" he asked.

"No, sir," I said.

"It's a law that sends faggots to prison," the captain explained. "In the old republic, the police had to catch you in the act of having sex or kissing another man. Now, it's different. Our leader gave the order to Heinrich Himmler to revise the law in order to protect the Aryan race from your sickness."

I was too young to think about things like due process and trials. I don't remember thinking about what rights I might have had. I just remember sitting there and letting this happen to me.

The captain held up Karl's letter. "Now, in the Third Reich, this letter is plenty of evidence. In fact, it's more than enough evidence. We have proof from the letter and from your own filthy mouth that you are a faggot. All we really need is the suspicion of a neighbor to convict, but we have much more than that here."

The Iron Words

"Sir"—I finally wanted to seek some help—"can I talk to my father?"

The Gestapo captain looked at me sharply and yelled, "Your father heard about his faggot son and hanged himself! I'm sure your mother will do the same."

I knew there was no way that was true, but it was the Gestapo's immature way of saying that I would not be able to see them. Finally, I began to understand that I was not going home that night. I would have to learn how to listen and speak to these people using their own warped version of German.

The captain then got up, walked over to the door, opened it, and yelled something out of it. He turned back to give me my sentence. "You will be taken to a work camp where you can serve your country by making supplies for the war," he said. "You will not be able to corrupt the youth of Germany in there, and our race will be safe from at least one more faggot."

"Sir!" I said to him rather loudly and desperately, "can I not choose to be seen by a doctor? In the letter, Karl—"

He held up his hand and turned his head away from me. "No!" he shouted. "Unfortunately, your father is not as friendly with the Reich. There will be no easy life of castration for you. We can get a confession from

Karl Schneider that you corrupted him into your sick ways. And, you filthy faggot, if you want to live, you'd better forget the name of Karl Schneider. Speaking another man's name in that manner will bring you instant death!"

By that time, the officer from the dining room returned and grabbed me out of the chair. As I was pushed through the door and into the kitchen, the captain tripped me, and I fell on the hard floor. I tried to get up and keep walking as the two of them were kicking me and spitting at me. Somehow, in a daze, I made it to the ballroom and saw the chandelier.

"How old were you at this point?" Riley asked as the car sped again through the southern Minnesota prairie.

"I had just turned seventeen," replied the aged voice. "Too young."

"Seventeen," Riley said in a low voice. He shook his head. "That was just two years ago for me."

"Fortunately," replied Jens, "times have changed. And despite what some may tell you, I believe that they have changed for the better."

"You must have been so angry in that office!" exclaimed Riley.

"The anger didn't come until later," Jens said. "I think I was in shock for some time until the finality of it all set in. I didn't feel real anger until probably twenty or thirty years later. Strange, I guess."

"Do you feel anger when you talk about it now?" Riley asked. "I don't want you to be mad that you are telling me about it."

"No, I'm not angry anymore," said Jens as he sighed. "No, now, at this point in my life, I'm just disappointed. You know, I've had a good life here in Minnesota, and I got to do a lot of things I wanted. I don't want you to think that I've been a miserable old man for the last seventy years. I guess, like most people, I have had some disappointments. Although, I could argue that my disappointments are perhaps greater than most because of the situation I was in back in Germany.

"But what I'm most disappointed about is that I never got to sleep with Karl. Now, I don't mean sex, Riley. I mean sleep. Sure, there was that one night in front of the stove, but a few feet separated us. To this day, I still want to know what it would be like to sleep next to Karl, naked and holding each other. That's all."

TWENTY THREE

"Mrs. Fredrichs, you need to calm down," said the voice on the phone.

"But you are telling me that our whole case is ruined," Dot cried. "You're saying that this is really all Jacob's fault, and there is nothing we can do about it."

"No," responded Jake's attorney, Ms. Mari Bender, "please don't put words in my mouth. I'm only telling you that we have to find a new approach. We cannot place all the blame on Klonopin, at least not in the way we were planning before."

"But Klonopin is dangerous, and that man let my son have it! Without the pressure from the Athletic Department, my son would be walking!"

"Mrs. Fredrichs, there is actually no evidence of that. You know that I want what is best for Jacob and his future; I know that you want that, too. We have to face the facts and the research. We will have no chance of winning any settlement if we don't—and I mean all of us—accept that Jacob had to have known he'd been taking Klonopin."

"But," Dot said, "what about the expert who said that people can take Klonopin without even knowing it? That doctor must have research to prove Jake's case."

"Mrs. Fredrichs, please listen carefully," replied the attorney. "That expert psychiatrist has just had his license revoked for negligence to patients. It turns out that he's had four patients kill themselves this year, because he is firmly opposed to any kind of psychiatric medication! His failure to treat patients led to their deaths. We will never get a court to qualify him as an expert witness when clearly he has a bias that costs lives."

"Is there nobody else who knows about Klonopin and how dangerous it is?"

"That's my point," Ms. Bender said. "There isn't anyone who will testify to that, because it isn't true. I'm very sorry, Mrs. Fredrichs, but there is no evidence that you can take Klonopin without knowing it. All the research, and all the physicians we can find, say that it is a safe drug and quite useful for treating anxiety when used properly."

"So that's it, then," Dot said dejectedly. "It must have been all Jacob's fault. We just deal with that and go on our merry way, right?"

"No, Mrs. Fredrichs, please listen," the attorney replied. "We just have to change our approach. We can no longer say that Jacob was taking Klonopin without his knowledge. However, we can still make a case that the Athletic Department provided the initial prescriptions of an addictive substance; they introduced it to the athletes. We will also pursue the fact that the university physician is not a psychiatrist and did not provide the correct education about Klonopin to Jacob. Basically, it is our case that it is their fault that Jacob had Klonopin in the first place and didn't know how to use it correctly. Jacob didn't know how to respect the medication, because he hadn't been informed about it."

Mrs. Fred was finally calm and listened carefully to the attorney's words. She was not an unreasonable person and began to understand the change in their case.

"All right," she said, "I understand. Let me do some more reading about it, and we'll talk again soon. I want to talk to a friend of mine and read a bit more about Klonopin."

"And Mrs. Fredrichs," Ms. Bender added, "you must get Jacob to admit he was using Klonopin. He had to know he was taking high doses of it. We can't have him lying, but that doesn't change the fact that he got the initial prescription from the team doctor. Do you understand that point? Our case is much stronger if Jacob fully admits that he knew what he was doing."

"I will talk to him," Dot responded sadly.

Dot ended the call without saying another word to the attorney. She was dreading the discussion she would now have to have with Jacob. Mrs. Fred thought that Jacob was doing a superb job by acknowledging his responsibility for his actions that night. But now, she believed that he must have been keeping his Klonopin abuse a secret. Once again, she was disappointed in her son and his behavior.

TWENTY FOUR

It was the first night I had ever spent away from my parents. After I'd been condemned by the Gestapo captain, without any sort of trial or testimony, I was kicked out to the big dining room and told to sit on the floor next to one of the large wooden tables. A Gestapo officer took a sort of primitive handcuff and put one end around my right wrist; the other end he locked around the leg of the table.

I was the only person chained in this way to a table. I thought it was strange that the others in the room kept working as if there was nothing unusual about a young man sitting on the floor in the midst of an elegant banquet hall with handcuffs on. As the night began to fall, three other men were brought into the room and chained, each to his own table. These men were all quite a bit older than me, and I wondered if they were being held there on the same charge. None of us spoke during the night because one officer, who had no doubt drawn the short straw, stayed and watched over us with a rifle. It was very dark in the room as all the lights were turned off. The officer occasionally used a flashlight to keep an eye on us.

I didn't sleep very much. However, at one point I must have fallen asleep, because the officer woke me when it was my turn to be escorted to the toilet. Other than that, the night was filled with thoughts of my parents. I was full of panic for what they must be going through while I was in there. I hoped against hope that they were not foolish enough to come to the restaurant to ask about me. I knew now that they would have been chained to tables as well.

So I am not sure if I woke up in the morning, or if I was already awake when the sun began to show through the high windows. Regardless, the four of us chained to tables began to stir when the other Gestapo officers arrived for their day of work. They went about their business as if nothing unusual was taking place. One officer even began working at the very table I was chained to without so much as a glance!

Before long, two new officers arrived with rifles and stood by the doors that led to the regular restaurant dining room. The officer who had been with us during the night came to each of us and unlocked our chains. He instructed us to go with the men with the rifles. When he came to me, I told him that I had to use the toilet. He yelled at me and said that there was no time. He grabbed my shoulders and brought me to my feet then pushed me toward the door. I stumbled and fell; he kicked me hard on the upper thigh with his big boots. Still none of the newly arrived workers paid any attention.

The four of us walked in a group, with one rifleman in front and one in back. We walked through the restaurant, where breakfast was being served to Gestapo officers. I'm not sure if the owner and cooks were doing this willingly or not. It was hard to tell who was friendly to the Reich, and who just wanted to stay alive and well.

We left the restaurant and walked along one of the larger streets in town. People stared at us; I'm not sure what they were thinking. I was not a religious person even then, but I found myself desperately praying that my parents would not see this parade. However, I knew that Konigswinter was a small enough town that they would surely hear about their son being paraded through town with three other criminals.

In about fifteen minutes we arrived at the small Konigswinter train station. A train was already parked next to the platform. I remember thinking how quiet it was. There was an engine followed by any number of box-cars, the kind that typically held freight. I didn't see any regular passengers, or even other civilians, around. Everyone standing beside the train was a uniformed soldier.

We were led down the platform to a man who was wearing a different uniform than the Gestapo. This was the first time I saw a member of the infamous SS; it would not be the last. I would later find out that this particular man was the lowest rank of SS and was probably attempting to prove himself for a promotion. Next to this SS officer, two of the freight cars were open.

We walked up to the cars. I was the first to be shoved in, and one of the other three was pushed after me. I assumed the other two were put in the next car, but I don't know that for sure. As he was pulling the freight car door shut, I saw the face of the young SS, not all that much older than me. I heard the chain and lock close us in.

It was quite dim in there. I went to one of the far corners and sat, leaning against two of the walls. I started to sob, but I tried very hard not to let the other man notice my despair. Only a moment after the door was closed, the train started to move. Aside from the normal noise of the train, it was very quiet. I didn't want to leave

Konigswinter, and my body lurched with the movement of the train as I silently sobbed.

I don't know how long I cried, but at some point I decided to pull myself together. I recited some poetry to myself that I had memorized; it was the only thing I could think of to do to get my mind off my situation. It didn't really work, because I kept thinking of the Gestapo captain, the kicking and spitting; my upper thigh hurt terribly from the last kick in the banquet hall.

Finally, I took this opportunity to look at the man who had been thrown in with me. He was probably fifty years old, although I'm not quite sure. Everyone looks fifty when you're seventeen. He was rather large, and by that I mean fat. He had no hair and a bushy black beard. He didn't look like someone I really wanted to get to know.

I'm not sure how far we had traveled when I began to notice that I very much had to use the toilet. The pressure was getting almost too much to bear, but I forced myself to sit and concentrate on poetry. Then I knew that I had no choice.

I shouted across to the other man, "Where do you suppose we use the toilet? Do you think they will stop?"

"Idiot, young idiot," he yelled back at me. "There's no stopping this thing. Do you know who you're dealing with? Do you know who is driving this train? The Nazis don't care about your piss. Just go over in that corner; we'll have to get used to each other's stench."

He gestured to a corner, and I went over to it. It was so dim in this part of the car that I was only a little self-conscious. I took my pants a little way down and did what I had to do. The strong urine smell was horrible, but there were much worse smells to come.

When I returned to my own corner, the man asked, "What are you convicted of?"

"I'm not sure," I said.

"Hmmm, that doesn't sound right," he said. "Even the Jews know what they're in for."

I sat silent.

"The three of us were in the regular jail. We're convicted killers," he said. "The Nazis decided to clear the jails and move us to the camps. Filthy pigs."

I stayed silent. I wasn't sure whether he was telling me this to have some kind of power over me, or to just plain scare me.

He continued, "I couldn't stand my wife's sister who was living with us. She pushed herself into my business one too many times. I lost my temper and stabbed her with a knife in front of my wife."

The Iron Words

I remained silent and did not respond to his morbid story.

"You're awfully young," he said as he considered me. "How old are you?"

"I'm seventeen."

"I think I know why you're in here," he said me in a very sly voice. "Sure, in Berlin there might be some seventeen-year-old killers, but not in a small town like Konigswinter. If you had stolen something, you'd be rehabilitating in the Hitler Youth right now. They would never put one Jew in with a convict, and you don't look Jewish anyway. You don't look like a Gypsy, either. But I saw the way you walked outside—a little too graceful for my taste. I think you're a 175-er."

I was shocked that he had figured it out but decided to play dumb. I told him that I didn't know what he was talking about.

He said, "You're a 175-er. A filthy faggot."

I told him that I was not.

I saw his shadow get up from his corner of the train car and heard the sounds of his prison-issued shoes as he walked over to me. He was even larger than I thought.

He said calmly, "Here, 175-er, make yourself useful."

He unzipped his pants and pulled out his penis. He grabbed me around the back of my neck with one of his disgusting hands. He shoved his penis in my mouth. It was repulsive, and I hated him. I have never forgotten his sounds and his taste. But I was so scared and had no idea what to do.

That was my first sexual encounter with another human.

The train rattled on for I'm not sure how long, but it seemed like an eternity. Every so often, we would stop. I'd see the same young SS face when he'd unlock the car and throw in two pieces of bread. There was no water, and I was getting extremely thirsty. I also grew very hungry because the man in the car with me always took my bread. The stench of his defecation was horrendous. I don't recall the train ride as a cohesive story anymore; I only see, smell, and feel the images.

But once more he stuck his penis in my mouth. I started crying loudly.

"What are you crying for, filthy faggot?" he asked me. "You're supposed to like this sort of thing. I'm the normal one in here. I'm the one who likes to have sex with women. You are a filthy faggot, but you will do."

He tackled me in the corner and tore off my pants. He had anal sex with me.

The rest of the train trip I was silent. I was not able to cry anymore. But aside

The Iron Words

from my thoughts about hunger and thirst, I
thought a lot about that horrible, fat man.
He said he was the normal one, although
he was the one who killed someone, stole
food, and raped a defenseless young boy in
a locked train car.

TWENTY FIVE

Abby was sitting on a ledge outside the entrance to Riley's dorm building when he walked up the concrete steps carrying his gym bag. He'd spent the afternoon with one of the team trainers and was hoping to take a nap. He had mixed feelings when he saw Abby sitting there.

"Hey, you!" she called as he approached.

"Hey."

"You getting back from training?"

"Yep." He smiled at her when he reached her level and opened the door for them both. They walked to his room in silence. Riley fumbled though his gym bag for his room key. His hair was still damp from the shower he had taken at the athletic facility.

As soon as he opened the door for her, Abby walked into the room, threw her phone on the desk, and flung herself on his bed.

"It's hot in here," she said. "Turn on the air."

Riley sighed and adjusted the thermostat next to the door. He didn't know how rare it was to have an air-conditioned dorm at the University of Minnesota, and how even rarer it was to be able to control it yourself. The perks of being an athlete were unappreciated unless the athlete spent time with regular students in regular dorms.

Abby studied him as he placed his gym bag on the floor and his keys next to her phone on the desk. She reminded herself how lucky she had been to be able to get him before some other girl swooped in. Not only was he a star player with good professional prospects, but also he was absolutely gorgeous.

Riley kicked off his flip-flops, walked over to the bed, and crashed on it. He pushed Abby to the side of the bed and against the wall. She grunted and laughed.

"I'm tired," he said. "I want to take a nap."

She said with a sly tone, "I'll help you relax." She laughed again.

Riley turned so he was lying on his back. Abby scooted her body up and sat on his thighs; she was not heavy. She bent over and massaged his chest and arms over his T-shirt. Riley took a very deep breath.

"See," she said, "you need me to help you relax. Don't forget that."

He gave a small smile as she sat straighter and pulled down his gym shorts. He breathed deeply again. But for the first time during sex, something strange began in Riley's mind. Instead of thinking about Abby, or some other attractive girl, Riley started to see a series of images in his mind. There was Jens, at seventeen, in the Gestapo office. There was Jens, again, listening to his mother tell him to be careful as he left the house. Another image of Jens, but this time in the train car with the disgusting fat man. And now, an image of Jake in his wheelchair being pushed by Mrs. Fred. In his mind, he saw the caring and compassion that Mrs. Fred had for her son.

"Stop!" he shouted. The force of his voice startled them both; he had used his hands to push her away.

"What?" she said, in a normal voice. "Did I hurt you?"

"No," he said, "I'm just not in the mood."

"Not in the mood? You're an American college boy with a hot body and an even hotter girlfriend. What do you mean you're not in the mood?"

"It's not going to happen, Abby," he said. "Please get out of here."

"Okay, okay," she said reluctantly. "I'll just stay and sleep with you."

"No, Abby, I want you to leave."

Riley looked at her and saw a different person. Instead of hot sex and playfulness, he now saw calculation and manipulation. He didn't want that anymore.

"We're done, Abby." He pulled up his gym shorts and got out of the bed.

"What?"

"I can't do this with you anymore," he answered. "It's just not going to work. I can't explain it, but I want to take a break from sex for a while."

Abby wondered what she had done wrong, but then she dismissed her thoughts as she fell back on her pride and her other prospect. "Fine," she said. She got up and grabbed her phone from the desk. "You don't know what you're missing. I would have been very good for you, but oh well. You're not the only fish in the sea, Riley Hunter. You're not the only hot-body athlete around here. Besides, I've got a football player who always likes it when I stop by!"

"Good," he said. "I hope the two of you are very happy."

She reached for the door handle and opened the door, then turned to face him one last time. Her face turned cold as she straightened her body and looked at him defiantly. "Oh, now I get it. This is because you're gay. Isn't it?"

"Get out!"

She turned in one quick motion and started down the hall. Riley crossed to the door and slammed it. Then he flung himself on the bed for a peaceful nap.

TWENTY SIX

"I hope it wasn't too much trouble to re-schedule your appointment," Riley said as he picked up Jens in St. Paul.

"It was not a problem at all. The Mayo Clinic has a system for my shots. I don't really make appointments."

"Good," said Riley. "I found out at short notice that I had a chance to practice with some former Olympians from the U.S. Hockey Team. My coach really wanted me to do it."

"How far did you have to go?"

"They have some great ice down in Colorado Springs at a training center. I took a flight to Denver and someone picked me up for the drive down there."

"Did you have a good time?"

"Yeah," replied Riley. "Practicing with those guys was great. Most of them are pros and I learned how intense the whole thing is. The traveling was terrible, though. All the security and being packed on those planes isn't fun. The airport in Denver sucks."

"Indeed things have changed," said Jens. "But I still think it's quite a miracle that we can hop on a plane and be half-way around the world in less than a day. Some things in this world are much better than they used to be. Traveling is definitely one of those things. Sure, there are some unsafe places and cramped planes.

But your generation has access to places that people my age never dreamed of. You can feel secure going to China or parts of Africa! My generation never had that. And flying in a cramped plane is still better than being on a ship for several days or trying to sleep while sitting up on a sixty hour train ride."

"Point taken," said Riley. He smiled and nodded at Jens.

Again, I'm not sure how long the train trip was. I had no sense of time, but counting the number of times that bread was thrown in the car, it was at least two days. The train stopped for long periods of unexplained time, so I didn't think the distance we traveled was very great. I assumed that the stops were to pick up new passengers, if you could call us that.

I was starving and dehydrated. I was also nauseated from the train's motion and sick from the man in the car with me. I had some pain where he'd had sex with me. I remember thinking that one of the positive aspects of not eating was that I would not need a bowel movement. The large man in the car with me did not have a problem with that. Because he'd been eating his food and mine, he defecated in the corner more than once. The smell was horrendous, and I just curled up into a tight ball, hoping that he would not come over to me anymore.

Then, finally, during one of the stops, the door to the car slid open, and the young

SS officer stood there. He did not have any food to throw at us this time. He took a moment to look into the dim car and let his eyes adjust.

"You"—he motioned to me—"get out here. This is your stop."

He told the other man to stay in the car and slammed the door shut. Another SS officer grabbed me. He pushed me ahead of him and told me to keep walking. The young SS officer gave him some papers that were folded and bound with a rubber band. That was the last time I saw the train.

The new SS officer and I walked around the side of a train station and toward a jeep that was parked alongside it. It was late afternoon. I could see that this was a small-town train station, but I couldn't find a plaque that would tell me which one. I didn't want to look around too much, in case the SS officer got mad at me.

When we approached the jeep, I saw that another man was standing behind it. He was dressed in normal clothes, like me, and his were equally dirty. When we got closer, I could see that his hands were bound together with thick rope; the rope was tied to the bumper of the jeep.

The officer grabbed my arm and forced me to stand next to the man who was already tied. He reached into the back seat of the jeep and pulled out more rope. I did not resist as he tied my hands tightly and strung the other end around the bumper. Then he walked over to the side of the building where there was a spigot for water. He turned it on and washed his hands.

I heard him say as he looked at me, "I touched you, faggot. I need to get that filthy faggot germ off my hands!"

I had to turn away my face and look at the ground, not because of what he said, but because I wanted that water so desperately. In that moment, nothing else existed. There was no Karl, no parents, no home, no rude Nazis. Only water. But he just turned off the spigot and jumped in behind the wheel of the jeep. There were no other occupants in the vehicle, so there was plenty of space for me and my companion to ride along, but we both knew that we were meant to walk. If the driver couldn't tolerate even touching me, he surely would not want me in the jeep with him.

The jeep moved, and we walked behind. By now, people in the small town were staring at us through windows and open doors. Some pointed and laughed, others turned away. We came upon a group of young kids playing with a ball in the street. The SS officer slammed on the gas pedal, and the jeep lurched forward, out of control. The other man and I fell to the gravel and were dragged, just a meter or so. The kids laughed hysterically. We got up and continued to walk. I did not feel anything toward the children who laughed.

Soon, we were out in the countryside on a dirt road. At some point, my companion must have felt that the noise of the jeep would allow us to talk. I was apprehensive about talking to him at first. Not only was I scared of the SS driver, but I wasn't sure if my tied-up companion would be as disgusting as the fat man in the train car.

Regardless, he turned and asked me, "What is your crime?"

I looked at him. He was probably midthirties, with dark hair and a slender build. He was about the same height as me and had a very pleasant face; I've never forgotten that face. He was dirty, but handsome.

"I don't know why I'm arrested," I lied.

He looked a little suspicious. "I'm in for Paragraph 175."

I was relieved to know that there were others like me. I was even more pleased to know that he was older, more experienced, and probably smarter than me.

"I am convicted of Paragraph 175, too."

"I thought so," he said. "It was clear by the way the driver acted toward you back by the train station."

"Do you know where we are going?" I asked him hesitantly.

He sighed. "We are going to the work camp at Buchenwald. I've heard rumors about it from a group of friends I had back in Frankfurt. It's not an extermination camp, it's a work camp to make ammunition for the army."

The terrain became very forested as we progressed farther from the town. The SS officer never bothered to look back at us and kept the jeep going fairly slowly the entire time. I was grateful for that.

My companion and I talked about our towns and the general situation in Germany for the rest of the journey. I asked him if he was hungry and thirsty; he had been on a train from Frankfurt, but was in a compartment to himself and had bread. He was quite disgusted to hear about the man I had been thrown in with. He looked very sad when I told him about the sexual encounters.

Now, under normal circumstances, it would have taken a long time for me to open up to someone about these private details. But this was a difficult situation, and we both needed to make friends fast, because we didn't have the luxury of history. Over the next years I learned that friends can be made and changed instantly. The same can be said of enemies.

Up ahead, I began to see lights through the trees. My companion gestured with his head at the tall metal fence that now ran beside the road. On closer inspection, we saw that the fence was made of barbed wire.

We came past a taller, narrow structure that had bright lights shining down from it; this structure stood just inside the fence. I assumed correctly it was a watch-tower. When we passed it, two large beams of light came from the top of it and focused on my companion and me. Finally, the jeep stopped in front of an enormous iron gate. It was black and thick. Two SS guards stood in front of it with machine guns. They exchanged words with the officer driving the jeep and then opened up the gates.

The jeep jerked forward, and we walked again. As we proceeded through the gates, the guard who stood on my side of the open-ing turned his head and spit in my face. It was warm and smelled, but I dared not to use my arm to wipe it off, because I was so afraid of them.

Then I noticed letters made out of bent metal and fused to the gate itself: *Jedem das Seine*. That means in English, "To each what he deserves."

TWENTY SEVEN

"Well, Riley," said Professor Weber, "I'm very glad to see you."

He smiled back at her over the desk in her office.

"The term finished last week," she continued, "and your coach has been e-mailing me inquiring about your grade."

"Yeah, he's kind of anxious like that."

"I had a talk with Mr. Jaenisch last night," she said. "I was sitting on my porch and saw him open the window in his kitchen, so I went over. Riley, I know you've been spending time with him. Does he look all right to you? He seemed to be very frail to me."

"I've been thinking that, too. Do you know I take him to the Mayo Clinic in Rochester every week?"

"Yes, we talked about that," Jade said.

"I think his treatments are making him a little sicker," Riley said. "He thinks so, too. Anyway, he told me that he feels worse. But he also says that he's glad to do it if it makes him feel better at the end."

"Well, I can understand that. He is very glad to know you, Riley. I'm really impressed as well. You have embraced this project all on your own, without the intervention of the Athletic Department, and I'm very proud of that."

"It's no problem, I actually like driving him down there," Riley said sincerely.

"He didn't tell me too much about what the two of you talk about over all those miles," she said. "I do not want you to share private information. But he did say that he's been able to talk to you about some things that he has kept hidden for a long time."

Riley did not feel it was appropriate to share with Dr. Weber that Jens was gay. He still had not asked Jens if it was all right to share. "He has a very interesting life," said Riley. "I don't know how I always feel about it."

Professor Weber's eyes shot straight toward Riley when he said this; she was quite glad to hear the words he chose. "Riley, did you just hear how you described his life?"

"That he has an interesting life?"

"Yes," she said. "I love that you said he *has* an interesting life, instead of he *had* an interesting life. This shows growth. Often, students think about people as old as Jens as if their life is already over. You just used the present tense to describe his life. Good for you!"

Riley smiled back at her. He understood the point she was trying to make and was also a bit proud of himself.

"What other big ideas have you learned?"

"There have been a lot of small things," he replied. "But I think the biggest is that when I look at him, I see myself."

"In what way?"

"Well, not that we are like each other. He has a completely different life, and we don't really have that much in common. But when I look at him, sometimes I imagine what I will be like when I'm ninety years old. I never thought about it before I started hanging out with him. But now I know that someday I'm going to be old."

"And how does that change the way you feel now?"

"It makes me want to treat other people, and myself, better. I never really thought about the day when I can no longer play hockey, but by watching Jens, I know that day will come. I also know that I'm not always going to look like this. At some point, my hair will turn gray—or maybe even fall out."

Jade was pleased. Of course, she realized that he had missed a lot of her course. There were entire lessons and chapters of readings that he had missed. However, she also knew that this young man had grown.

"Very good, Riley. You passed."

"I did?" he asked. "You mean that's it? No paper or anything?"

She said, "If I assigned you a paper, you would ramble on and on about some topic in order to fulfill a number of words. That is not what this course is about. You have learned some valuable lessons that will serve you well. More important, you have learned some things that will help all the older people you encounter, and you learned about yourself. That is the real goal of education. You passed."

"Thanks!" exclaimed Riley. "Do you mind if I go? I thought this would take longer, but if I leave now I can get some ice time in before I pick up Jens. He has an appointment this afternoon."

"Of course," Dr. Weber said. "I hope to see you around."

"Me, too." He got his things together and left the office. Riley was relieved that it was over, and he'd passed the course. The coach would be relieved as well. He had also been sincere when he told Professor Weber that he hoped to see her around. Aside from hockey coaches, he had not been close to any teacher in high school or college; this was a nice change for him.

Jade smiled after he left and went back to her computer. She began to craft an e-mail response to Riley's coach then stopped to consider for a moment.

In front of her was a class list for the course Riley was taking. The students on this list had spent many hours in class with her; they had completed the readings and participated in class discussion. *Is it fair that Riley should get the same good grade as the others?* She decided that fair was not always equal. The most important thing in undergraduate education was the growth, not the time spent sitting in a chair.

She went back to her computer and typed, "He got an A."

TWENTY EIGHT

"**E**very time we pay for parking that woman complains about the cash drawer being on the wrong side. Do you think she does that for every car that goes through here?" asked Riley. They had just pulled out of one of the Mayo Clinic parking ramps and were heading back to St. Paul.

"I noticed the same thing. Today I looked and saw that she does have to reach all the way over herself to get the change. She probably has a legitimate complaint."

"But why tell us about it? We can't do anything about it. She should complain to someone who can help her."

"Well, Riley, when you're older and have a job, you might understand. I worked in a hierarchical setting for a long time. It's difficult to change things. No doubt she has complained to her supervisor. But we don't know the politics of what has to happen to move the cash register to the other side."

"Seems like it should be easier."

There were many different kinds of SS all over Buchenwald. When I arrived that day, I didn't know the difference between any of them. In time, I would learn who was still climbing and who was scheming with whom—not unlike the atmosphere of the faculty of the University of Minnesota. When we were finally untied from the jeep, my companion and I were told to follow a guard. I would learn later that he was one of the lower ranked of the group.

We followed him into a building that was near the iron gate. We were put in a small concrete room that had no windows, only a wooden table in the middle. There was a drain in the corner of the room, and a hose was connected to a spigot coming out of the wall. I wanted to run over and get something to drink from the hose, but I didn't dare.

The same SS officer who brought us to the building entered the room and closed the door behind him. He kicked a large metal bucket ahead of him.

"Take off all your clothes, shoes, and anything else you have, and throw it in this bucket," he ordered.

My companion and I obeyed quickly. I was quite dizzy from having not eaten, and I was extremely thirsty, but I found the energy to take off my shoes and put them in the bucket. I remember being a little shy to take off my clothes in front of another 175-er, but I was more scared of the SS officer. Remember, besides Karl, I had never met another homosexual before.

The Iron Words

The SS officer yelled to us, "Get over there!"

He pointed to the corner where the drain was and kicked that metal bucket back toward the door. My companion and I walked over to the corner and stood next to each other; neither of us looked at the other. The SS walked over to the spigot and turned it on. I saw a fast stream of water come out of the end of the hose.

He opened the door and shouted something that I did not hear. A man dressed in a prisoner's uniform entered with a small pail. He walked over to us and threw a lot of white powder all over us. Then, he set the pail on the table and went to grab the hose.

"No," said the SS officer to the prisoner, "you can leave. I'll do it."

The prisoner took his pail and walked out, grabbing the metal bucket with our clothes on the way. The SS officer closed the door and walked over to the hose. I didn't know how sadistic the SS were; the Jewish people knew, but I did not.

The SS sprayed our fronts with the high-pressure water. Actually, I didn't mind this. It felt good, and I was able to even get some swallows of water inside me. At least, I could get the smell of the man from the train off me.

He told us to turn around and put both hands against the wall. He sprayed our backsides, and I closed my eyes for a minute. Then, suddenly, I stopped feeling water on my back. I heard my companion yell in pain. I turned, and I could not believe what I was seeing right next to me. The officer had taken the hose with the high-pressure water and inserted it into my companion's rectum.

"What are you screaming for?" the officer asked. "I thought you filthy faggots liked this kind of thing."

As the water filled his colon, my companion yelled louder. Finally, the SS took out the hose with a laugh. I will never forget the laughs of the SS.

"Did you like watching that?" he asked me when he noticed my shocked expression.

I didn't say anything and immediately turned back to face the wall. My companion was breathing hard, but he was silent.

"You better learn this lesson now, filthy faggot!" he screamed in my ear. "When we ask a question, you answer!"

When he yelled into my ear, I pressed myself against the wall and clung to it tightly. At that moment, I just wanted everything and everyone to go away.

"So did you like watching that?"

I told him, "No, I didn't like watching it." I was new to the camp, you see, and didn't know the sadistic ways and mind manipulation of the SS officers.

Because he had not liked my answer, he took the hose and quickly jammed it into my rectum. I was still sore from the train ride, and at first, the water felt even clean. But then, intense pain started as the pressure inside me grew.

"You liked watching that, didn't you!" he screamed again.

I still had not figured out his mind manipulation and replied, "No!"

I was now very nauseated, from the pain and from not eating. I started to vomit a yellow liquid, but the SS officer didn't stop.

"Hey! You filthy faggot!" he yelled at me. "Did you like it when I shoved that hose up his ass?"

Just then, I heard my companion say, "Yes, you liked it."

Now, I finally got the point and shouted through the pain and nausea, "Yes, I liked it!"

"How much did you like it?" the SS yelled back.

"Very much!"

"Will you think about it when you masturbate?"

That was the most depraved thing I had ever been asked, but I had no choice. I desperately wanted the water to stop. "Yes! I will think about it all the time!"

He removed the hose, and I collapsed on the floor. Without saying anything more, the guard dropped the hose, turned off the spigot, and left the room in a hurry. I was in the corner of the concrete chamber, wet, naked, and crying. I was embarrassed when the water started coming out of me.

My companion helped me up to my feet. "You're going to have to start thinking differently," he said to me in a very calm voice. "Even if the opposite is true, always tell them what they want to hear."

I didn't respond but knew that his advice was good to follow. He supported me with his arm around my back. We were both still naked and quite uncomfortable.

Then the same prisoner as before came into the room with a pile of folded prison garments. He put them on the table and told us to wait; he left the room and returned shortly with a wooden box. "These are your clothes," he said as he gestured to the pile. "But before you put them on, you have to stitch on your badge."

He pushed the clothes toward each of us and grabbed a sheet of paper from the box. "Which one of you is Jens Jaenisch?"

I raised my hand. He looked on the list to check something, then reached into the box and handed me pink fabric in the shape of a triangle. He took a small rectangle of white fabric and a large black marker from the box. He checked the piece of paper again and wrote "1973" on the white fabric.

He explained as he handed them to me, "This is your badge, and this is your number. Stitch the pink triangle on your left chest. Make sure the point of the triangle is going down. Then stitch the number underneath the triangle."

He grabbed some coarse white thread and a needle from the box and handed them to me. Now, for the first time, I noticed that he was also wearing a badge. Stitched onto his left chest was also a triangle, but it was purple and smaller. Using his badge as a guide, I started to sew. I had no experience with needles and threads, so I'm afraid I did a poor job. I remember worrying about whether my sloppy stitches would bring me more pain.

Curiously, in addition to his number, my companion was given two badges: a pink triangle, exactly like mine, and a large yellow triangle. He was instructed to stitch the two together, with the pink one on top, creating a mixed-color Star of David. He was both a 175-er and a Jew.

I didn't know if it was okay to ask questions of other prisoners, but my companion suddenly asked, "What does your purple badge mean?"

"It means I am a Jehovah's Witness," he said.

I was not familiar with the faith. I was absolutely shocked at what the prisoner said next.

"And don't ask questions, you faggots," he said to us. "You will learn that in here, even we prisoners have a rank. You pink bastards are on the bottom. You faggots don't speak to any other color unless you are spoken to."

That was my first initiation into the cruel hierarchy of the camp. Not all prisoners were equal at Buchenwald, and I would soon discover how hated we pinks were. It may be disappointing to think about oppressed people being oppressive. But we prisoners were. We were treated like animals and treated each other like animals.

The greens were on top; they were actual criminals sent to the camp from real prisons. I quickly got over the fact that those who actually deserved to be punished received the benefits from being on top of the pyramid. I hated that the man who raped me on the train was probably in some other camp wearing a green badge.

The red triangle was for political prisoners, the blue for immigrants. We didn't encounter too many with the black triangle of the mentally ill, because they were in a special hospital building. The atrocities those blacks must have suffered! Very few of them lived more than a couple of days in the camp.

After the purples there were three colors left, and these three were treated the harshest. The brown triangles, Gypsies, were punished for their reputation as beggars; the yellows, Jews, were imprisoned because they were so hated by the Nazis. Last, were the pinks. We were next to the lowest in the camp.

"You said there were only three colors left," said Riley. "The browns, yellows, and pinks. So, if the pinks were second to the bottom, who was lower than them?"

"My companion was the lowest," Jens replied in a very sad voice. "He was the despised half-pink, half-yellow. But it wouldn't be until the next morning that I'd learn just how hated he was."

TWENTY NINE

By the time we had finished stitching on our badges, it was quite dark outside. The SS guard who had used the hose came back into the room and explained that we had missed the dinner and the evening assembly. We would be taken straight to our block.

My companion and I followed him out of a different door, and for the first time we saw the camp stretched out before us. Bright floodlights mounted on tall wood posts illuminated the land and buildings. In front of the first building we were in, which sometimes we referred to as the main building, was a large expanse of gravel. The guard called this the parade grounds and told us that we were to assemble there in the morning and evening. At the far end of the parade grounds, a row of long single-story buildings came into view. This was the first row of what we called blocks.

We crossed the parade grounds behind the SS officer and came upon the first row of blocks. Each block was a separate building that housed roughly two hundred men. I would soon discover that all the blocks were a mix of colored badges, except for ours. We followed the SS to the last row of blocks, and indeed, to the very corner block, which housed all the pink prisoners. It was near one side of the barbed-wire fence, and a bright light shone on the building.

I was having a hard time walking, because my shoes were way too big for me, but I made do in an attempt to draw as little attention to myself as possible. I would also soon discover that I was quite lucky to have received shoes that were too big; many in the camp were forced to cram their feet into shoes that were way too small. Also, I was lucky that my pants and shirt basically fit. I saw many in the camp who had pants that were way too short or shirts that hung to the floor.

We reached the block, and the SS opened the door on the very end of the long, rectangular building. We stepped inside, and I saw how crowded it was. A single row of lights hung on the ceiling through the middle of the building. The lights lit two long rows of bunk beds, one row against each wall. A narrow aisle of about one meter separated the two rows. Most of the beds already contained a single prisoner; it was very quiet.

I would learn later that being a pink only had one advantage, although it was a large one. We were the only block where there was just one man per bed. It was common to hear of two, three, or even four men in one bed in the other blocks. The SS thought that the temptation would be too great to put two of us homosexuals together.

Finally, the guard broke the silence and yelled, "Rudolf, come here!"

Immediately, a man came running from the middle of the block. He was very tall, probably over six feet, about thirty years old, with a shaved head. In fact, I now noticed that every man in the block, except for my companion and me, had a shaved head. Rudolf was also wearing a black band around his arm. I quickly scanned those around me for other black bands but did not see any.

"I have two new ones for you," said the SS officer to Rudolf. "This one is a regular faggot, and this one is a special half-breed Jew faggot." He pointed to each of us in turn.

Rudolf replied, "Yes, sir." Rudolf did not have a pink triangle; his was green.

The SS officer said, "This is your capo. You will obey him. Rudolf, show them where to sleep."

Capo is an Italian word for chief. You see, the SS appointed a prisoner, always a green, to be in charge of each block. They were marked by a black band of fabric tied around their arm. The SS officers were mostly lazy, stupid men who liked their evenings free for drinking. With a capo in charge at night, they could do just that. Oh, of course, they kept their eye on things and loved spontaneous inspections to keep the capos on their toes.

Rudolf turned to an upper and lower bunk that were vacant behind him and pointed at one for me and one for my companion. I caught Rudolf's eye and noticed that he'd started staring at me. It was not an angry stare, but not pleasant either; it was if he knew me or was contemplating something about me. I wasn't quite sure what I thought of Rudolf, because I didn't yet know the politics and structure of the camp hierarchy.

"Get in bed," said the SS officer to us. "Rudolf, I will stay here and keep an eye on these two for a while, especially the Jew faggot."

Some of the other prisoners looked over when he said this, but most of them had stayed perfectly still since the SS officer arrived. I also didn't dare to look around at them too much.

I walked over to my top bunk bed and discovered that you could hardly call it a bed at all. It was merely a wooden platform suspended on four wooden posts. There was no mattress, no pillow, only a heavy, brown wool blanket. A second wooden platform was fixed below it and was already occupied by another prisoner. I used all the strength I could find to grab onto the platform and pull myself up. I was so weak from lack of food and all the trauma I'd been through.

As I was stretching out on the wood and pulling the blanket over me, I heard the capo say to the officer, "What about their hair?"

"They arrived too close to assembly time," the officer replied. "Take care of it tomorrow before I see them again!"

"Yes, sir," responded Rudolf.

Suddenly, the SS officer looked at me, growled loudly, and ran to my bed. He stepped on the lower bunk and grabbed me with one hand. I heard the prisoner below me grunt; the officer must have stepped on him. He pulled me to the side of the bed and with his other hand, took his rifle and slammed me on the shoulder. The intense pain shot to my brain.

"You never sleep with your hands under the blanket!" he shouted at me. "You hear me? You filthy faggot, we won't have any masturbating in here! You got me? You never sleep with your hands under the blanket!"

The Iron Words

He hit me again with the rifle and stepped off the bed. I heard his footsteps walk away, but I did not look. I squeezed my eyes tight and tried desperately not to cry. I wasn't hungry anymore, because I was so scared of doing something wrong again. However, I was very careful to keep my hands and entire arms on the outside of the blanket.

I don't know how much time passed as I tried to sleep. At one point, I slowly opened my eyes and turned my head up and down the block. Indeed, all the men were sleeping with their arms and hands on the outside of their blankets. The Nazi's fear that we would masturbate was so strong that we were the only block that kept the lights on all night. I discovered later that these precautions had been ordered from the highest officials in Berlin. I clasped my hands together tightly over the blanket.

I waited for sleep but it was difficult. I tried with all my strength to not feel any emotion. Then, sometime during the night without warning, a loud bell began ringing throughout the whole building. I sat up in fear and looked at the prisoner in the upper bunk next to mine. He gestured that I should put my head back down and be quiet. I thought it best to follow his lead. The bell did not ring long, and when it stopped we all heard a loud conversation.

"Which one, Rudolf?" I heard the SS officer shout down the block.

"This one right here."

I did not know where Rudolf was indicating, but I hoped beyond hope that it had nothing to do with me.

"Come here, you filthy faggot," said the SS officer.

Then, I heard another voice say in a pleading tone, "No, it's wrong! I wasn't! Rudolf, tell him!"

"Don't listen to him," Rudolf shouted back. "I clearly saw him sleeping with his hands below the blanket. I'm sure he was masturbating!"

The voice of the prisoner continued as the guard dragged him over the floor and toward the door. "Rudolf, how can you do this to me? No, it is a lie! I was not. Rudolf, how could…"

The prisoner's voice faded away as he was thrown outside the door. After a moment, a shot from a rifle tore the night and my soul. I sat and opened my eyes, but immediately the prisoner next to me gestured again, and I lay back down on my platform. It was the first of many deaths.

And now, I did allow tears to stream down my face. I looked up at the light, clasped my hands on my empty stomach, and thought about Karl. Castration would have been so much better.

THIRTY

Riley turned to Jens, who was sitting in the passenger seat, and said, "So, I want you to know that because of you, I've started paying more attention to things."

"How do you mean?"

"Well," Riley replied, "I've been reading the news and what's going on in the world; I never did that before. I feel that I should be more informed about things. I just never realized before that what goes on in the world can have an impact on my life."

"And where do you do this reading?" Jens asked.

"Mostly on the Internet," Riley responded.

"Just make sure you always consider the source," Jens advised him. "The Internet is a wonderful tool, but remember that anyone and everyone can access it and add to it."

"Yep," answered Riley with his hands on the steering wheel. "I'll remember that."

Although there had been several nice spring days, this was the first real hot day of the year. It was only the last week of May, not even technically summer yet, but the temperature rose to eighty-four degrees as they made their way across the prairie.

"Did you know they have gay marriage in Minnesota now?" asked Riley. "I'll bet you're pretty happy about that. I thought we voted on that before, but it turns out, we were just voting on whether to make gay marriage constitutionally illegal. The governor made gay marriage legal in the middle of May, just a few weeks ago."

Jens was glad to see that Riley was becoming more informed, even if he had some of the facts wrong. "Actually," Jens corrected him, "same-sex marriages can start on August first. The legislature voted to grant same-sex marriages, and the governor signed it on May 14."

"It's pretty good news, right?" responded Riley.

Jens hesitated for a moment, and then said, "Yes, it is good news. I have to say, Riley, I was a little bittersweet about the whole situation. Of course, I'm very glad for the people who can get married and have the security that they deserve. But I have to admit, every time I see happy gay couples on the news, it makes me a little sad."

"Why?" the young man asked, a little astonished. "Aren't you happy for people like you?"

"I'm ashamed to say it," replied Jens in a softer voice, "but I guess it boils down to jealousy. When I see these couples, it's a reminder of what I could never have."

"But aren't you glad that we have come this far in accepting gays? Especially considering what happened to you?"

"Oh, of course. In fact, I watched the vote in both houses of the Minnesota legislature and got quite a thrill thinking about how Hitler and the rest of those thugs would have reacted. If there were real justice in this world, all of them would have lived long enough to realize how meaningless they all were. Wouldn't it be great to see Hitler's face when he realized that Jewish people and homosexuals have thrived?"

"That's interesting." The pair remained silent for a few minutes as Riley thought about Jens's reaction to gay marriage. The young man was able to understand the frustration coming from Jens. It must be very hard for Jens to know that he was just born too early to be married. However, he was not born too early to be in love. "Do you still think about Karl?" asked Riley abruptly.

"Hmmm, that's an interesting question," answered Jens. "I guess, yes, I think about him a lot. But I'm not sure it's the real Karl that I think about; it's more like the ideal of Karl that I formed in my mind after knowing him such a short while. When I was in the camp, it was thoughts of Karl that got me through a lot of horrible things. But these thoughts were not reality; I know that.

"So, yes, I fantasize about what life would have been like if Karl and I could have grown old together. I think about where we would have lived, and what we would have done. I wonder if we'd have married women in order to keep the facade alive. But again, it is all a fantasy because the Karl I knew died when his father caught us kissing."

THIRTY ONE

I never knew how long I slept. There weren't any clocks in the block, and we lived by the sound of the loud bell. One thing I know for sure—on that first night I didn't sleep at all after the commotion. The lights, my hunger, and the rifle shot kept me awake. Also, there was the noise of all those other men snoring and breathing together.

At some point, the loud bell rang again and instantly everyone sat up in his bed. I did the same and knew that I needed to learn quickly from all the others. The man from the next top bunk, who had gestured for me to keep quiet during the night, climbed down next to me as we both got on the floor. We were wearing our prison uniforms with pink triangles; they served as pajamas as well.

"Make your blanket like this," he told me. I watched him make the wool very straight and neat on the wooden platform.

I turned to my bunk and did the same thing with my blanket. I was extremely careful to be quite exact, because I now knew how fierce the punishments were in the camp.

Then he turned to me and said, "Now, follow me to the parade grounds, and I will help you get through the morning assembly."

He was much older than me, and very skinny. I noticed that his collarbones stuck out from his skin. I already had my shoes on, because I was so scared of the SS from the night before. The older man slipped on his shoes, then bent over to shake the man who slept on the bunk under him.

"Wake up," he said, "hurry."

He shook the man hard then stopped and studied him. He breathed a heavy sigh and looked me straight in the eyes.

"Help me get him up," he said to me. "He is dead."

"What do you mean?" I asked, not really wanting to know the answer.

"He is dead. Sometime during the night. We have to bring him with us to the parade grounds. Everyone must be accounted for, even the dead."

"How did he die?"

"Who knows? Probably from starvation. People die all the time here. You'll get used to it."

As you can imagine, I was very weak, but I helped the old man get the dead body and prop it between the two of us. We started walking toward the door; the others were leaving as well. A few of them stopped to help us, but the older man explained that it was better to let the new young prisoner take the burden so that they could save their energy. As hungry as I was, I already understood that I didn't even know the meaning of hunger. Looking around, I could see real hunger everywhere.

Most of the weight of the dead body was on me, but there really was not much there. The body did not even feel human, and I couldn't tell which part of him I was holding onto. He was nothing but bones. As we walked outside, another pink came to us and asked if he could have the dead man's shoes. The older man paused our progress and allowed him to take the shoes.

"Now, listen carefully," said the older man as we walked among the others toward the parade grounds. "We will wait in lines according to our block; I will help you find your place. You just stand there without moving or making any sound. Each man will call out his name, number, and reason for being here. Our block will go last. When it comes to your turn, yell your name and number, and then say, 'Ich bin eine warmer Bruder.'

The commandant of Buchenwald attends every assembly and hates us pinks the most. He makes us say that when it is our turn."

Warmer Bruder was a slang term for homosexuals back in that time. Literally, it meant warm brother. I'm not sure how it got associated with homosexuals, but it was like calling someone a faggot, I guess. Growing up in Germany, I'd heard the term often and even used it myself to taunt other children at play. Now that slang term would take on a whole new meaning in my life.

We reached the grounds and progressed to a line on the far side; it was the last line forming. When we got there, we dumped the dead body at the end of the line and started walking to our places. I was still with the older prisoner from the next bunk.

Now that it was beginning to be daylight, I saw that the parade grounds was not entirely bare; there was a structure in the middle of the gravel. A wood platform had been built, about ten meters by five meters and a half meter high. On each corner was a wood post that reached up and held a flimsy plywood roof.

I gasped. On one of the posts hung a body; I could see that he had a pink triangle stitched to his chest. I immediately remembered the scene in the block and the rifle shot that followed during the night.

"Is that the man who was dragged out of bed last night?" I asked the older prisoner.

"Yes," he said. "And, you know, it's your fault."

"What?" I said quite astonished.

"It's your fault. I expect you'll know why during breakfast. Here is your place."

I was bewildered and didn't know what kind of game he was playing with me. He left me in my place and took his own, three people in front of me. Now I didn't know if I could trust the old man, who seemed to have been friendly and willing to advise me.

Before long, a row of SS officers came out of the front building and walked toward the platform. The officer in front was wearing a full uniform that was extremely clean. He was the same height as me, but much more muscular. He looked angry. They reached the platform and stepped up onto it; the grounds were silent.

"This faggot was caught masturbating," he shouted as he pointed to the man on the post. "Let this be a warning to all you faggots over there. The next time, we won't kill first; we will cut off your dick and leave you to bleed. Count off!"

Somewhere, way across the grounds, I heard the yelling of names, numbers, and positions within the camp. I hadn't expected that each block would take a turn, one by one, with the attendance. Now I realized that this ritual would take at least an hour. Everyone stood silent and straight. The other officers held their rifles and walked among the rows. Every so often, I could hear them strike someone who wasn't standing correctly.

My eyes went to the corpse that was hanging on the post next to a man I assumed was the commandant. How could I be responsible for this man's death? I studied his limp body, shoeless and still. I noticed that he was not nearly as emaciated as the other men I'd seen; in fact, he looked quite well fed. I thought this was odd.

Before long, it was my turn. I was anxious and concentrated in my foggy mind to make sure I said it correctly. "Jens Jaenisch, number 1973, Ich bin eine warmer Bruder!" I shouted.

That was the first time of many, many times that I yelled that phrase into the unfeeling air of the parade grounds.

THIRTY TWO

When the morning assembly was complete, we stayed in our block lines and formed one long line that moved toward a building on the side of the front building. I assumed we were going to finally eat, but I was disheartened to see that the pinks would be the last group to enter the building.

As I followed the man in front of me, I felt a tap on my shoulder. I turned and saw that it was Rudolf, the capo from our block. He already had my companion from the afternoon before with him and instructed me to follow. We left the line and walked toward the front building.

My companion and I shared a glance, although we did not talk. Rudolf brought us through a side door and into a concrete room that was similar to the one we had been in the night before. However, I was very glad to see that there was no hose in this room, although there was the same spigot attached above a drain in the concrete floor.

The Iron Words

Against one of the walls was a wooden chair; lying on the floor next to the chair was an electric razor that was plugged into a crude electric outlet bolted to the concrete. I noticed some hair around the floor of the chair, but not a lot.

"Sit down in that chair," Rudolf commanded me as he pointed to the chair.

I started to slowly walk toward the chair, but Rudolf told me to move faster. I didn't find out until later that there was a very good reason he was so anxious to get me into the chair as quickly as possible.

Rudolf took the razor, turned it on, and quite gently shaved all the hair from my head; I saw it fall over my shoulders and to the floor. Then, Rudolf asked me to stand and take down my pants. Of course, I immediately thought this was a horrible request, but I knew better than to question anything anymore, so I obeyed.

"The SS like to keep you faggots clean," Rudolf said to us.

Rudolf took the razor and shaved off all my pubic hair. I wasn't as embarrassed, because my companion had already seen me naked, and I guess I just wasn't feeling much of anything after the events of the last two days. Rudolf was quite gentle with the razor, and I was glad for that.

Just then, the door sprang open and in walked the SS officer who had raped us with the hose. He noticed Rudolf shaving me and got very upset.

"What are you doing?" he said.

"I was told by the commandant to take care of these two right away," Rudolf replied.

The SS officer hesitated, and I could tell that he wasn't quite sure if Rudolf was telling the truth. Years later, I would become politically astute enough to read their expressions and figure out what was going on.

"Let me do the Jew faggot!" He pushed Rudolf out of the way.

I pulled up my pants and stepped aside; my companion sat in the chair. No sooner had the electric razor started, then my companion started making small cries. I looked over and saw blood running down his face. The SS officer was not being as gentle as Rudolf was with me; he was butchering my companion's head. I felt sick and sorry for him.

The SS officer forced my companion to stand up. He yanked down his pants. The officer grabbed my companion's penis and scrotum quite hard. He pulled down with great force, and my companion cried out in pain. The officer began to roughly shave off my companion's pubic hair. I saw blood dripping down to the floor; it was hard to tell which body part the blood was coming from.

Then, without any expression, the officer dropped the razor on the floor while it was still running and left the room quickly. He left just as quickly as he had when he raped us with the hose the night before. Rudolf bent over and switched off the razor, then told us to follow him. My companion had tears on his face as he pulled up his pants and looked at me. I wanted to help him clean up his bloody parts, but I dared not.

We followed Rudolf out of the building and diagonally across the parade grounds to the commissary. I noticed that my companion had a hard time keeping up as his groin still hurt from the harsh shaving.

"You won't get any breakfast today," Rudolf said to us as we walked. "We get only coffee at breakfast. You are to save part of your bread from dinner and eat that in the morning. Make sure you hide it on yourself so that nobody steals it during the night."

I was not only heartbroken to know that I would not have breakfast, but I was also starting to panic. I knew that I needed to eat something very soon, or I would faint and probably be killed. I also desperately needed water; I was glad that Rudolf mentioned something about coffee.

We entered the commissary, and Rudolf told my companion to get in line with the other pinks. Then he told me to follow him. I was curious why I was not getting in line, but again, I was not going to question. As I followed Rudolf up to the kitchen, I noticed that many of the other pinks were staring at us. Some were smirking, others shaking their heads.

Rudolf and I walked through the kitchen and entered a hall that contained many doors. The doors were all solid wood and closed.

"These are storerooms," Rudolf told me, "but the capos use them for offices."

He opened one of the wooden doors and gestured for me to enter. Inside, the very small room contained shelves of imitation coffee; it was the best-smelling place in the whole camp. Rudolf entered behind me and closed the door. He leaned himself in one of the corners, and I took the opportunity to save some energy and did the same, leaning in an opposite corner.

"So," Rudolf said to me, "you will save half your bread from dinner for breakfast, provided that nobody steals it from you in the night. For lunch, you will get a small bowl of soup that is basically water. For dinner, a piece of bread and a small sausage. Sometimes we will have cheese."

The Iron Words

I nodded my head to acknowledge that I heard. Rudolf stared back at me and smiled. His look was making me uncomfortable. I had a sense that something was not right with him.

"Are you hungry?" he asked.

I told him that I was very much hungry and thirsty. To my amazement and great hope, he turned to the shelf behind him and gestured to a large piece of bread, a hunk of cheese, and a tin cup.

"I got these ready for you this morning," he told me. "I had a feeling you would like it."

"Thank you, sir," I said gratefully and started to walk toward him.

"In here, you must always call me Rudolf," he informed me. "Out in the camp, you will always call me capo."

He handed me the tin cup. It was full of cold coffee, but I didn't mind. I drank it quickly.

"Your name is Jens, correct?"

"Yes," I replied, "Jens."

"Jens, I need an assistant. I need a helper to work with me in here during the dinner. Of course, you will do your normal work detail during the day, but at dinnertime, would you like to help me?"

"Yes," I said, because it was the only response I thought appropriate.

"Good. You see, my last assistant is now hanging on a pole on the parade grounds. So, I need someone new to help me."

I did not respond, but I was now afraid to be with him.

"Do you know why I was so quick to shave you myself?" he asked rhetorically. "I knew that SS butcher would want to draw blood, and I didn't want to see your young head damaged. The commandant didn't say anything to me this morning, but it was a lie I was willing to tell, because I really want you as my assistant. I wanted to protect you from what happened to the Jew faggot this morning. Are you happy that I protected you from that?"

I didn't say anything in response. Rudolf now crossed the small room slowly and grabbed my left arm with his right hand. He gently caressed it and put his left hand behind my neck.

"Jens," he said to me softly, "you are young. I liked you from the moment you were brought into the block last night. Will you do this for me? Will you be with me during dinner?"

He pulled my head forward and kissed me. I fought back and pushed him away.

"You're not a pink! Why are you kissing me?"

"I am not a faggot," he said. "But in here, I have needs."

I finally figured out what kind of assistant he wanted, and I told him, "I don't want to be your assistant if it means having to have sex with you."

Rudolf took a moment to look at me, and I could see that he was trying very hard to stay calm. He turned slowly away from me. "I'll let you think about it for a day," he said as he stepped back into his corner. "Just remember, my assistant gets paid with a lot of extra bread and cheese every day. Do you want to become as bony as the others? When it comes time for dinner tonight, I'll ask you again. I hope you are smart."

He grabbed the bread and cheese from the shelf behind him and started to eat them in front of me. I had no choice but to stand and watch. Now I knew why the prisoner hanging on the post had been so well fed.

THIRTY THREE

Minnesota Daily is the campus newspaper of the University of Minnesota. It is the largest student-written daily newspaper in the United States and has the third largest circulation in Minnesota, behind the papers of Minneapolis and St. Paul. Riley's quest to be better informed led him to pick up a copy daily from the stand in the entrance of his dormitory. Today was no exception.

He sat on a concrete ledge near his building. Certain student athletes were given the opportunity to stay on campus during summer and concentrate on training; Riley accepted that offer. He wouldn't have been able to hold down a regular job with his training schedule, and there wasn't much reason to move back to his parents' home in Hastings.

On the front page of the paper was another story about the recent action to allow same-sex marriage in Minnesota. This story featured a photo of two female students who had become engaged. Riley thought about Jens and his reaction when they spoke about the subject. He felt sad for Jens. He imagined how it would feel to want to play hockey, and to be able to play hockey, but to be suddenly told that hockey was off-limits. *How would it feel to watch others play hockey without me?*

Riley opened the paper and saw a headline that immediately took his mind away from Jens. "Jacob Fredrichs Family Sues Athletic Department and U Doctor." Riley dropped his head and pounded twice with his fist on the concrete ledge as he read it. Their claim was that the doctor introduced Jacob to a prescription medication that he became addicted to and abused. Apparently, a large amount of the medication appeared in Jacob's blood on the night of his accident.

The article continued by sharing an interview with the university spokesperson, who defended the school. According to the university, there was no negligence unless the doctor had provided too much of the medication. Since he had not, and Jacob Fredrichs acquired it on his own, there was nothing the school could be held responsible for.

Riley threw the paper on the sidewalk below and pounded his fist again. He swore loudly and then put his head down on his crossed arms. He stayed in this position, trying hard not to think or feel, until it started raining.

THIRTY FOUR

Another bell rang, signaling the end of breakfast, and Rudolf took me down the hall and shoved me outside without saying anything. All I had to do was make it to lunch, and I could get the watery soup he had spoken of. The other prisoners were exiting the building and heading in a long line toward a gate in the back of the camp, behind the blocks. This gate opened on a well-guarded path that led to the ammunition factory. I could not see the actual factory from the camp, but I could see the billows of smoke and steam rising above the trees.

I began to walk toward the line when the young SS officer who had driven our jeep the day before, came out of the commissary with my companion. He saw me and gestured for me to run over to them.

"All new pinks get a special job to do here," he told us when I ran over to them. "You will do this job until a new group of pinks arrive. You two are the only ones in the group who arrived yesterday."

Up to this point, because I had not eaten or had much to drink for several days, I did not have a need to use the bathroom. Besides, with the pain from the man on the train and the discomfort of the water hose, I'm not sure my body would have been able to tolerate a bowel movement. So, I had not wondered where the prisoners went to relieve themselves, but I would soon find out.

We followed the SS officer and approached a building opposite the commissary on the other side of the front building. The building was long and narrow and much smaller than the commissary.

As we got closer, a horrendous odor hit us in the face. The officer stopped to tie a handkerchief around his nose, and then we continued. He made my companion open the door, and we all stepped up on a concrete foundation and entered the stagnant building.

Running the entire length of the structure was a large concrete table that was one meter high. There was a space on either side to walk along it. We soon discovered that the concrete table was really one large container for human waste. Along the top, cut through the concrete, were many holes that were equal distances apart; there were no seats or covers on the holes.

"So, here is your work assignment, faggots," said the SS officer. "This was designed so that the shit and piss would run downward and into a large septic tank. But it doesn't work because the grade was not done correctly. The inmates here are allowed to use this toilet twice each day; your job is to clean it."

I didn't dare look at my companion's expression, but I knew mine was full of disgust. The officer walked us over to one of the far corners and pointed out a couple of disgusting brooms that were caked with feces. Next to the brooms were a spigot, a metal bucket, and a large pile of dirty rags.

"First," he said to us, "you start on this end, because it is the higher end, and sweep through each hole, pushing the shit downstream. You do that in the morning. In the afternoon, you fill up the bucket with water and climb in through the end hole. Use the rags to scrub the sides and bottom of the long toilet. You don't want to know what happens if it is not clean enough. Got it? We SS are very creative with our punishments. I will inspect your work carefully before dinner."

He started to walk toward the door. My companion and I each reluctantly took one of the brooms.

"I can't stand the stench in here," the officer said to us. "I'm going to be sitting right outside with my rifle. Get to work, faggots!"

He left the building, and the door closed behind him.

I was not going to waste time, partly because I was scared of not doing a good job, and partly because I was glad to have something else to think about other than hunger. Even though the work promised to be awful, at least it was a task I could focus on.

I took my broom, inserted it into the first hole, and started to sweep the disgusting deposits that lay on the concrete base. My companion began by walking with his broom down the entire length of the building. I was not sure what he was doing, but when he returned to my end, he announced that there were exactly sixty holes through the concrete top.

He started to work behind me and swept up anything I had missed. We continued this way down about a fourth of the holes.

"Do you think he would know if we took a little water out of the spigot?" my companion asked me.

"I'm scared," I replied, "but I'm also desperate. I really need some water."

He walked over to the spigot, got on his knees, and very slowly turned it on. He immediately stopped turning when just the slightest stream of water began to flow unto the concrete floor. He stooped over and put his mouth right on the spigot. Since it was barely running, I didn't hear any noise.

He drank for a long time and then motioned for me to come over. I quietly walked up to him, still holding my broom, and bent down. He got up and I quickly put my mouth on the metal ring. It was as good as any beverage I've had before or since! The word refreshing was made for that moment. I drank a long time, then carefully turned off the water and joined my companion at the holes.

I don't know if it was the actual water, or the fact that we had defied the SS that made us feel good. But for the first time since our arrival, I relaxed a little. Something about my companion let me know that I could trust him, and I absolutely needed someone I could trust in the camp. We talked quietly as we worked through the stench and hunger.

"You must do whatever you can to avoid the commandant," he said to me. "I was walking with another prisoner to the parade grounds this morning who told me that the commandant is ruthless. He is attracted to public beatings and executions. And he absolutely hates us pink triangles. Did you notice that our pink triangles are bigger than the other colors?"

Actually, I had noticed that when I was talking to Rudolf in the storeroom. His green triangle was not nearly as large as my pink one.

"The commandant ordered that the pinks be larger so he can see us coming," my companion explained. "He thinks we might want to have sex with him, and he wants to avoid us."

I kept working and assured him that I had every intention of avoiding all the SS officers as much as I possibly could.

"Where were you for breakfast?" he asked me. "I saw you go with the capo Rudolf from our block."

I told him about Rudolf and exactly what had transpired in the storeroom. I did not leave out anything, even the part about his former assistant hanging from the post on the parade grounds.

"What are you going to do?" he asked me in a concerned voice.

"I don't think I have much of a choice," I answered. "I really must have something to eat, and Rudolf can make that happen."

"But aren't you afraid that after a while he'll just find some other new young prisoner and do the same thing to you?" he asked. "Remember, you could just as well be caught with your hands inside the blanket when the next new group of pinks arrive."

I had not thought of that and was now too perplexed to respond. We worked in silence for a while longer.

"Let me try to steal extra for you," my companion said after a long time sweeping through the holes. "I'm from a very poor family, and I'm used to going without. You are young and growing. This way, you won't have to be his sexual slave, and you won't have to worry about someone new coming."

"Why would you do that?" I asked him.

"Because," he said to me sincerely, "it breaks my heart to see someone as young as you in here. And it would break my heart to know that you were being forced to love him."

We worked in complete silence for the rest of the morning. Fortunately, we were just finishing the last hole when the young SS officer opened the door from the outside.

"It's time for lunch," he announced. "I won't check the toilet until after you are finished this afternoon, but I hope for your sakes it will be clean!"

He turned and left through the door. We assumed that we should follow and set our brooms against the wall. The sun was bright, and my eyes hurt for a bit as we walked across the parade grounds to the commissary.

"Most of the others eat at the factory," the officer told us. "The few who work in the camp will eat with you; there will be a few capos in there, so behave. I'm going to have real food with people who don't shove their small Jewish dick up other men's asses." He looked at my companion when he said this and walked to the front building.

The two of us continued into the commissary and got in line with about one hundred others who had jobs inside the actual camp and not at the factory. As we approached the front of the line, I noticed one table with bowls and another with a large metal pot. Each prisoner took a bowl from the first table and proceeded to the next. A brown triangle was scooping very liquid-like soup with a ladle into each bowl that passed by. However, as I began to pass, a capo from a different block came up and shook his head at the brown triangle. I stood and waited for my soup; the prisoner with the ladle just stood as well. After only a moment, the capo pushed me aside using his arm that was wrapped with the black band.

So, still hungry and without food once again, I followed the line with my empty bowl. The prisoners each took a seat, in the order they were in line, on long benches that ran the length of the building. There were no tables, so each held his own bowl in his hand. They sat and slurped the soup with no utensils.

My companion, who was in line behind me, now sat next to me. I was holding my empty bowl with trembling hands. He reached over and steadied my shaking bowl, then began to pour some of his soup into it. I smiled at him. However, no sooner had we brought the bowls up to our lips, than they were both knocked out of our hands and onto the floor.

I looked up and saw a capo standing over us; he was the same capo who had told the brown triangle to deny me any lunch. He didn't say anything, just kicked our bowls farther out of reach and walked away.

"Hey, you," said a voice from the other side of my companion. "Listen to me."

I leaned forward, trying very hard not to cry, and looked at the face that was speaking to me. He was not that much older than me, and I noticed that his clothes were far cleaner than most of the others in the camp. He was a pink.

"I know you had a talk with Rudolf," he continued. "You will find that word gets around fast in here. Do yourself a favor and be Rudolf's assistant. Do whatever he wants you to do and act like you enjoy it."

The Iron Words

My companion interrupted. "I cannot stand by and watch this young man do that."

"Then, you will both be dead within the week," the clean prisoner said. "Listen, all the capos have assistants. I am the assistant to a capo from one of the front blocks. I do what I can to make him happy, and he makes sure I have lots to eat and clean clothes. Look around! Do you see all these bones and skin? I still have meat on me!" He lifted his shirt to reveal a normal-looking stomach and chest. "You could do much worse than Rudolf. He gets the pick of us pinks, and you should be jumping for joy that he set his eyes on you."

I was reminded of what my companion said earlier and asked, "What happens when he finds someone new? I'll be hanging from the platform on the parade grounds like the prisoner from last night."

"Eh," he said, "that guy was a jerk. He was only here for a few months, and Rudolf knew he couldn't trust him. He was always shooting off his mouth and telling on someone. Rudolf had been looking for a new assistant for a while. Look, make Rudolf see that you are trustworthy and become his friend. Make him like you. Do whatever depraved sexual thing he wants. Then, if someone new comes that he wants instead, he will set you free with no problem."

I looked from him to my companion and then to the floor.

"Look, kid," the clean man continued, "you have youth, vigor, and pretty good looks. You can use them, or die. It's that simple. Also, you smell like shit. Rudolf is not going to like that, and that is exactly why he will have fresh clothes for you tonight when you meet him during dinner."

Just then, the capo who had kicked our bowls returned and walked up to the clean prisoner. "You have a talk with him?"

"Yes," he replied. "Tell Rudolf that the new kid will meet him in his office tonight."

"Good," said the capo to the clean prisoner. "Come with me. I only get a few minutes of office time today."

The clean prisoner winked at me, got up, and followed his capo into the kitchen. My companion did not say a word or move a muscle. I sat quietly. I didn't know it then, but that clean prisoner was my salvation, and his advice is the only reason I'm alive today.

THIRTY FIVE

"**Y**ou know the guy you walked to the camp with? What was his name?" Riley asked as they drove home from the Mayo Clinic. "You always call him your companion and never by a first name."

"He had a name, of course, but I never found out what it was. People were a bit odd about names inside Buchenwald. I knew the names of some of the prisoners, but not many. I think that some people didn't want to bother with names because it would make it harder to deal with the inevitable deaths. Other people probably wanted to be known as a number so that they could keep their real life on the outside separate. I'm not sure, perhaps everyone felt different about it. I, however, liked it when people said my name. It was just a small reminder that at one time, I had a home and parents.

"My companion never shared his name. I really believe that he thought our relationship was too special to involve names. That in some odd way, we could be closer, because even something as important as a name was trivial to us."

"What about the SS?" asked Riley. "You've talked about the young SS and the SS with the hose. Did they have names that you knew?"

"The SS had rank," replied Jens. "We knew some of their names, but mostly, we referred to them as *untersturmführer*, *obersturmbannführer, standartenführer,* or the like. I thought it would be easier for you to keep them all straight if I associated them with what they actually did. Honestly, it's been so long since I've thought exclusively in German that even I get the ranks mixed up."

"Sometimes I think that sports teams get a little out of control with nicknames," Riley added, a bit out of the blue.

"How so?" asked Jens.

"Well, the cool kids get cool names, but sometimes people get to be known by something stupid they did. In high school, I was called 'stealth' because of the way I skate. But there were also nicknames that I don't want to say, because they are sexual, or they are making fun of a guy's family."

Riley, for the first time, began to realize the various privileges he had been given because he was one of the two best on the team. In high school, he had been on top, like a green capo who roamed the halls of Hastings High with plenty of bread and water.

After that first lunch, I was still starving because of the message that Rudolf delivered to me through the other capo. But my companion and I were quickly ushered out by the young SS officer and brought back to the toilet building.

Again, he waited outside after having reminded us of our task. My companion and I went inside and filled the bucket with water. Like before, we drank from the spigot, although this time we weren't so quiet because the officer sitting outside knew that we needed to run the water. We took the bucket and a few rags and walked over to the holes.

"Why don't you just stand there and let me climb inside," I said to my companion. "I'm going to get new clothes at dinner and that way you don't have to sleep in your smell."

"So," he said, "you've already made your decision. You're going to trade sex with Rudolf for favors."

"Yes," I said, "I've decided that I want to live. And I don't see why you can't benefit from that as well. Seriously, look at yourself. You have dried blood on your face from your shaved head. I don't want to look like that, and I don't want you to have to go through that again, either. Just let me do this."

He didn't say anything, and we began our job in silence. I don't think he was judging me, but perhaps he was just very sad that he was powerless to help a young man in need. Anyway, the scrubbing of the long toilet was a terrible assignment; I probably would have vomited if there had been anything in my stomach to come out.

Suddenly, the door of the building was flung open, and the commandant entered, still wearing his full uniform. He was alone. I was not sure what happened to the young SS officer who was waiting outside. My companion was filling up the bucket with fresh water, and I was standing in one of the holes. The commandant slammed the door behind himself and stepped loudly into the building.

"Get out of there!" he yelled in a very deep and loud voice. "Get out of that hole!"

I used the sides of a hole to climb out and slid down on the concrete floor. My companion set down the bucket and walked over to me.

The commandant was fear personified. Many people think that someone who is large and angry is the person to be most afraid of. However, I know from my experience in the camp that it is the person who is irrational and quick to make decisions who causes the most damage. The commandant was one of those people. I could see it in his eyes.

"A faggot and a Jew-faggot," he said to us and shook his head. "I want to see you work. Take off your clothes! Now!"

My companion and I just stood there and glanced at each other. The situation was too bizarre for us to comprehend as quickly as the commandant would have liked.

"Take off your clothes!" he bellowed at us once more.

We both kicked off our shoes and removed our clothes, tossing them to the concrete floor. I had been there less than twenty-four hours, but already I was used to having people see me naked.

"What happened to your head?" the commandant asked my companion.

"I hurt myself falling out of bed," he said.

"Why is your tiny Jewish dick bloody?"

"Same reason."

My companion was one very smart and quick fellow. His response surely saved him a beating, or maybe even worse.

The commandant just stood there and continued to stare at us. We both also stayed still because we weren't sure what was happening, or what we were expected to do next.

"Both of you," he said after a long while, "get in there and start scrubbing."

My companion went and grabbed the bucket. I climbed into the hole that I had gotten out of and took the bucket from him. If I thought the task was horrible before, without shoes it was thirty times worse. Even though we had already swept most of the bigger pieces away, the toilet was still littered with feces that squished between our toes.

"Get down in there and work!" the commandant ordered again.

He came over the toilet and peered at us through the holes. In fact, he watched us the entire time, walking along and looking through whatever hole we were near. My companion and I squatted in the dank stench and scrubbed; we took turns getting fresh water when it was needed.

At the time, I didn't know why the commandant wanted to watch us scrub naked. I remember wondering why he had nothing better to do. Now, I have come to understand that he had a terrible personality defect; he received great pleasure from knowing the power he had over us. Unfortunately, it was a personality defect that most of the SS shared. Today, I often wonder if it was the ultimate power of their position that made them this way, or was it that the Nazis sought out this kind of person in the first place? Probably a bit of both.

Finally, we were done with the toilet. We climbed out and walked back to the spigot with the bucket. I looked at my companion and saw that his body was streaked with brown; I assumed I looked the same. The commandant, however, without a word, simply opened the outside door and left.

We tried very hard to clean ourselves with water from the spigot. Fortunately, we discovered that underneath the pile of rags was a drain in the floor. I filled a bucket and poured it over my companion's head, and he did the same for me. We also washed our feet.

The young SS officer entered the building just as we were getting our clothes back on. He walked over to the toilet and used his flashlight to check through the holes. Then, without saying anything or acknowledging our work, he gestured for us to follow.

My companion's clothes were still fairly clean, but mine were caked on the bottom with feces. I remember getting quite anxious hoping that all the promises from Rudolf would come true. We walked into the commissary; my companion and I did not speak. He got in the line, and I walked alone through the kitchen.

Rudolf was waiting for me at the rear exit of the kitchen. I followed him back to his office, the same storeroom where he'd brought me for breakfast. We stepped in, and he closed the door behind him.

"I am very glad to see you," he said. "I know about that awful thing they make you new pinks do, so you should change clothes."

He turned to a side shelf and gave me a new stack of clothes with shoes. I took them, set them on a shelf near me, and started to take off my old shoes.

"Just throw your stuff in the corner," Rudolf said. "I'll have an old faggot take care of it later."

I started to take off my shirt, and oddly, Rudolf turned around and faced the door. It was clear to me that he didn't want to see me naked. I thought this was quite bizarre. I threw my old clothes in the corner and put on the fresh ones.

"Don't put on your shoes, yet," he said to me. "In one of your shoes there is a spool of thread with a needle stuck through it. Don't forget to rip the badge and number from your old shirt before you leave. When you get to the block, sew them back on your new shirt. Then, make sure you hide the needle and thread underneath your blanket. Be very careful. Before you got here, an assistant was caught with needle and thread; the commandant made him stitch a pink triangle to his balls. He died a week later of infection."

In my mind, it was just another thing to worry about. The casual mention of death was still shocking to me at this point, but before long, death became a normal part of every day. That's sad to think about.

Anyway, Rudolf took off his own shoes, took a large sack and a metal jug from the shelf behind him, and sat on the floor.

"Come down here," he said.

I got down on the floor and sat with my back leaning against a shelf. Rudolf opened the sack and gave me a large loaf of bread. I took it and began to eat it voraciously.

"Don't eat so fast," he said with a chuckle. "You don't want to get sick. We have plenty of time."

I started to eat slower, and I have to say, I'm not sure I have ever enjoyed bread that much again. I took a few deep breaths and allowed myself to relax against the shelf and breathe.

Rudolf handed me the jug. "It's water."

I drank, although not as quickly as I had been eating because of the water I'd already had from the spigot in the toilet building. Rudolf reached into the bag and took out a few small pieces of cheese. I'm not sure what kind of cheese it was, or if it was even fresh, but in that moment it was the best cheese in the world.

He began to eat as well and shared the water from the jug. He took out another loaf of bread and told me to keep it for breakfast. Rudolf explained how to hide it in the waistband of my pajamas and to sleep with it in my armpit. The other pinks would know that I was his assistant, and they would try to steal the extra bread from me.

Then we were both finished eating, and it came time for me to pay the fee associated with the fresh clothes and food. I sat still and waited for him to tell me what to do.

"Jens, just come and spread out next to me," he said. He pushed a few things out of the way and completely stretched out on the floor. He was quite tall and barely fit. I stretched out next to him; our sides were touching. Then, he rolled over to face me. His dark eyes looked into mine, and he smiled.

I had to remind myself that this was the same man who had basically killed someone the night before. He was also the man who used starvation and intimidation to get me to be with him. I made myself promise within, that whatever happened between the two of us, I must always remember the depravity he was capable of.

Now, Rudolf put his arms around me and squeezed hard. He rolled me over on top of him; my face was in his neck. He kissed my forehead.

"We have nothing but time in here," he said to me. "I like to take my time."

We stayed like that, him holding me in the storeroom, until the bell rang. Then we both got up, and he gave me my breakfast bread, which I hid in the waistband of my clean pants. He opened the door and I walked, alone, back through the kitchen to the line of other pinks leaving the commissary. Some of them looked at me, and I knew they were thinking about what I had probably just done with Rudolf.

After dinner, we all assembled on the parade grounds and once again stood very still while each man announced his supposed crime.

Riley asked, "The SS must have known what the capos were doing. Why didn't they care?"

"That's a very good question," answered Jens. "You see, the SS were supposed to be doing a lot more work. The higher-ranked Nazi officials in Berlin thought that the local camp SS were watching us all night, supervising during meals, organizing work details, and a lot of other things. But as I said, the SS were lazy; they needed the capos to do their jobs while they were drinking and gambling. The SS were willing to allow the capos some slack in order to make Berlin believe that the SS were working hard.

"Also, plenty of the SS officers were wanting sex themselves, and with no women around, they used a pink triangle from time to time. As long as Rudolf was happy, the SS didn't worry that he'd say anything to the commandant. Again, I was lucky that Rudolf was my capo, because it meant I was off-limits to the SS. Yes, it was hardly mutual with Rudolf, but the SS were sadistic and especially cruel when they had finished. Many pinks were shot in the back as they walked to our block after sex with some SS scum."

THIRTY SIX

I've heard actual prisoners in the United States speak about the boredom of being in prison; they talk about the rigid repetition that seems to go on forever. When I hear this, I want to slap them. First of all, we were not actual prisoners; we were unjustified victims who had no reason to be there—well, except for the greens. Second, I craved the type of repetitious boredom that people in modern prisons complain of.

You see, even though we had a strict schedule that never deviated, there was always some kind of disruption to our lives. Someone would die. Someone would get beaten. Some SS officer would slam his rifle on someone's head for no reason. We would go for days without food, then be told to gorge ourselves on moldy bread before it grew worse. It is hard to be bored under the constant threat of death and pain. In the camp, change was never good and uncertainty meant pain.

The Iron Words

My companion and I continued to clean the toilet for about another month. While Rudolf made sure I stayed healthy, my companion was beginning to grow thin. I asked Rudolf for an extra loaf of bread, beside my own, to take with me each dinner. Rudolf, who I think was trying hard to buy my affection, obliged and gave it to me. My companion never asked about the bread when I passed it to him during our morning broom sweep; he took it and ate quickly. I'm sure he knew where it came from.

Even if my companion had asked what I had to do to get the bread, I would not have answered. The number one priority in my life was making sure Rudolf could trust me. Watching those around me grow thin and die, I knew that my only hope was to make sure Rudolf continued to need me.

Though it had been about a month since I became Rudolf's assistant, we still had not done anything sexually together. I wanted to begin hoping that it would stay that way, but hope was a dangerous thing at Buchenwald. Rudolf continued to want to hold me on the floor and kiss my forehead. A few times he asked me to take off my shirt and he would gently rub my arms. That's all we had done together.

I knew which of the other pinks were assistants to other block capos; I could tell because we assistants were the only ones with meat on our bones. I wanted to find another assistant and ask about the sexual part that was not happening with Rudolf, but I knew that I could not betray him. If the other assistant told his capo, Rudolf would be devastated. I could not take that chance. However, I lived with the fear that Rudolf might have lost interest.

When our first four weeks were coming to an end, our sleep was interrupted one night as the young SS officer brought some new pinks into the block. I remember hearing a loud commotion when the door opened, and the officer marched in with five new men behind him. I did not dare to sit up, but my heart was beating rapidly. What would Rudolf think of them?

I heard the SS officer and Rudolf assign the bunks; I heard the officer kick them around a bit. While this was happening, I was able to sneak a peek and was quite relieved to see that all five of them were at least forty.

Every time new pinks were brought in, I had this same panic. However, because most of the young men were fighting the war, the new homosexual prisoners were almost always middle-aged or older.

I went to sleep that night relieved, but also a bit happy—well, as happy as could be expected under the conditions. With the new men starting work the next day, I knew that I would not have to clean the toilet building anymore. I looked over and down at my companion. He must have been thinking the same thing, because I caught his eye. We both smiled quickly and went back to sleep. That night, I made extra sure to keep my hands over my blanket; I didn't want to give Rudolf any reason to replace me.

I must have slept better that night because it was the first morning that the bell didn't wake me; I awoke with my companion shaking me. I climbed down, put on my shoes, and walked with him to the parade grounds.

This time, one of the new pinks had not gotten the message about how to announce himself. Either he was too tired to pay attention, or he just didn't want to, but either way, he simply announced just his name and number when it was his turn. The commandant didn't waste any time and did not give second chances. Remember, this was a man who acted first and thought second, if at all.

The commandant blew a whistle to stop the attendance roll call. I stood extremely silent and could tell that all the pinks were afraid; we hoped he would not take it out on all of us. The commandant himself stepped off the platform and marched our direction. Rudolf had now located the man and pushed him out of our line; he fell to his knees. The commandant came up to him, grabbed him by one arm and yanked him to his feet. He then pushed the pink ahead of him toward the platform.

The other SS officers stood at attention on the platform. The commandant gave one more big shove to the new pink, and he fell on the ground in front of the stage. "This faggot doesn't think he is a warmer Bruder!" He then bent over and yelled into the new pink's ear, "Are you too cold to be a warmer Bruder?"

There was no reply. I desperately hoped that the new pink would answer him in a way that would stop the commandant.

"Answer me!" shouted the commandant, even louder. "Are you too cold to be a warmer Bruder?"

Suddenly, the new pink screamed, "I am not a warmer Bruder!"

The commandant kicked him very hard with his thick black boots. He kicked him several times; the new pink curled up in a ball. Then, the commandant signaled to the young SS officer to join him. The commandant said something to the young officer that only those closest could hear. The young SS took off running, very fast, toward the front building. The commandant kicked the new pink several times. Then he marched back up on the stage and leaned against one of the poles.

All of us remained silent and still; nobody knew what was in store for the new pink. We only knew that he was a dead man. As he waited against the pole, the commandant took a pack of cigarettes and a lighter out of his pocket. He took one cigarette, lit it, and started smoking. We all waited.

After a few minutes, the young SS officer came running back, this time with a metal can of gasoline. Finally, the blocks of men in formation started to figure out what the punishment would be and how it fit the crime.

"So, if you are too cold to be a warmer Bruder," said the commandant, still smoking from the stage, "then you need to be warmed up!"

The commandant nodded at the young officer, who began to douse the new pink with the gasoline. Then, as we all had foreseen, the commandant jumped from the stage and bent down to the man. He inhaled one last time then took the cigarette out of his mouth and pushed it into the man's clothing. The commandant sprang back as the new pink burst into a ball of flame. The doomed pink screamed loud and long; his screams still are in my mind. He got up and started running around, full of flame and pain. Those in the front of the formation made room for him. Finally, after just a few moments, he stopped and dropped to the ground. His body was made to stay there for several weeks, charred and still, until some animals must have hauled it away.

THIRTY SEVEN

"Come in, Professor Weber," the head of the Sociology Department said when she saw Jade walk through the office door.

"Good morning," replied Jade with a smile.

"You can close the door if we need to be private," said the department head. "You didn't tell me in your e-mail what you wanted to speak about."

Jade closed the door to the small office and sat in one of the chairs opposite the desk. "I'm going to get right to the point," she said. "I'm afraid that I may have committed an act against academic integrity, and I have to report myself."

The department head remained quite calm. She had learned not to react until all the information was given. This was not the first time she had dealt with faculty who had made a mistake, and it would certainly not be the last.

"Tell me what you did," the department head said.

"Well," began Jade, "I had a student athlete in my course on aging, and he was failing. Of course, the Athletic Department intervened, and I decided to grant a large extra-credit assignment in lieu of missed sessions and homework."

The department head interrupted, "Are you comfortable with that?"

"Of course I'm not," Jade said. "But we've both been around here long enough to know how things work. No, I'm more bothered by the assignment I gave him."

"How so?"

"I have a neighbor in St. Paul who has always intrigued me," continued Jade. "He is a former professor from this campus. He's advanced in age, and I just knew there was a story that he desperately needed to tell."

"And you thought that you were the person he needed to tell it to?" the department head interrupted once again.

"I know," replied Jade, quite embarrassed. "My husband has accused me of the same thing in this matter. I just wanted to help him, so I arranged for the student to work with him."

"Was there a story?" the department head asked.

"Yes, a very worthwhile story," responded Jade. "But I'm proud to say that the student didn't tell much of it to me. I think he feels some loyalty to my neighbor."

"He maybe also didn't appreciate being a spy," the department head added in a straight tone.

"Well," said Jade quickly, "that's it exactly. I asked a student to be a spy, didn't I?"

The department head sat back in her chair and took a minute to think. Jade glanced out the window at the summer sun as a window air-conditioner blared in the small room.

"Let me think about it," said the department head, "but my initial reaction is that you would have infringed on the student only had you made him tell you the story. Because you decided the act of gathering the story is what's important, rather than the story itself, I think you are in the clear. If you had made the student break the neighbor's confidence, then we would be having a different discussion right now."

Jade was relieved that she need not face a faculty committee. However, she was still a bit disappointed in herself. She did not know the great good she had done for two needy people.

THIRTY EIGHT

While the winters in Minnesota were notoriously long and cold, the summers were heavenly. A summer day in Minneapolis was as nice as anywhere on the planet. However, even though it was perfection outdoors, it was cool and dark inside the hockey practice facility.

Riley was skating, very fast and alone, around the rink. He had fallen into a pattern of just skating, even though he knew the team coaches and trainers wouldn't approve. He was wearing jeans, a sweat shirt, and his hockey skates. He was not wearing pads, a helmet, or any other piece of equipment. Riley was fairly sure this was the first time in his life that he'd ever just skated for the fun of skating.

In fact, the new pattern was so strong that he had skipped his weight training for almost two weeks. He loved the simplicity of going to the ice without a huge duffel of stuff. He swerved and glided through the middle of the rink and raced around the outside. He knew that he was neglecting work on the swift maneuvers and strength that made him great, but Jens's horrible tale made him want to have fun while he was young and capable.

For the first time in his life, Riley understood what it meant to have privilege. He was not going to squander his opportunities any longer. He was ready to start the next school year with a new attitude. If only he could get Jake out of his mind. Riley was very afraid that Jake would haunt him the rest of his life.

As Riley swerved backward around the south curve of the rink, he saw a familiar shape coming down the steps across from him. He had been avoiding this person for over a month, but now it was time to face the music.

The coach saw immediately that Riley noticed him as he approached the edge of the ice. He gestured for Riley to join him on the north end of the rink. Riley kept his fast pace, backward around the side of the rink, then switched to forward and skidded to a fast stop in front of the coach. He'd had enough practice over the years to know how to avoid spraying the coach with the small chunks of ice that flew from his skates.

"Hi, Coach," Riley said as he attempted to gain control of the conversation by sounding upbeat. "I'm just getting some ice time in."

"Doesn't look like that me," responded the coach in a gruff manner. "Looks like you're figure skating to me. I don't see any pads or pucks on the ice. I don't even see a stick."

"I have hockey skates on, Coach," replied Riley and held up his foot for the coach to see.

"Hmm," said the coach. The coach did not look happy. But then, oftentimes it was hard to tell. "You haven't returned my calls," the coach said. "I was worried about you, but now I'm just plain mad. I got a message from your professor that you got an A in her class. So what's wrong now?"

"Nothing's wrong," answered the young man. "Just spending the summer training."

"You've missed a lot of training sessions," said the coach, "and I see that the rumors are true. Your ice time is spent fooling around without any equipment. Why are you wasting time?"

"I'm just taking a few weeks off," said Riley. "I'm actually still doing the project from Dr. Weber's class, and I just wanted to take a break."

"That's not what I heard," said the coach matter-of-factly.

"What?"

The coach took a step back and cleared his throat nervously. His expression looked odd to Riley. "The guys on the team are saying that you are staying away from them because you're gay," said the coach bluntly.

Riley was surprised. "What?"

"Well," replied the coach, "I've heard it from more than one person. Are you gay?"

Riley immediately knew that it must have been Abby who was spreading this gossip. She had left several angry voice mails and texts over the past weeks. Riley just shook his head and cursed her silently.

"I want to know," implored the coach. "Are you gay? I have a right to know; I've invested a lot of money and time in you. If you're going to do something that screws with the chemistry of this team, I have the right to know about it. Are you gay?"

Riley was just about to answer, but then he paused. He knew that he was not gay; he had always known that he was attracted to women. It wasn't something he thought much about. Normally, he would have shouted the truth at the coach and then taken it up with Abby and the guys on the team. But now, with the images of Jens and Buchenwald in his mind, he stopped himself from reacting.

"Maybe," said Riley in his regular voice. "I don't see how that makes any difference to the chemistry of the team."

"It makes all the difference in the world!" The coach lost his temper. "Do you think the other guys are going to pass the puck to you? Do you think they're going to want to hang out with you? Who wants to shower with a faggot? I don't! And what about the donors to the program? Those rich bastards are old as shit. Do you think they're going to part with a dime if a faggot is on the ice?"

During the coach's tirade, Riley did not see him as the respected coach of a Division I hockey team. In his mind, Riley saw him as just another homophobic Nazi. However, there was one crucial difference: Jens was forced to stand and listen to this crap; Riley was not.

In that moment, Riley experienced how it felt to take complete control of his life; he liked it. As the coach began to yell louder, Riley simply skated away.

THIRTY NINE

My new job in the camp was very different from cleaning the toilet. It was also different from the task assigned to my companion. I watched him go with the other pinks that morning to the ammunition factory. I followed Rudolf into the front building.

The front, or main, building had two floors. We walked up the wooden steps to the top floor. I had assumed this area was off-limits to prisoners, but apparently I was wrong. We were above the rooms where the daily arrivals were cleaned, clothed, and shaved. Even though we only got new pinks every couple of weeks or so, new yellows were arriving every day. Up until this point, I had not wondered why us pinks never left the camp; we just died there. However, the Jewish people arrived each day, and each day, a truck would take old and sick Jews back to the train station. Something different was happening to the yellows that was not happening to the rest of us. I hoped my mixed-colored companion would be safe.

Rudolf and I walked down the hallway that ran through the middle of the second floor and stopped midway. "Look here," Rudolf whispered into my ear, "through this door is the commandant's office. You never go in there and stay very quiet out here. You're going to work in that room, across the hall from him. You stay out of his way, you hear me?"

"Yes," I whispered back, "of course."

Rudolf opened the door across from the commandant's office and motioned for me to go inside. I saw a room with many rows of filing cabinets. A large window overlooked the entrance gate to the camp. There was only one other person, a red, in the room.

Rudolf closed the door and walked me over to the red. The wood floor was not well built and creaked as we walked. "This is Otto," Rudolf said to me as he pointed to the red. "Otto will show you what to do. I will see you at lunch." With that, Rudolf left the room.

Otto looked at me with disgust and shook his head. I was used to that reaction by now. "So, you are Rudolf's assistant?" he asked me bluntly.

"Yes."

"Some SS officer must owe Rudolf something very big for him to have secured you a job up here."

"I wouldn't know," I said.

"Of course not," he answered. "You're the first pink to be allowed up here. You should be in the ammunition factory with the others!"

I apologized for not being at the factory. But he was a red and needed to respect the green who symbolically stood behind me. I looked indifferently at him from that point on.

Otto explained that the room was a paperwork collection point for the camp. In his opinion, the only good thing the Nazis had ever done was insist on well-maintained records. I think, as a political prisoner, he was hoping Germany would lose the war so that he could be a hero. The records would help to prove that.

Each new prisoner had to have a record created and filed. Consequently, each departure was also noted on the original record. The forms of those who died were then separated from the forms of those who had been sent away. Also, any infraction a prisoner committed was noted and filed.

Otto took care of the arrivals and departures; it required him to make two visits downstairs each day to collect the

information. I was responsible for collect-
ing the infraction slips that were depos-
ited in a box outside the building.

Except for the deaths, it was fairly
easy for Otto to deal with the arrivals and
departures; it was straightforward work. My
job, however, required me to put up with
an endless string of lies. The records of
infractions were a complete joke. The SS
simply made up stuff to make it look like
they were doing something. When they really
discovered an infraction, they just shot the
prisoner but were too lazy to write about
it. I noticed that most of the infraction
slips were in the same handwriting, which
would change from time to time. I had a
suspicion that whoever lost a game of cards
was the officer who had to waste his time
writing bogus slips.

But I never complained about my job to
anyone. I was always very grateful to Rudolf
for securing it. In addition, when I saw
the condition of my companion after his
first day of work, I knew that I was receiving special treatment.

He met up with me as I was leaving dinner
with Rudolf that day; we walked together
toward the block. He was looking rough, and
I gave him an extra piece of bread. He took
it from me, and I noticed that his hands
were like raw meat. Red welts and blisters

were spread all over his palms, and his fingers were swollen and black.

"What happened?" I asked.

"All of us pinks work in the foundry for the ammunition plant," he said. "It's our job to process the molten metal before it's made into large sheets. Then the sheets get stamped and turned into something. I'm not sure if it's bullets or what."

"I've seen a lot of pinks who work in the foundry," I told him, "but I haven't seen hands like yours before. What's happening to you?"

"Well," he said, "the others have gloves. I found out this morning that my job is to stir the hot liquid as it pours out of a basin. It's very hot and splashes on my hands. There were several SS officers over there whom I hadn't seen before; they must not work inside the camp. One of them even gave me gloves. But they got taken away."

"What? By whom?" I asked.

He explained, "Some of the other pinks taunted me about being Jewish. The officers were not around, so one of the pinks held me from behind while another took my gloves."

I was astounded. Not only was it bad enough to be treated this way by the SS, but to be hated by the other prisoners was unthinkable. It was even more unthinkable that the other prisoners were pinks and should have had more understanding. But in a dog-eat-dog situation, everyone turns into a dog. My companion was just unfortunate to be on the bottom.

"Hmm. You can't talk to the SS about it. That will bring trouble to the whole block."

"I know," he said dejectedly.

"I'm going to get some salve from Rudolf. He had a blister on his foot. He stole some from the main building and has it under his blanket."

"I can't ask you to do that," he responded. "I know what you have to…"

"Of course you can ask me to do that," I interrupted. "You and I are together in this, from the train station to the end of the war."

That was the first time I had spoken aloud about hoping for the end of Germany. Of course, we all thought about it all the time, but none dared to speak of such hope.

"Also, I will make sure you get some gloves. If anyone has a problem with that, you tell them that Rudolf is going to catch them with their hands under the blanket. I might as well get even more benefit from my arrangement. If I'm going to survive, then you are, too."

Michael Fridgen

My companion never refused my help again,
nor did he question Rudolf and my relationship. I was committed to using my body and
mind to get out of this alive.

FORTY

It got cold in the fall. There were no calendars in the prisoner areas of the camp, but I passed a calendar mounted on a wall whenever I went to the filing room. Also, the prisoners with nonfoundry jobs in the ammunition factory could easily find calendars in various offices. By the time the end of October approached, I was glad for the scratchy wool blanket but was increasingly worried about the winter.

The block as a whole was not heated. There was a very small woodstove in the corner near the door; however, it was only used when an SS officer needed to stay through the night with us. Needless to say, that was not often. The worst part about the lack of heat was having to keep our hands above the blanket. It was impossible to get warm when one part of your body was always blue and freezing.

Rudolf told me that there was no use getting me an extra blanket; it would get stolen quickly, and there were not many to go around. There was always some rumor that the blankets of the pink triangles were to be given to the greens and reds anyway. By the time the first snow fell, the prisoners were desperate to grab any type of cloth they could find. And believe me, they somehow managed to find some. Through Rudolf, I was able to get extra layers of clothes for my companion and me. We wore them constantly and creatively, often wrapping shirts and pants around our feet.

I'm not sure how Rudolf actually felt about me asking for extra supplies for my companion. However, he always followed through and seemed happy to get them for me. I was very honest with him about who they were for, and he didn't seem to mind they were given to the multicolored star. In these early days, Rudolf went out of his way to make me happy. It was a bizarre courtship.

My companion's hands had finally healed with the help of the salve. The others never bothered him again when he showed up for work with gloves. I never had to say anything, either. I imagined that Rudolf got through to some of them and scared them into compliance. Rudolf puzzled me because he was just so nice to me; again, I reminded myself of what he had done and was still capable of doing.

The Iron Words

Rudolf continued his habit of just holding me on the floor during dinner. Sometimes, he would feel my arms and chest, but mostly it was quite innocent. However, that was about to change.

It was Christmas Eve, 1942, and everyone in the camp was aware of the approaching holiday. It had become known that the Nazis wanted to stop all work on Christmas Day. Normally, we worked seven days a week, because the war effort did not stop, so, we were surprised to know that we could spend a whole day in the block. I remember thinking it was good of the SS to do this for us, until my companion reminded me that it was just another way of poking at the Jews. It was an insult to make the Jewish people work on all their holidays, but then give them the day off for a big Christian celebration.

Otto and I continued to have very little conversation as he ignored me day after day. When we were finished work on that Christmas Eve, I wished him freedom for the New Year. He ignored me, as he always did.

I walked to the commissary and got ready on the floor of Rudolf's office. He entered, not too far behind me, with his usual sack of food. However, this night he was able to smuggle in some actual gingerbread! I was elated and savored each bite; I remember hoping that nobody in the block would smell the strong scent on my breath. Apparently, one of the SS officers received the treat from his wife, and he hated it, so he gave it to Rudolf in exchange for something I probably didn't want to know about.

Rudolf talked some, but not much. Normally, we chatted about the weather or mundane things as we were on the floor together. Of course, politics and the war were never mentioned.

So, it surprised me when he suddenly said, "I have a wife and kids, you know. It's Christmas, and I'm thinking about them."

"Oh," I replied, "where do they live?"

"In Dresden, with her parents. At least, that is where they were the last time I heard from them. We were poor, and my wife was starving. I stole some money from a man I was working for, and he caught me in the act. Because I was so afraid of going to a work camp, I killed him. I was caught doing that, too, and now I'm here."

I didn't react; I was not sure what to say. I was glad he trusted me enough to tell me this, but at the same time, I didn't really want to know all that.

"So, you see Jens, I really am not a faggot."

It didn't make any difference to me whether he was or not; I assumed the outcome would be the same. But I wanted to be nice to him, especially at this time of year. "I'm sad to hear all that," I told him. "You probably miss your kids a lot, especially on Christmas."

"Oh," he replied sadly, "I miss them, but I'm afraid they do not miss me. I was bad to them. I beat them. But never my wife. No, I always put her on a pedestal."

I began to figure out that Rudolf was warped somehow when it came to family relationships. His own upbringing was probably not very good, and now he had a need to privately show affection and publicly show power; it's what drove him.

Rudolf started kissing me, and I knew that he was thinking of his wife. I did the best I could and was finally starting to earn the many favors I had been granted that fall. At least, because he was pretending I was a woman, Rudolf was gentle during sex; I was happy about that. As you can tell, I was also becoming quite warped myself. I somehow believed that Rudolf deserved to do this to me.

When we were through, he left me to clean up. My clothes needed to be changed, so I ripped the badge and number off and pinned them to the fresh clothes that Rudolf had in the sack. I had been able to grab a few pins some weeks earlier and found it much easier. The SS officers never looked close enough to notice, and I was good at hiding the pins in the cloth. I was able to sleep much better knowing that the needle and thread were not in my bed.

After the evening roll call, as was customary, we all marched back to our block and settled down, under the bright lights, for our first night before a holiday. But suddenly, when we had only been in there for an hour or so, a loud clanking woke all of us up. I was startled and sat up quickly.

Coming through the door were the young SS officer, the officer who had raped us with the hose, and two others who had not been there very long. The officer with the hose banged on a pot with a metal spoon.

"All right, you faggots!" he shouted. "Get your asses out of bed. The commandant wants to see you!"

These SS officers were extremely drunk. Some of the prisoners started getting out of bed and jumping down from the bunks. I wasn't quite sure what to do. I looked to the middle of the block, where Rudolf normally slept, and saw him walking toward the SS officers.

"Go back to bed, Rudolf," the young one said to him. "You're not needed in this. Faggots only! Hurry up, you pink bastards!

The Iron Words

And no shoes—the commandant says that you warmer Bruder are too warm anyway, and some snow on your feet will do you good. Hurry up!"

One of the SS got his rifle from his shoulder and shot at the ceiling; they all laughed hysterically. We started running out of the door and into the darkness. Yes, it was very cold on my feet, but I was too scared to notice too much. I was very afraid of the drunken SS with their stupidity and rifles.

We could hear them shooting into the sky behind us as we all ran toward the parade grounds. The prisoners from the other blocks were peeking out of doors, attempting to see what was going on. It became apparent that only the pinks had been summoned this night.

The commandant was already on the platform, surrounded by about twenty other SS officers. Some I recognized, some I did not. We ran to our normal place at the very end of the grounds and began to form our usual single line.

"You faggots!" the commandant yelled at us. "Get your asses over here, in front of the stage."

We ran in a large group and stood right in front of the platform. Now, I could see that all the officers on the platform were completely drunk. The four who gathered us from the block joined the others on the stage. There was a lot of loud talking and staggering about.

It was our habit to form a straight line for the roll call, but the commandant didn't want that. He walked to the front of the platform and yelled at the other SS to quiet down.

"You faggots, just make a large group right here!" he shouted and pointed to a general area in front of the platform.

We lost the shape of our line and huddled together. Now, I was starting to feel the pain of the snow on my bare feet. We all wanted to rapidly switch weight from foot to foot, but none of us did that because we were afraid.

"It's Christmas, you faggots!" The commandant's speech was slurred. "I have to work tomorrow watching you bastards, while you get to loaf around all day!"

When he said this, cries of agreement came from the others on the platform. A few shots rang through the night.

"So, tonight," the commandant continued, "you faggots are going to help us celebrate Christmas. I want to hear *Stille Nacht!* And it better be good. You faggots are supposed to be good at this sort of thing, and the Jews don't know the damn song!"

The Iron Words

We all stood in silence. I had heard what he said, but I didn't know how to respond. I don't think any of us did.

"What are you waiting for?" he shouted. *"Stille Nacht!"*

Again, we were silent. I don't think we were trying to be belligerent, but nobody wanted to be the first to sing. What if this was some kind of cruel joke?

After a few moments of him looking at us and us looking at him, the commandant turned around and grabbed a rifle from an officer behind him. "I said sing!" he shouted and pointed the rifle at a pink in the front row. He shot, and the man's body fell to the ground. It was sad to see that there was no gasping of surprise from our group; we were all used to this sort of immediate death.

I don't know who, but someone among us started singing *Stille Nacht*. I joined in the singing immediately. We all knew the beautiful words and simple melody we'd grown up singing. My feet hurt badly, and I was shaking from the cold and fear, but I managed to keep singing.

Strangely, the SS officers, including the commandant, just stood still and listened. They were quiet for once, and maybe even respectful. You might think it made me happy to see that the SS were listening to us, but on the contrary, I was furious. You see, we were being forced to do this; they had even killed to get us to do this. They were quiet, because they wanted to seem normal and even spiritual. Here they were, using us to provide them with some sense of humanity on Christmas Eve. They were using us in the worst way possible. I don't believe I've ever felt so violated since then.

When we had finished with the three verses that were customarily sung, we stood silent again. After a few moments, the drunkards took over once more, and the normal crude SS officers were back.

"Who wants to hear another?" shouted the commandant.

And so, with our feet killing us, we stood in the snow and sang German Christmas carols for I don't know how long. I wanted to go back to the block badly, but I would have stayed there all night to avoid what happened next.

We were in the middle of *O Tannenbaum*, when one of the SS shouted, "Hey! He's not singing!"

It was clear that the officer was pointing at my companion. I had completely forgotten that, because he was Jewish, he did not know any of these songs.

"Bring him up here!" yelled the commandant.

The Iron Words

The young SS officer went to the front of our group and dragged my companion to the platform. Oh, how I wished that I had remembered him and shoved him into the middle where he might have remained hidden. My companion now stood there, looking terrified.

"You are a Jew-faggot," said the commandant when he noticed the multicolored Star of David. "The Jew side doesn't know shit, but surely the faggot side knows something, huh?"

I wanted to close my eyes, but I couldn't. The SS officers were drunk and trigger-happy. I saw little hope in this situation.

"I'll tell you what," continued the commandant, "you sing one verse of *Stille Nacht* perfectly, and I'll let you go. Hell, I'll even get a piece of turkey from our dinner tomorrow and bring it to you! Now you sing—perfectly—not even one wrong word."

I didn't know how much of the song, if any, that he knew. He was Jewish, and of course he had not learned it from home or church. However, he was from Frankfurt, so perhaps he had picked something up from going around town during the Christmas season.

"I'm waiting," said the commandant in a pretend sweet voice. "Won't you sing for us? Please?"

I saw tears begin to stream down my companion's face. He was breathing heavily and fidgeting with his hands. Softly, he began to sing, "Stille nacht, heilige nacht, alles schlaft, einsam…einsam…einsam—"

"Oh," interrupted the drunk commandant, feigning sadness, "what a pity."

The commandant shook his head and turned to look at the other officers. I closed my eyes and waited for the shot that I knew would come. I was having trouble breathing and started to shake.

"I'm not going to deal with you now," the commandant said, and I opened my eyes. "I want the whole camp to see this, and only the faggots are here now. Take him and tie him up. Put him in the SS dining room so that he can watch us eat the feast tomorrow. I will deal with him after Christmas. Now, you faggots get back to your block!"

Everyone started running, except for me. I stood and stared at my companion who was weeping profusely on the platform. I wanted him to look at me; I wanted that so desperately. But it was not to be. My sense of survival kicked in when some rifle shots began. I started running like all the others.

How many times did cowardice save me? Many times. What could I have done anyway?

The Iron Words

My companion was already pretty much dead.
Now that I'm eighty-eight…well, some days
it was worth it to live. Other days, not so
much.

FORTY ONE

Riley stood in the shower and felt the cool water wash over him. He had expected to be alone on the ice and was not pleasantly surprised when he discovered that four others from the team were there. Since he had spent the summer avoiding organized hockey, this was the first time in a long while that he had practiced with other guys from the team.

It had not gone well on the ice that morning. Riley could tell that something was not quite right with the other guys. Their skating was aggressive and fast. Too many times Riley was hit with a stick or jabbed by an elbow. These impromptu practices were usually more relaxed which made Riley frustrated and confused.

By the time the guys decided to stop, Riley was hot and sweaty from the intense activity. He noticed that the others looked just as tired. Riley was in great shape and could make them at least work hard to harass him. He still did not know why the guys were so rough that morning.

When they walked into the locker room and threw down their gear, Riley, in his routine, stripped and jumped into the shower. Now, as he felt relieved from the water, he wondered what the other guys were still doing in the locker room. Usually they would all be in the shower by now, especially after an intense morning. Riley grew suspicious of the other guys. He questioned if Abby had been spreading more rumors about him. *Maybe the coach told them to give me a hard time.*

Hoping to avoid them, he stayed in the shower as long as he could. Then, he got tired and turned off the water. Riley grabbed a towel from a shelf at the end of the shower room and dried off. He tied the towel around his waist and walked to his locker. He heard some laughter from the team lounge on the other side of the bank of lockers. He ignored it.

Riley approached his locker and noticed that a piece of paper had been stuck into one of the metal air vents in the door. He pulled it out and noticed that it smelled badly. The paper had been folded into a makeshift envelope and a message was scribbled with blue ink on the outside.

Dear faggit,

Please do not bring AIDS into the locker room – its bad enough we have to shower with u – we left a gift in this note. If u can't help urself and want to rape us – please use it.

Thanks,

The Managment

Inside the folded paper was a used condom. Riley was repulsed. But he did not think about the snickering guys in the team lounge. Instead, Riley's first thought was of Jens being forced to sing barefoot in the cold snow.

Riley tossed the paper and gift into a nearby trash can. He took the towel from his waist and threw it on the floor. He quickly dressed and, ignoring locker room rules, left his practice clothes and gear on the floor. He grabbed only his skates.

When he passed the team lounge on his way out, he glanced at the four guys. They noticed him and diverted their eyes. On the outside, they looked like his teammates and guys he used to hang out with. But on the inside, Riley saw them as being four young SS officers. He shrugged his shoulders and shook his head. He was not mad, just very sad.

The Christmas Day holiday was not a joyful time. Because Berlin decided we were not working that day, the SS decided that we didn't need to eat either. I, like all the others, rationed what was supposed to be my breakfast bread for the whole day. Most in the block spent the daylight on their wooden beds, curled up in blankets and rags; there were no SS officers around, and we took the chance of sleeping with our hands inside the blanket. I guess that was the only Christmas gift I ever got at Buchenwald.

I was very worried about my companion and knew that it would be at least another twenty-four hours before I'd see him. If he really had been tied up in the SS dining room, he would be hungry, but at least warm. However, there was no doubt in my mind that the officers spent the day drinking. I couldn't imagine what horrors he would have to endure the drunker they became.

I'd never had this much time before to just sit and look at the other prisoners. It was a terrible sight; the prisoners looked more like ghosts and less alive every month.

The Iron Words

Loose skin, jagged bones, bruises, scabs, and sad eyes were everywhere. The lack of hair was horrific. The block smelled of every human odor combined.

I have to say that I was glad when that day was over. At least in the filing room I was warm and had something else to think about. The holiday had become much more of a curse than a blessing. Since then, I've never been able to hear Christmas carols and enjoy them; all I think about is singing for the SS with frozen toes.

The next morning, with a nervous stomach for my companion, I made my way to the parade grounds. I expected to see him hanging from a pole or lying dead behind our line. However, there was no sign of him. The SS officers, including the commandant, acted as if nothing had happened on Christmas Eve; they stood on the platform as usual. I kept expecting my companion to be dragged out of the front building, but that didn't happen, either. Not knowing was far worse than knowing, and the panic inside of me grew more intense.

I had no choice but to go to work; I attempted to sneak a look in the various rooms in the front building as I made my way to the filing room. There was absolutely no sign of my companion. As I got busy updating the records, I became afraid that perhaps they had been so rough with him in the SS dining room that they had killed him and already disposed of his body. I asked Otto if I could see the death notices from Christmas Day, but he just snorted at me and sneered.

We had the normal lunch of watery soup. I looked around for Rudolf but didn't see him. I was very much looking forward to seeing him during dinner so that I could hopefully get some information. If anyone knew what happened, it would be Rudolf.

We went back to work, and I was still very nervous. Then, after three hours, Otto and I were interrupted in the middle of the afternoon. Rudolf, quite quietly, entered the filing room and closed the door behind him. He walked straight over to me. I could tell that Otto was both annoyed and curious.

"Jens," Rudolf said to me as he handed me a sack, "I brought you some food. There is not going to be any dinner again tonight."

"What? That will mean that most of us will not have eaten any real food for over two days."

"I know that, but there is nothing we can do."

"Rudolf," I said as I looked directly into his eyes, "what is going on?"

I know he could tell how anxious I was. I'm also sure he knew why I was acting that way and how much I wanted to find out information about my companion.

"Jens," he answered, "I know you are close with the Jew-faggot they tied up two nights ago. I heard all about it from some of the other pinks. I don't mind that you were close to him, and I've even helped him through you. Remember, I've given extra food, clothing, and medication for you to give to him."

"I know that," I said, "and I appreciate that. Rudolf, I'm very sincere and I thank you for all of that. But you have to tell me what happened to him."

"Jens, listen," he continued, "you must forget that you knew him. Forget him entirely. Instead of dinner tonight, they plan an exhibition that involves him and the entire camp. I don't know what they have in store, but the rumor is that it will be horrific. Just close your mind, Jens. I will see you tomorrow at dinner. Forget him, Jens. He is already dead."

With that, Rudolf left as quietly as he arrived. As I watched him go, I contemplated what he had just said to me. I took a deep breath and promised myself that I must survive, not just for me, but for my companion. If that meant he was already dead to me, then that was how it was going to be.

I opened the sack Rudolf gave me and saw two small loaves of bread and a hunk of cheese. I began to stow them between the multiple layers of waistband I was wearing. Then, I noticed Otto. He was just standing and shaking his head at me; I knew he was judging me, and I didn't care. I took one of the loaves and offered it to him.

"No," he said, "I don't want this food from a whore. I know what you do to get it."

"No matter who it's from," I said. "It's still bread. Stale, yes, but bread nonetheless."

"I don't want it."

"Are you telling me that you would rather starve than take food from a pink?"

"Yes," he replied, and we never talked about it again.

As dinner approached, naturally I was quite sick to my stomach. I kept repeating Rudolf's words and tried hard to forget that I ever knew my companion.

Finally, the bells rang, and we cleaned up the projects we had been working on. Otto and I, without speaking, went out the door and into the hallway. Suddenly, the commandant himself came down the hall and toward his office. Now, this happened every once in a while and we knew to stop immediately, place our backs against the wall, and lower our heads until he passed.

The Iron Words

The commandant walked past us and put his hand on his doorknob. Then he stopped, paused for a moment, and turned to us.

"You, red," he barked at Otto, "get out to the assembly. You, pink, get in here."

I was in an intense panic. Did he know that I was a friend of the Jew-faggot? Was this the end for me?

Otto took no time to run to the stairs and get out of the building. I followed the commandant into his office.

"Close the door," he commanded me.

I obeyed and stood very near it.

The room was about the same size as the filing room. It contained a large desk that was quite messy with papers and miscellaneous stuff. A large chair for the commandant sat on the opposite side of the desk and faced the door. Two regular chairs were off to the side. There were a couple of empty bookcases, and there was a rifle of some sort in the corner.

Directly opposite the door was a huge window that overlooked the parade grounds. I had seen this window often as I stood for roll call and wondered what the commandant was doing all day.

He unbuttoned his uniform coat and removed it, hanging it on a hook next to the window. Then he walked to the middle of the window and stood, looking out.

"Come over here," he commanded again.

I walked over and stood about a meter away, also looking out of the window. I could see the entire parade grounds stretching out before me. The first row of blocks was also in sight. From this vantage, the commandant had an excellent view of the wooden platform.

The entire SS contingent, minus the commandant, was assembled on the stage. The prisoners were almost finished making their usual lines. I wondered if they knew that dinner had been canceled.

Then, I noticed something new to the usual scene. In front of the platform, placed on the ground, there was a wooden ladder that was about four feet tall.

"Do you like my horse?" the commandant asked me.

"I'm sorry, sir, but I don't understand. I don't see a horse," I said, hoping it wasn't another cruel trick.

He laughed. "No, that wooden ladder in front of the stage. We built it yesterday. I call it my horse."

I did not respond and remained staring out of the window. He must not have expected me to respond, as he also remained still and quiet.

From the back of the assembly came the young SS officer pulling on a rope that was tied around my companion's neck. He was naked, bloody, and shaking. I reminded myself to forget he was my friend, but I couldn't. It was just too difficult.

The officer brought him to the front of the platform and made him stand up. Even from this distance, I could see that they had attached both a pink and yellow triangle to his bare skin; blood streamed down his torso from the badges. Because the blood look dried, I assumed they had done this to him on Christmas Day. Later, I would learn that they had actually poked nails through his skin to attach the two triangles.

Next to me, in the upstairs office, I could hear the commandant begin to breathe deeply. I remember thinking how the commandant loved this sort of thing. Why wasn't he down on the grounds? And what was I doing there with him?

Surprisingly, there was no condemnation. None of the SS officers started screaming about what the man had done; perhaps the bloody pink triangle was condemnation enough. The young SS officer took my companion and made him step onto the bottom rung of the ladder. Then, he forced him to bend over the top of it. Next, another SS officer helped the young one grab my companion's arms and pull them straight down toward the ground.

My companion was now bent over the top of the horse, with his buttocks in the air. The young officer used heavy rope to tie each of his hands to the bottom of the ladder. Then, the other officer helped him pull my companion's legs through the rungs. They tied his feet on the same side as his arms, just a little farther up. All of his weight was supported by his stomach resting on the top of the horse. I don't know if you can picture it, but it was a very painful position to be in.

The commandant now reached for the window and slid it open. The cold December air came into the office, but I knew not to react.

The officer who had violated us with the hose now stepped forward. He carried a standard horsewhip. He jumped off the platform and came up to my companion. Without warning, he took the whip and gave a harsh blow to the buttocks. I jumped a little and then reminded myself to stay calm. I saw blood appear as the first blow ripped the skin.

He waited a bit and then struck a second time. My companion screamed in pain. A third time, a fourth time. With each strike the screams of my companion got worse. I desperately tried not to get sick; I didn't want to give the commandant any excuse to harm me.

Then I heard an odd noise next to me. The commandant's breath was quicker, deeper, and he was making a small moaning sound. First, I looked out of the corner of my eye, and then I actually turned my head because I could not believe what I was seeing.

The commandant was masturbating while the torture was occurring down below. Each scream of pain from my companion fueled his maniacal act. The commandant was one very sick person, if you could even call him a person at all. I've never hated anyone like I hated that man. I still hate him.

"Finish me!" he commanded and pulled me over to him.

Finally, I knew why he wanted me in the room. I became a soulless entity and did what he asked. It was terrible and disgusting. The screams from my companion haunt me every night with the images of the commandant.

I'd like to say that this was an isolated incident, but it was not. The commandant enjoyed it so much that at least once a month some pink was tied to the horse. And every time, I was there in his office to finish him.

When he was finished this first time, he pushed me aside and left the office quickly. I cleaned myself up and ran down to the assembly. The whipping had stopped when I got there, and Rudolf had asked some of the pinks to get my companion down from the horse. Yes, my companion was still alive, and I gave myself permission to care for him again. I followed as the same group of pinks brought him to his bunk and set him on the wood. He turned over onto his stomach. I found the salve and began to put it carefully over his open wounds; there were many.

At one point, he gently grabbed my hand and said, "Please, be careful. Don't get caught doing that."

He was right, it would be instant death to nurse a man like this. I worked quicker, and with one eye on the door.

Night fell. I saw my companion wince with pain as he now had to roll over on his back. He painfully pulled up his blanket and put his hands over the top. He was still naked and must have been very cold. I wanted to at least get him dressed, but Rudolf was already staring at me and warning me with his eyes to stay away.

Now that my companion was on his back, I could clearly see the two triangles and streams of dried blood that came from the six nails poked through his skin. My heart was broken and I wasn't even able to cry. I closed my eyes to try to sleep. In my mind, all I could see was the SS taunting him over their Christmas dinner. I had a suspicion that one of the SS came up with the idea of nailing on the triangles to payback this Jew for the crucifixion.

I thought it was all over, and he could rest, but again, nothing was predictable at the hands of these animals. Sometime during the night, the door burst open, and cold air surrounded us. The young SS officer entered, carrying an armful of wood. We all watched carefully as he bent over and put the wood in the stove. He grabbed a rag from his pocket and lit it with his cigarette lighter. We all knew this meant that he would be spending the night in the block with us. But none of us knew why.

"Where is the Jew-faggot?"

My companion answered weakly, "Here."

"Get over here!" the officer shouted.

I heard my companion get up and painfully climb down to the floor.

The SS said loudly, "The commandant thinks that you warmer Bruder need some cooling off. You will sleep outside. I will watch to make sure you don't sneak back in."

I wished they would all get over the whole idea of the warmer Bruder. It was a terrible slang that gave them such an easy excuse for causing misery, especially in the winter.

I heard some footsteps, and the door closed. I shut my eyes and once again tried to forget about him.

The next morning, Rudolf woke me before the bell. I saw that the young SS officer was gone. I did not see my companion on his bed.

Rudolf said slowly and softly, "Jens, he's dead. His body is outside. I want to help you bring him to the assembly, but I can't risk being seen as soft in front of the other capos. Can you understand that?"

I just looked at him, not speaking or feeling.

He continued, "You'll have to bring him yourself because nobody else will touch him. This block has been through enough, and I'm not going to let the SS catch us with one short on the count. Jens, you have to do this."

The bell rang. Rudolf left, and I got out of bed. I was the first to open the door, feel the cold, and see the body of my companion in the snow. He was curled up in a tight fetal position; his skin was red, blue, and hard.

I walked up to him and knelt down on the cold ground; I turned him over. Immediately, I saw the pink and yellow triangles, and the nails that affixed them to his skin. I wanted so badly to yank the nails out of him and throw the triangles over the fence. But even now I dared not, because I knew that my companion wanted me to survive.

The Iron Words

I really had not realized how skinny
he'd become until I lifted him with ease. I
was sick for his death, but also sick for
my own strength. I did not deserve to be
treated so well when the others were starving. It was all a lucky circumstance for
me, and that made me sick, too.

I brought him to the parade grounds and
gently placed him at the end of our line.

Now I had a lover and a rapist, but no
companion.

FORTY TWO

"Hello," she said into her phone.

"Hi, uh, Dr. Weber?"

"Yes, what can I do for you, Riley?"

She was glad that he had called. Over the past weeks, she and her husband had seen Riley drive Jens to his appointments. Jade didn't want any details of Jens's life, especially after the discussion with her department head, but she did want to know that Riley was doing well.

"You said I could call you at this number. I hope that's still okay."

"It's fine," she responded. "This is a good time for me."

"Have you seen Jens lately?"

"I've seen him getting in or out of your car; I've seen him get his mail a couple of times," she answered. "That's probably all I've seen of him lately."

"I'm kind of worried about him. Does he look okay to you?"

Jade answered, "My husband was just saying the other day that he looked thin and weaker than normal."

"I think so, too," Riley said. "Every week it seems to be more of an effort to get him from the car and into the clinic. Last week, I had to get a wheelchair to bring him back to the car."

"Have you asked him about it?" she asked.

"Yes," he replied, "but Jens doesn't like to answer questions about his health. He just tells me that everything is fine. I've been doing some reading on his condition, and I don't think he's responding the way he is supposed to. By now, he should either be much better, or he should have died from paralysis in the muscles that make you breathe."

"When you go to the Mayo Clinic," Jade asked, "do you go inside with him?"

Riley said, "Yes, but it never takes too long. I get him from the parking ramp and into the right building. He checks in, we wait for about ten minutes while they get ready, then he gets called back for his injection. That's it. I don't go back with him for the injection."

"So you've never been able to talk to any of the doctors or anything?"

"Nope," answered Riley. "I'm not sure they would be able to tell me anything without Jens wanting them to."

"I think you are doing a very good thing, Riley," she said. "Even though the spring term is more than finished, you continue to look after him. I like that. But as for this situation, I think you have to let him take the lead. He will tell you if he wants to, or if he feels you really need to know. Just keep doing what you are doing and make things as easy as you can."

"Okay," Riley said, "that makes sense." He paused a bit on the phone; they both sensed that he wanted to say more. It took a few moments for him to begin. "Dr. Weber, I want to thank you for introducing me to Jens," Riley said in a most sincere voice. "He's made a big difference in my life already. I don't think that I will ever be able to share with anyone what I've learned from him; at least, I haven't asked him if I should. His life makes me want to completely change mine. I never realized how much time I was spending on things that don't really matter. So, I want you to know that I'm glad this all happened, and I want to thank you for giving me a chance to improve my grade."

Professor Weber wanted to craft an elaborate response about sociology, mentorship, and responsibility, but all she said was, "Riley, learn what you can and be the person you want to be. That's really all any of us can do."

FORTY THREE

"How many times do you have to say that number?" Riley was pushing Jens's wheelchair away from a clinic building and toward the parking garage.

"Oh, the Mayo Clinic number?" said Jens. "A lot. They ask it constantly."

"I've heard you say it to everyone you meet in there," Riley inquired. "Is it the same as your social security?"

"No," answered Jens, "I asked a nurse about it once. There was an actual patient number one, a man from Canada, when they started keeping records at the Mayo Clinic over one hundred years ago. My number is 7,001,740; I guess they've had a lot of patients over the years. Of course, I have it memorized because they ask it so much. I guess we all get to be known by more numbers than our names. I have a university ID number that I haven't been able to forget, even though I haven't use it since I retired."

"What was your concentration camp number again?" asked the young man. After the weeks of hearing about the intense happenings of Buchenwald, Riley grew comfortable asking more kinds of questions. It felt good to not have to filter every word as he had to do so many times in his life. He liked what his relationship with Jens had become.

"I was 1973," Jens responded. "I guess I'll never forget that number either."

"Don't you have one of those tattoos on your arm?" asked Riley. "I thought all concentration camp survivors had those."

"No," Jens answered, "Hollywood likes to show those tattoos. Actually, I think only Auschwitz and maybe some of the other larger camps put tattoos on people. Buchenwald was small enough that they relied on the numbers sewn to our shirt. American culture, thanks to Hollywood, thinks that the camps were all the same. In reality, camps were quite a bit different from one another. Buchenwald was a work camp; it was quite unlike the horrible death machine that was Auschwitz."

The death of my companion was very hard to take. The day after, when I looked out the window of the filing room, I saw the black iron sign that read, "To each what he deserves." What a lie that was! My companion did not get what he deserved. He was a very nice man and deserved to be back in Frankfurt with a job, food, and warmth; he did not deserve to be put in a wheelbarrow, naked, and taken to the incinerator with fabric triangles nailed to his body.

Otto seemed particularly grumpy the day after the exhibition on the horse. When I arrived, he smirked and grunted at me even more than usual. I was never quite sure what his problem was, but this day I could tell he wanted to argue with me. Several times he tried to antagonize me that morning until I'd had quite enough.

"What?" I said loudly after he called me a warmer Bruder under his breath. "What is it today, Otto? Obviously, you want to say something to me. So, let's have it out."

"I want to know what you were doing with the commandant," he replied. "Why were you in his office after I was told to leave?"

So that was it. Otto was bothered that I was getting special attention from the commandant. If only he knew what really happened in that office he might not have been so bothered by being left out.

"It is none of your business," I answered. "And if you ask again, I'll tell him that you want to know. Believe me, you won't last long after that."

I had no intention of ever talking to the commandant about anything, but Otto didn't know that. At last I had something that I could use to scare him.

"You know," said Otto as he stood straight up and looked directly at me, "that faggot yesterday deserved every crack of the whip."

He held up a paper from his collection that morning and added, "I also see that he didn't make the night."

I was in no mood to hear these things; I was tired and frustrated. Remember, it had only been a few hours since I'd carried my companion's bloody body to the parade grounds.

"How can you say that?" I asked him. "How can you be happy for all that pain and wave his death around in front of your face? Don't you know that we are all in this together? We are all prisoners in Buchenwald!"

"We are not in this together!" he shouted.

"Shh," I whispered. "They will come in here, and we'll be next."

"We are not in this together," he hissed back at me in a loud whisper. "You faggots deserve to be in here."

"I never hurt anyone," I said. "And what about the Jews? Do they deserve it, too?"

"No, of course not," Otto retorted. "One of the reasons I became a political activist was to stop all the injustice that was being done to the Jews. I was one of the only Christians in Berlin to see what the Nazis were doing to the Jews; I worked to stop all that. The Jews were born into their faith and are just as equal as me. But you were born into humanity and threw it all away to be unnatural."

"What do you know about homosexuality, anyway?" I asked. I knew it would do no good to explain how I had always felt homosexual. It never ceased to amaze me how imprisonment made people turn on each other.

The Iron Words

"I don't want to know anything about being a faggot," he snapped. "Listen, I saw you faggots running around Berlin for the last twenty years. I saw you drinking and singing in the cabarets, wearing women's clothing, and sucking on every man you found. Where were you when they closed the Jewish shops? Where were you when the Jews started disappearing? Where were you when the Weimar Republic was falling apart, and Hitler was standing there, ready to take over? You weren't of any help, because you were too busy running around Berlin in silk stockings."

"That was not me," I boldly said to him with a slightly raised voice. "I have never been to Berlin, and I have no idea what you are talking about. All I did was get caught kissing another boy my own age in a dark hallway behind a store. That's it. Don't blame me for what other people did or did not do in Berlin."

"But what are you doing with Rudolf now? You do unnatural things to get what you want."

"We are all doing unnatural things!" I shot back. "We are in a concentration camp!"

"You faggots deserve everything you get. Let me tell you this. When the German army falls and the Nazis are gone, it will be us reds who will be the heroes. We are the ones who were smart enough to speak against the Führer from the start. When we grab power, the first thing we are going to do is put all you pinks on a ship and send you to America, where you belong. You can run around New York and Los Angeles in your high heels."

At the time, I couldn't figure out where all his hate came from. Now that I'm so much older, I think that maybe he was gay himself and was frustrated with his life. It would explain why he hated us so much that he couldn't listen to reason. You have to admit that there was a decent quality to anyone who spoke against the violent Nazis in defense of the Jews. I also now know that there was some truth to what he was saying about Berlin. I can see how a passionate activist could get extremely frustrated when nobody would listen.

But back then, I didn't see any of that. I worked that day in silence, upset that Otto believed my companion deserved the events of the previous day. By the time dinner arrived, I was fuming and told Rudolf all about it.

Rudolf was especially nice that night. Because of Christmas and all the missed dinners, it had been a few days, and I knew he wanted to have sex for a second time. But he must have realized the mood I was in, and we just ate on the floor that night.

Rudolf listened intently as I described the conversation with Otto.

Remember, Rudolf was not a pink, and the greens hated us as much as Otto. Rudolf would often refer to us as faggots, and he would even call me that. But now I wonder if it was just because he didn't know what other word to use. In any case, I think he would have been deeply upset if I ever wanted to discuss homosexuality with him. He didn't want to see what he was doing and who he was doing it with; in his mind, our relationship had become as normal as his with his wife.

The next morning, after assembly and breakfast, I went to the filing room. To my surprise, Otto had not beaten me there as he always had before. I turned on the lights and got to work. Strangely, Otto did not show up, and it was getting to be quite late in the morning.

Then, when it was almost time for lunch, one of the capos opened the door and entered the room. He took just a few steps forward. "Otto is dead," he told me. "He tried to escape last night and was shot."

I heard the words and took a moment to comprehend what they meant. You see, there were often escape attempts from Buchenwald. The forest was very near, and it was extremely tempting to find a way over the barbed wire and run. I spent many nights thinking about how I would do it, and where I would run. I imagined myself surviving in the woods until the war was over. But we all knew that to attempt escape was to commit suicide. There were always SS officers in the watchtower and others patrolling the perimeter. Even someone who just got a little too close to the fence was shot instantly. There was no questioning.

It became known that any officer who shot an attempted escapee was granted extra time off and a meal outside the camp. Often times, the SS would get so anxious for this reward that they would force a prisoner to try to escape. I myself, on more than one occasion, saw them tackle a prisoner, take one of his shoes, and throw it against the fence. Then they would make the prisoner go and get his shoe. When he got too close, they would shoot him.

"You can just do your job and his," the capo told me. He left the room and closed the door, leaving me alone.

First, I was happy to know that I would be alone. There was absolutely never a time, not even in the toilet, when prisoners were alone. I was happy about this privilege. But then, I remembered that I would be alone in a room next to the commandant. I didn't like thinking about that.

The Iron Words

As I worked that first day without Otto, I couldn't help but contemplate why he had tried to escape when his whole purpose was to wait things out and be a hero. I must have completely misunderstood who he was. That night, I learned what had really happened.

"Otto is gone," Rudolf said to me when we were on the floor of the storage room. "You can have some peace now. You don't have to listen to his rants about the pinks anymore."

"I can't believe it," I replied. "I never thought he would do something so stupid as to escape."

"Oh," Rudolf said frankly, "he didn't do it. The Obersturmführer owed me a favor. I didn't like the way Otto was talking to you. So, Otto lost a shoe last night and now the Obersturmführer gets to have a nice meal. Maybe he still owes me. I'll have to think about that."

Rudolf grabbed me and kissed me on the floor. It was devastating for me to think that I, in a way, caused Otto's death. Otto did not deserve what he got, either. Even though he said some terrible things about homosexuals, I had to give him credit for being one of the few to speak against Hitler.

As far as Rudolf was concerned, I had been very nice, accommodating, and trustworthy.

Michael Fridgen

But I had done nothing to earn this level of
devotion from him; we'd only had sex once.
I think he was just one of those men who
liked punching a guy in a bar who insulted
his wife.

FORTY FOUR

Time went on; when I think of it now, it's a bit bizarre how mundane pain and death can be. I remember the odd events and the deaths that were more important to me, but the whole place was so horrible that despair became the common emotion. I once read a book where a woman had seen a murder and it haunted her everyday of her life. I'm not haunted by every death I saw because they were too normal.

I turned eighteen in the spring of 1943. By summer I had been there for a whole year. It was hot for those months, but nobody dared to complain about it for fear of the relentless winter that was surely coming. I remained at work in the filing room, but all alone, as Otto was never replaced. Some days, it was quite hard to get all the filing done; it depended upon how many arrivals and departures there were.

I believe it was in August of that year when I noticed that some of the Jewish

prisoners were constructing a new building in the very rear of the camp. Instead
of working in the factory, this contingent
was busy behind the blocks on some sort of
structure that was very near the rear fence.

I was suspicious and afraid. There were
always rumors flying around the camp that
Buchenwald would be turning into an extermination camp. It was easy to start rumors
that spread quickly through the prisoners.
When I saw the new wooden structure going
up on a concrete base, I grew nervous.

Normally, I did not ask Rudolf for news
from SS officers. I believed that I was better off not knowing most of their plans.
Every once in a while, Rudolf would warn
me of something, but mostly I just asked
him for things, not gossip. However, this
time I was too afraid of the building, and
I really wanted to know if we'd be in more
danger because of it.

"What are those Jews and their capo
building behind the blocks?" I asked him
during dinner.

"Oh," he told me, "you wouldn't believe
it if I told you." He shook his head and
even chuckled a bit as he said this.

I grew more skeptical. "Is it something
bad?" I asked bluntly.

"Some will think it's bad," he said, "but
others will love it. I just found out from

a hauptsturmführer three day ago. It seems that Buchenwald is getting a brothel."

"A what?" I asked in surprise.

"Yes," he said, "they are constructing a building to house a few women for the SS officers to have sex with. Don't ask me who ordered it or how they got permission from Berlin, but apparently many of the work camps are getting them."

"Where are they getting the women?" I asked.

Rudolf looked at me like I was missing the big idea. Then he must have figured out that I really didn't know.

"They are getting them from the Jewish extermination camps, of course," he said. "They're offering the prettier women a chance of freedom after spending a few weeks in a brothel."

Now, I had gotten the picture. The SS had found an unending supply of new women to rape.

"But," I said knowingly, "there won't be any freedom for the women, will there? I've been around long enough to know how the SS work."

"I suspect you're correct," he said. "You will probably have to file the women as they arrive and then as they depart for Auschwitz."

I didn't say anything in response to this, and there were a few moments of silence.

"Maybe the SS will be in a better mood, huh?" Rudolf said. "It can't hurt, anyway."

"Well," I answered, "the pinks will like not having to worry about servicing the SS and getting shot. That will be nice."

Then a terrible thought entered my mind. I'm ashamed to admit that I was more concerned about myself than the women who were to be raped countless times.

"Will the capos be able to visit there?" I asked bluntly. I was afraid that Rudolf would go to the brothel and stop needing me. In my mind, nothing in the camp was greater than the fear of losing Rudolf's aid.

"Yes," he said, "the hauptsturmführer told me that the capos were welcome. But don't you worry, Jens, I could never go there. If I went there, it would remind me of my wife, and I couldn't handle that. Besides, I love her and took vows with her."

I was relieved, but I was confused about Rudolf once again. For some reason, I wanted him to be all bad or all good. But in this very confusing place, Rudolf was a mix of everything. He beat his kids but loved his wife. He called me faggot, but was gentle during sex. Now, he was telling me that he would be breaking his marriage vows by having sex with a woman, but not with me.

"And here's the most interesting part," Rudolf continued. "The commandant is

interested to see if he can cure you faggots of your sickness. He's going to order
that every pink triangle visit the brothel
at least once each month. As the pink capo,
I've been told to keep a ledger to make sure
that everyone goes and does their duty."

"I don't think I could do that," I said.
"I feel badly for the Jewish women."

"You won't have a choice," he answered.
"Jens, you should go and give it a try.
I won't care if you have sex with them.
Maybe it will work. It won't change any-
thing between us."

"I don't think it will work," I said.

We didn't talk about it again. However,
not a month later, I received several
arrival slips to file. These forms contained
the names of Jewish women. Almost immediately, gossip flew through the camp about
which SS officers had visited the brothel
and how many times.

As the weeks went on, I also began to
notice that some of the capos had let go
of their assistants. I could tell because
the former assistants were starting to grow
thin; their services were simply not needed
anymore. There were more pinks being sent
to the foundry now, and fewer with camp
jobs like mine.

Then one night as we were preparing for
bed, Rudolf informed me that it was my night

to visit the brothel. I put on my shoes and made my way outside and across to the brothel. I think it was mid-November. The cold night air had returned.

I really didn't know what I was doing, but I opened the door of the new building and stepped inside. Apparently, the SS didn't much care for anything nice; they were there for only one reason and that was not to clean.

The brothel already smelled terrible. It was really just a long hall with several small rooms opening into it, each with its own door. A few of the doors were open; the others were closed. I still didn't know what to do, so I stood by the outside door.

Then, a man came out of one door and left it open. As he approached, I could see that it was another capo, a good friend of Rudolf.

"Ah," he said when he saw me, "you pinks have no idea what to do, do you? Just pick a door and go in. The rest is easy!"

He laughed as he walked outside. I didn't want to risk running into any SS officers, so I quickly walked up to the first door that was open and went in.

The room was quite small, with no window and just a small wood platform for a bed. However, I noticed quickly that the platform had an actual mattress. I was more impressed with this than anything else I saw that night. Sitting on the bed was a very pretty woman with long black hair. She had a blanket thrown on top of her.

"Hello," I said. I stood there for a moment, took a deep breath and sat next to her on the bed. I had absolutely no intention of doing anything with her; I don't think I could have even if I wanted to. The situation was just way too bizarre. "Listen," I said, "I'm here because I have to be. I'm just going to spend enough time sitting here, and then I'll be on my way."

She sat up to look at me. "Oh, you have on the pink triangle." She pointed at my chest. "Some of you have been in here before."

I found myself desperately wanting to talk with her. I wanted to know about her life and what her name was. I wanted to make her feel better by lying to her and telling her that she would be free soon. I think I just really wanted a friend, and it was so nice to be able to talk to a woman for a change.

But I couldn't partake in a discussion. The thought of her being raped thousands of times and then killed was too much for me to handle.

"How long does it usually take," I asked her after a few minutes.

"You should probably be done by now," she said. "But will you just sit in here a couple more minutes?"

I sat as long as I felt was safe and then left. Obviously, she hadn't requested more time to enjoy my presence; she just wanted to get a break and put off the next visitor.

In the filing room, I knew that the women changed quickly. I made my monthly visits and they were always the same, even though the women were different each time. I never made the friend I wanted, but the silence gave us both a pause.

FORTY FIVE

It was winter again, sometime in January 1944. The horrible cold returned, as did the practice of finding whatever you could to keep warm during the night. Rudolf had wanted a lot of sex lately, and he repaid me with layers of clothes that I was grateful for.

One morning, I awoke to shouting in the block. This was nothing new, and I slowly stirred, wondering how much time until the bell rang. But then, I suddenly realized that the shouting was directed at me.

Two SS officers were standing at my bunk. "Get down, filthy faggot!"

I had seen these two around for a couple of months; the young officer and the one with the hose had left sometime in 1943. I sat up quickly and jumped down onto the cold floor. Then, one of the SS officers threw my blanket on the floor and started looking all over my platform. I was very glad that I did not have anything in there, especially the needle and thread.

"Here they are," said the SS unexpectedly while holding up two packs of cigarettes. "The filthy faggot stole cigarettes from the SS. Not smart, you filthy pig!"

Of course, I had done no such thing. It is possible that the cigarettes could have been on the platform while I slept, or the SS might have brought them along that morning. Either way, I was being framed for something I did not do.

"Faggot 1973," said one of the SS officers as he wrote my number on his small pad. "Tell the commandant that we'll have one on the horse tonight."

Fear swept through my body. After having survived so far, I knew that I would probably not survive this. I could get through the horrible pain of the whipping itself, as most did. But also like them, it was unlikely I'd survive the wounds. Very few victims of the horse lived another month.

You see, it was so dirty all over, and we had no medical supplies. The open wounds would get infected; then the fever set in. We all got colds quite often, as we lived in close quarters. Stomach flu and other viruses would get passed around. The men would often die of these things, but I was still young and strong. I had survived all this, but I knew there was little chance I could survive the many wounds of the horse.

The Iron Words

I had no choice but to gather myself and try to have a normal day. I walked, with my many layers, toward the morning assembly. I was not very far from the block when Rudolf came running up to me. He was crying. Now I was in shock both for my situation and for seeing the emotion coming from Rudolf.

"It's my fault," he said to me through tears as we walked. "I have failed to protect you."

Rudolf tried to conceal his emotions and spoke quietly, but a few others walking in our vicinity started to stare. I was afraid on multiple levels.

"What do you mean it's your fault?" I asked quickly.

"It's the brothel," he said. "It has ruined everything."

I couldn't understand what the brothel could possibly have to do with me. "What are you talking about?"

"The other capos don't need me anymore," he said. "I used to be on top because the capos needed access to you faggots. But now that they have the brothel, they don't need me, and I'm at the bottom. Now, I'm the filthy capo who sleeps with you filthy pink faggots. Do you know the capo from block eight?"

"I know who he is, but I don't know him personally."

"We got in a big fight yesterday," Rudolf said. "I ended up punching him. He framed you with the cigarettes to get back at me. He knows how much you mean to me."

I realized that he was still seeing me as an extension of his wife; the masculine role inside of him dictated that he protect me. Rudolf continued crying, and I was once again reminded that I would have to face the horse. We walked in silence for a few moments. I realized that I would need to completely give in to his delusion. It was the only way I had a chance of survival.

"Rudolf," I said, "listen, you can help me survive this. Get me a lot of salve and clean bandages. If I keep the wounds clean so that they heal, I can survive. Rudolf, please stop crying, because I need you."

That was exactly what he needed to hear. Rudolf desperately wanted to know that he could still protect me. I could almost see the passion return inside of him when he knew he had a purpose.

He stopped sobbing and said, "Yes, I will get all the supplies, and more. I will make sure you have good food, even vegetables. Leave everything to me."

Knowing that Rudolf would take care of me and that I might have a chance to survive, I relaxed a little during the day. However, I was still in fear of the terrible pain of the horse. I was very glad that Otto was not there to see this.

The time came for the assembly, and as the bell rang I reluctantly walked out of the filing room. As was customary on days when the horse was to be used, the commandant was waiting for me in the hall. Without speaking, he motioned for me to come into his office. Up until this point, I had completely forgotten about the commandant and his customary behavior when someone was on the horse.

I took a few steps into the office and began to wonder how I was going to handle this situation. Surely, I needed to tell him that I would be on the horse and not able to service him. But how much else should I say?

"Commandant," I said, "I can't be with you today because I am the accused to be on the horse. I must go quickly."

Even after this long together, we had barely spoken, and it felt weird to talk to him.

He looked at me in surprise. "What did you do?"

"The SS found cigarettes in my bunk, they think I stole them," I said.

"Did you?"

"No," I said, "I was framed by someone trying to hurt the capo in my block."

I don't know why, but somehow I got the idea that I should be honest with him. I told him about the brothel and its impact on Rudolf. I also told him about the other capo having a fight with Rudolf and framing me.

I think there are several reasons for what happened next. First, the commandant owed Rudolf a lot. Who knows what seedy plan Rudolf helped him with? Next, I think the commandant was looking for a way to display more power over the capos, since they had become a bit unruly. Last, as unfortunate as it was, he liked the idea of the pinks having to service the capos.

"Do you go to the brothel every month?" he asked me.

"Yes, sir."

"Is it working? Are you getting rid of your sickness?"

I knew it was his idea to send us there, so I said, "Yes, my sickness is leaving. Every time I go, I enjoy it more. I think I will be normal someday."

He stood for a moment and considered how smart he was, and then he said, "Good. That's very good news. Of course, you will still suck my dick when someone is on the horse, no matter how normal you get."

That was such a typical uninformed statement coming from someone so undeniably stupid. He wanted to get rid of the homosexual side of me, while at the same time enjoying the symptoms of that side.

"Wait here," he said to me and left.

I stood near the office door then moved to the window in order to see what was going on down below. The prisoners had made their lines and I could see that the SS officers were attempting to find number 1973; they were getting upset. The commandant arrived and marched straight up onto the platform. I wanted to hear what was going on, so I opened the window a crack, despite the cold air that rushed in.

"Capo block eight," the commandant yelled, "come forward!"

Under penalty of being struck, none of the prisoners ever showed any kind of reaction on the parade grounds. But I could imagine the shock and gossip that was forming in their minds. The capo walked forward. I strained to hear every word coming from below, as they directly impacted my well-being.

"You are being punished for spending too much time in the brothel," shouted the commandant. "You will be on the horse. Capos are no longer allowed in the brothel. Because the treatment is working, the pink faggots will take the extra time from the capos!"

With that, I knew I had done the correct thing. Now order would be restored among the capos; Rudolf would be on top once again. In addition, more pinks would need to service the capos, and consequently, they could obtain extra food and clothing.

The commandant quickly jumped off the platform and marched back to the front building. In no time, he was back in the office and capo block eight was stripped and tied to the horse. The commandant and I did not speak, and the usual occurred among the cold air and terrible screams coming from the grounds.

Rudolf was melancholy for a few days after that. I think he was upset that I ultimately had to save myself without him. But as his status returned to normal in the camp, he got over it.

"You've never talked about the shower," said Riley. "How did you get so scared of gas coming out of your shower? Did you have those at Buchenwald?"

"Well," Jens answered, "we didn't have any shower facility when I arrived. Everyone smelled awful, and we did our best with whatever water we could find. It was much easier during a rainstorm, and if it was warm, we often ran outside naked in the rain when the SS were drunk at night. But I think it was sometime in the fall of 1943, a shower building was added to the toilet building. Rudolf said that the SS officers were worried about being visited by some kind of international humanitarian inspectors; these inspectors would want to see a shower. But we all had a hard time believing that.

"See, Riley, we didn't get much news from the outside world. However, as the Jewish prisoners were rotated from camp to camp, we learned a lot about the other sites. In an odd way, the camps became our world. It's not unlike how the freshmen at the University of Minnesota know nothing about foreign policy, but they know that the dorms at Hamline University are a lot nicer.

"So, we had heard all the terrible details of the extermination camps. We knew all about the showers at Auschwitz. None of us, not even Rudolf, ever dared to use the showers at Buchenwald, just in case. Obviously, it scared me enough to avoid showers until I moved into my house in 1994."

"Do you know the people in the pictures that are in your shower?" asked Riley.

"No, they are just photos from a book I had about the Holocaust. I know that they all survived, and that is enough."

FORTY SIX

❝I read an article last night about the records you had to keep while working at camp," said Riley, sincerely showing increasing interest in Jens's history.

"Oh? What did it say?"

"It was about how the Nazis were really good at keeping records. They were completely crazy and believed that the Third Reich would last for at least a thousand years. They thought that they would be seen as huge heroes and saviors of the human race. They wanted to keep records, so that they could prove all the good things they did."

"The whole thing was just one big delusion," said Jens. "What a load of crap."

One particular piece of camp news spread faster than any other, and that was the rumor of medical experimentation being conducted on prisoners. So far, we had not had any of that happen at Buchenwald, but it was something we were all afraid of.

We pinks were especially concerned about the news we'd heard coming out of Dachau, a camp near Munich. There was a large contingent of pinks being held in Dachau for the purpose of finding a cure for homosexuality. Nazi doctors attempted to change sexual orientation by introducing various hormone treatments and the like.

One of the more popular approaches used by Dachau doctors was to insert a capsule containing a hormone mixture into the scrotum of a pink triangle prisoner. The idea was that the hormones would be released slowly and absorbed by the body, thus curing the sickness. Of course, in reality these things never worked. However, the real problem with these experiments is that the men themselves had a high interest in saying that they did, in fact, work. If you knew that you would get to remove the pink triangle and stop having treatments if you said you were cured by a capsule, then that was exactly what you'd do. There was no way to prove that someone really changed at all.

Unfortunately, most of the pinks at Dachau died. Many perished from various infections or problems related to the hormones they were given. And those who said they were cured were then exterminated, because they were of no use anymore. We were terrified of that scenario happening at Buchenwald.

So, you can imagine the fear that shot through me when I was informed in the spring of 1944 that I was to share the filing room with a nurse. Apparently, they didn't want her to see the processing of prisoners on the first floor, or the shaving room, so they put her with me. They also didn't want her to see what occurred on the parade grounds, making my workplace the perfect location for her office. Of course, I was always worried when anything changed in the filing room, because it put my situation in jeopardy.

They brought her up there one morning. She was slightly shorter than me, but just as skinny. When I saw her, I wondered what the food situation was like on the outside; it had never occurred to me that it was possibly as bad as what we had in the camp. She had short blond hair and was probably around thirty.

All the SS officer said when he brought her was, "You don't have to worry about the prisoner working in here. He's a faggot, so you'll be safe."

"Thank you, I'll remember that," she said and shot me a glance.

The officer left, and I sat for a moment, not knowing how to respond. I wasn't sure if I was to be afraid of her or to help her. After being in the camp for almost two years, I had completely lost the ability to relate to people in any normal sort of way. But I would soon learn that she was certainly not someone to fear.

"I'm Bertel," she said to me. She crossed the room to set the white box she was carrying on one of the filing cabinets.

I told her that my name was Jens, and I would help her arrange the room to the way she wanted it. She saw the rows of filing cabinets, however, and probably realized there was little we could do to create more space.

"Some of the prisoners will be coming up here to get an inoculation," she said. "I'll need a space to do that, and also a place to do the paperwork."

We spent some time figuring out how best to arrange the room and then moved the pieces of furniture. I was surprised that she seemed quite at ease working with a prisoner, and I didn't detect that she had a problem working with a faggot. Perhaps she didn't know what it meant.

We only exchanged a few pleasantries during those first days, but we became more comfortable as the weeks went on. Finally, she received her boxes of supplies and the inoculations would begin.

"Jens," she said to me one day, "I want to inoculate you, but I don't want you to tell anyone about it. Nobody else, all right?"

"All right," I said.

"You agreed so fast"—Bertel sounded curious—"Don't you want to know what I'm giving you, or why I'm insisting on it?"

"I'm not used to asking questions, I guess," I responded.

"Well," she continued, "Buchenwald is a testing site for a typhus vaccine. Many of the prisoners will get the vaccine, and some will not. None of the pink triangle prisoners are to get it, but I want you to have it. You seem like a nice reasonable person."

"Does it work?"

"It worked well at the camp where I came from," she said. "Jens, you don't really have a choice. The Nazi doctors will introduce typhus into the camp, and without the inoculation, you likely won't survive. However, with the shot, you have a good chance."

"Thank you," I replied. "Can you tell me if the capos will get the shot?"

"Yes," she answered. "The SS officers make sure that all the capos will be inoculated."

I was quite grateful to her for thinking of me, and I hoped beyond hope that she was truthful, and the vaccine would work. Also, I made sure to tell Rudolf about the situation. Not only did I want him to make sure to get inoculated, but I also knew that he had a way to get more pinks the shot. Of course, the other capos wanted to make sure that their assistants would be safe.

The Iron Words

Over the next few days, a long line of prisoners arrived after assembly each morning for Bertel to inject them. I could see the intense fear in their eyes. They simply had no way of knowing what was in that syringe, and their imaginations ran wild.

I grew to like Bertel and the way she systematically approached her task while showing a slight bit of care at the same time. There was precious little care at Buchenwald, and it was very nice to watch.

"Were you a nurse before the war?" I asked her one afternoon when we were alone. "Or did you become a nurse because of the war?"

"I'm not a real nurse," she answered. "I mean, I wouldn't be able to save anyone in a hospital or anything. I'm a Reich nurse; I joined just before the war. I received training only in very specific tasks, like giving these inoculations."

I didn't say anything. My opinion of her changed when I learned she'd volunteered to help the Nazis.

She must have noticed my attitude because she immediately walked toward me. "Jens, I'm not a Nazi. I'm just doing this to feed my family. I hate them and all they do. I hate these camps; they make me sick."

I took a few moments to consider her situation and knew that she must not have a husband to provide for her family. Normally, I would never pry; but as I said, I had lost the ability to relate in a conversation. "Did your husband die in the war?" I asked bluntly. "Is that why you're having trouble feeding your kids?"

"No." Bertel took a long look at me and paused. I think she must have heard how bad it was for us in here. Regardless, she must have thought she could trust me. "Jens," she began, "I'm like you."

"I don't know what you mean."

"I should be wearing a pink triangle."

It took me a moment to understand what she was saying. Of course, I knew about lesbians, but I had never thought about them the whole time I was at Buchenwald. How sad that it never occurred to me that women were in the same state as me. "Were you released from a work camp?"

"No," she explained, "it doesn't work that way. There are no women like me in the camps; no women wear the pink triangle."

I didn't know what question to ask next, but I did know that I was hungry for information. I continued to look at her, hoping that my interest would let her know she could trust me.

"Women aren't as much of a threat to the Nazis," she said. "They won't let women do anything important, so they don't worry about us being homosexual as much. They know that no woman will rise to power and threaten the Reich."

"Do they know about you?" I asked.

"Yes," she said, "I am from Berlin. Ten years ago, in the summer of 1934, Hitler decided to rid the Reich of anyone who was rumored to be homosexual. This became known as the Night of Long Knives. Not only did they go directly after specific people within the Nazi party, but they also sent the Gestapo to raid the homosexual areas of Berlin. I was apprehended with a friend of mine at a place called the Magic Flute Dance Palace. It was a place where a lot of women like me would congregate."

"What happened? Were you sent somewhere?"

"No, women like me are more use to the Nazis on the outside of the camps. I don't know how much you men in here know about what the Reich is doing on the outside, but it's horrific. There is panic among Hitler and his top men that Germany may run out of young boys to fuel the war machine; it's been like that from the start. So, when a woman like me is apprehended, they make us stay put and have babies. It's either that or an extermination camp. I am among many women like me who have been forced to give birth multiple times."

"How many babies have you had?" I asked.

"Seven, since 1936," she answered. "We all live in the same one-bedroom apartment I had before the war."

"So, they are back in Berlin?" I asked.

"Yes, fortunately my mother is still around and looks after them. But it is very hard for both of us. It's hard for the children, too."

"Who is the father?" I asked, before I thought how impertinent that question was. "Bertel, I'm sorry for asking that. I apologize."

"Don't apologize. It's not your fault they did this to me. Jens, none of the children have the same father. Because I have naturally blond hair, they supply blond men. But the worst part is that they provide no support for us. Not even any financial support. The men leave when they are finished with me, and I am left to birth and raise the offspring. Of course, they don't like women working, at least working for any sort of decent wage, so I was left to become a nurse."

"I've seen many horrible things in here, Bertel," I said, "but your story is the saddest."

The Iron Words

"Oh," she replied, "I've seen a lot of things in the camps, too. I suspect you've had it worse."

"We're all in this together," I said. "I don't think there is such a thing as better or worse for people like us."

FORTY SEVEN

Bertel was with me through the entire summer. The typhus vaccine was a series of inoculations that each of us had to be given at specific times. One day in early August, Bertel informed me that the SS had begun forcing some prisoners to spread typhus-infested lice on the blankets in several of the blocks. This was supposed to be completed in secrecy, but of course, we all knew what was happening. I could see great fear in the eyes of the pinks who had not been inoculated. In addition, the ones that had been given the shot were hardly any less afraid. Nobody knew what was going to occur.

Typhus hit Buchenwald fast and hard. Daily, I noticed more and more men ill during the morning roll call. However, the vaccine worked quite well. Neither Rudolf nor I got sick.

Many of the pinks were quite ill; some became delirious with fever. The SS officers, under orders of the Reich doctors, didn't care about the sick prisoners at all. They were only concerned with the inoculated prisoners and if they were getting sick. So, there was no need to waste resources on prisoners that contracted typhus. As soon as a capo identified a man with the illness, his number was checked with Bertel. If the ill prisoner had not received the vaccine, as was most often the case, it was noted in a record, and he was shot. Then I recorded the departure.

As you can imagine, our filing room office was quite busy. Not only was Bertel constantly checking the records of ill prisoners, but I had a backlog of deaths to record. The Nazi rule of meticulous record keeping was fully enforced during this time, and Reich doctors appeared daily to check Bertel's work.

As the illness progressed, I found that Bertel did not want to hear anything about the details of what individual prisoners were facing. She spent her days in the filing room checking on the inoculated prisoners to see how they were feeling. I don't blame her at all for the distance she kept from the conditions in the blocks. I believe, in a way, she felt some responsibility for the horrible disease ravaging the camp. I found her to be a very caring individual, and it must have killed her inside to know the part she played in the whole ordeal.

Several times during Bertel's time at Buchenwald, a prisoner would get sentenced to the horse. Even though the commandant knew Bertel had seen her share of atrocities, he did not want her to witness this punishment, so the commandant asked me to lock her in the filing room when this punishment occurred. Remember, the window of that room looked onto the iron gate and not the grounds. I, of course, would still go and perform my duty to the commandant across the hall, while Bertel was locked in our filing room.

Obviously, she knew that something was going on. It was summer and the windows of the whole building were constantly open; she told me that she could hear the screams. I decided to tell her about the sick commandant and where I went during the punishment. I didn't leave out any of the details.

"That doesn't surprise me," Bertel said matter-of-factly. "Jens, did you know that I live in one of their rooms?"

"What do you mean? You live with the commandant?"

Throughout this whole time, I hadn't wondered where Bertel lived. I knew she was not in the camp, but I suppose I thought she had a hotel room provided by the Reich in town.

"Yes," she answered, "I live in the village with the commandant and his wife."

"He has a wife?" I was astonished. It had never occurred to me that he would have any sort of family.

"Yes, the commandant has a wife in the village," Bertel replied. "The Reich forced him to give up a room for traveling workers. Jens, it's terrible. His wife is probably the most horrid person I've ever met. The first night, she came into my room and told me that her husband never wants to have sex with her. I'm sure they had been told why I was forced into being a nurse; his wife started saying disgusting things to me."

I was sad to hear what was happening to Bertel on the outside of the camp. Many times, I found that I had a warped picture of how nice it was on the outside, probably because it was so miserable inside. I didn't like knowing about the terrible things Nazis were doing to those outside the camps.

"I'm sorry, Bertel," I said, "but there probably isn't much you can do."

"Well, I lock my room when I'm there. It does keep her out. So far, neither one has tried to enter with a key. I'm sure they have one. I think, perhaps, they are a bit afraid of me because I'm from Berlin; they don't know who I may know. So I lock my room and hope for my time here to end."

"I'm surprised he's married," I said, "but I'm not surprised that he's married to someone like her. The commandant is a vile human being, and no normal person could ever live with him. I'm also not surprised that he doesn't have sex with her, because he gets plenty of that in here."

"Listen, Jens, it gets much worse. I don't want to tell you this, but I feel that you and the other prisoners in the camp have a right to know how bad she is. His wife is more horrible than you can imagine; she collects things from the prisoners. He brings them to her."

Bertel was silent. I knew she wanted to say more and was attempting to find the words. But she started crying instead. I think she had been thinking about this for a long time and wanted me to know. I imagined that she was going to say that the commandant's wife collected jewelry, or even gold teeth. But I was not prepared for what Bertel was about to tell me.

"She collects tattoos," Bertel said through her tears.

"What do you mean?" I asked.

Bertel took a moment to collect herself and then said, "The commandant inspects the bodies of the dead prisoners before they are incinerated. When he sees one with a tattoo, he skins it off and brings it to her. She dries it like leather."

"Have you seen these things?" I asked in complete disgust.

"Oh, yes," Bertel said. "She is not shy about showing them off. Right there, in the kitchen, she cleans the bloody skins and works on them. They hang all around. She makes lampshades from them."

With that, Bertel broke down in a fit of sobs. I quickly walked over and hugged her, muffling her cries as best I could. I had seen many unjust and painful things inside the camp, but perhaps this woman from the outside was the most unfortunate victim of the Nazis.

Riley asked, "Do you know who Alan Turing was?"

"I think I've heard of him," answered Jens, "but remind me." Jens was fully aware of Alan Turing and his terrible story, however, the teacher in him wanted to discover what Riley knew.

"Well, he was this guy during World War Two that lived in England. He was incredibly smart. He was technically a mathematician, I think, but he knew a lot about a whole bunch of different subjects. Anyway, he basically invented computers and artificial intelligence. We wouldn't have any of our computers today if it wasn't for him.

"Also, he pretty much saved England during the war. He was so smart that he built a machine that could break the German secret codes."

"What happened to him?" asked Jens the professor, fully aware.

"Okay, here is the sad part. He was arrested in the 1950's for being gay. It was illegal to be gay in England at that time. He was forced to have some kind of injection to cure his homosexuality, but it didn't work. He died when he was forty-one from cyanide poisoning. Some say he killed himself, but others think he was murdered."

"What do people think of him now?"

"He's basically a hero to a lot of people, especially in England. I read that there was a huge movement to get him pardoned of any crime. The Prime Minister apologized to his family a couple of years ago. A bunch of people are trying to get the Queen of England to give him a pardon. I guess she is the only person in England who can do that."

"Remind me how old he was when he died," said Jens.

"Forty-one."

"The saddest part of this story is thinking about all the missed years," said Jens. "Who knows what kind of advances he may have made if he had lived longer?"

"Who knows what things those that were killed at Buchenwald might have done?" replied Riley. "Someone you saw die on the horse might have cured cancer."

Jens could not reply with words. He just made a small hum and slumped back in the passenger seat.

FORTY EIGHT

In early September, I entered the filing room to find Bertel quickly packing all her medical supplies and records.

"Jens, I'm leaving. My work here is finished. I'm going back to Berlin to my family."

"Did something happen at the commandant's house?"

"Nothing any more bizarre than what typically goes on there," she answered. Bertel looked at me and set down some file she was packing. She smiled, tilted her head, and walked over to me. Then, she wrapped her arms around me and squeezed me hard.

"You will get through this Jens," she said quietly into my ear. "I will miss you. You will survive. You have to survive, for me. I have to know that I saved at least one person, and I want that person to be you."

"I will miss you, too," I said as I hugged back. "I know that I am alive because of the vaccine you gave me without permission. I am grateful to you. But also, I'm thankful for the good memories I have of you in this office. You treated the prisoners with respect and gave me hope that not all is lost."

We had only known each other for a summer, but I think we were both starved for someone to know. When we separated, Bertel walked back and picked up the last bundle of files. She dropped them into a box that sat on one of the filing cabinets.

"I hope your children are okay and that you'll be able to feed them," I said sincerely.

"I'm not sure what I'll find in Berlin, Jens. Even though the circumstances of their births are terrible, I am still their mother. I want to take care of them and see if there is anything I can do to make the world better for them. My time with the commandant and his wife has taught me that I get to have a choice in the kind of world I want. Oh sure, they can have all the power and kill and rape, but I decide what happens in my mind, and I know what I want to happen in there."

"Please take care," I said.

"Jens," Bertel added softly as she approached the door, "one more thing. I'm not supposed to tell you this. Nobody in Germany is supposed to know this, but I overheard one of the Reich leaders from the village talking with the commandant. I needed some water and crept out of my room because I wanted to avoid his wife. They didn't know I was listening to them."

She was speaking so softly that I had to strain to listen. By the way she spoke, I could tell this was no mere piece of gossip; Bertel wanted me to know about something important that had happened in the world. My eyes squinted, and I turned my head to listen better. Bertel had not yet opened the door.

"Last week," she began in an intense whisper, "the Allied Forces took Paris back from the Nazis. I'm not sure what that means, exactly, but it seems to be a huge defeat for the Third Reich. France is a country once again. Perhaps, before too long, you will be a person once again. Take care, Jens."

FORTY NINE

The autumn of 1944 was full of gossip, rumor, and perhaps some truth. It seems as if every prisoner had heard some new bit of information about where the Allies were and how quickly Germany was falling, but you wouldn't have known any of that by observing the SS. On the contrary, the closer the Allies came to victory, the more determined the SS became.

The conditions around the camp grew tighter and harsher during those days. I believe it was for a variety of reasons. As instructions from Berlin arrived less often, the SS officers grew more concerned about holding onto what they could control. Remember, these weren't men with much experience making decisions based on facts. They were simple people who could only see their very small version of a world, so they were desperate to maintain Buchenwald and the power it gave them.

Also, I believe they were still deluded about winning the war. No doubt Hitler continued to send messages about the triumphant German force, and the SS were uneducated enough to believe them. I often wonder when they finally got the point. How far did the Allies need to push into Germany before the SS realized that all was lost? But disappointingly, all the news of the Allies made time go much slower. Hope is quite odd that way. To make matters worse, there was always some green or red prisoner shooting his mouth off about how we'd all be home by Christmas. When that didn't happen, it made Buchenwald even more depressing.

On Christmas Eve, 1944, the commandant ordered a huge Christmas tree to be cut from the nearby forest and displayed on the parade grounds. He even had strings of the new electric Christmas lights strung onto the tree; it was the first time I'd seen such lights. The tree should have looked quite bizarre in such a horrific place, but I liked it very much. It was probably the novelty of it all; after two and a half years, I'd seen everything there was to see at Buchenwald, and it was nice to have something new to look at. Rudolf told me that the commandant ordered the tree to harass the Jewish prisoners. Apparently, the commandant thought he could introduce new ways of harassment now that Berlin seemed to cease caring about the camps.

The calendar soon turned to 1945. I would be twenty that spring, and more than ever, I wondered where I'd be on my birthday if I were still alive. In February, for the first time, we saw an American plane fly over the camp. News spread quickly. By the end of February, Allied planes became more common, and we could finally hear the war happening at night. At least now we had some confirmation of the rumors that had been going around for months.

Not much changed between Rudolf and me that winter. Even though a few younger and better-looking pinks entered our block that year, Rudolf never gave an indication that he wanted a new assistant. "Jens," he said to me one night in early March, "when the Allies get close, if we are still around and the SS flee, I'm going to run."

"What do you mean?" I asked. "If the Allies get to Buchenwald, of course we will be around and freed."

"I think you have been listening to too many rumors," Rudolf said. "Everyone suddenly has a fantasy of dining with the Americans on cakes and cookies. It might not be like that."

"Of course it won't be exactly like that," I said. "But it will mean freedom from the Nazis."

"Maybe," he said with a heavy sigh. "Haven't you thought about what the SS officers will do when the Allies get too close? Do you think the commandant wants the Americans to see the horror of this place?"

"What? Do you think they will destroy the camp first?"

"That's exactly what I think."

I grew sad when I realized that I might have lived through all this, only to be killed at the last moment. It was very depressing to think about.

"I'm also worried that the Allies might not know what this place is and bomb it," he continued. "The ammunition factory has to be a big target. Surely they know about that."

"I hadn't thought of either of those things," I said sadly.

"Anyway, Jens, listen," he said sincerely, "if the Americans do show up and free us, you will not see me. I'm going to run into the forest and disappear."

"Why?" I asked. "They will have relief trucks and food, clothing—"

"I'm a criminal," he interrupted me. "I killed a man, and I still have a lot of time to serve. I can't take the chance that they won't capture the greens and send us to a regular prison."

"Where will you go?"

"The Americans are coming from the west, the Russians from the east," he responded.

"There have been several rumors that Dresden was recently bombed. Too many rumors to not have some truth. I'm worried about my wife. I will try to get to Dresden to see if my family is healthy and if they will come with me south to Bavaria. We can't stay in Dresden because too many people will know me and my crime."

"How easy will it be to move?" I asked.

"I don't know," he told me. "It will take a long time for stability to return. We won't even know what country we live in for a while. I hope they won't make the same mistakes that they made after the last war; they left Germany crippled, and we had no choice but to follow our destiny toward Hitler. I hope the Americans, British, and Russians will realize what they did and make a different plan."

"They are all marching toward Berlin, aren't they?" I asked as I thought about Bertel and her family.

"Of course," he answered, "they will punish our whole country for what we tried to do."

"What they tried to do, you mean," I corrected him. "I didn't have anything to do with it."

"Jens, you are so young," he said with a chuckle. "You will someday learn that Hitler never did anything illegal. As odd as that sounds, it is the truth. Hitler's power came from democratic elections. Anyway, stay far away from the SS officers during this time. They have run out of liquor, and they are ten times worse sober than they were drunk. They are scared and still have all the power their machine guns provide."

In the middle of March, during the day, the Allies bombed the ammunition factory. That night, not including Rudolf, there were only seventeen others that slept in our block. All the other pinks were killed in the foundry.

FIFTY

"**J**ens, wake up!" I heard a voice whisper loudly in my ear during a night in early April.

I opened my eyes and saw Rudolf standing next to my bunk. None of the others in the block could hear us as we were all spread out, now that so few remained. Of course, the lights remained on all night, and we continued to sleep with our hands outside our blankets; the SS were still around and armed.

"Jens, quickly," he whispered, "follow me. And be quiet."

I quietly got down from the bunk and followed him to the door. I continued to sleep with my shoes on, because it was still cold in the spring. Rudolf quietly opened the door, and we both stepped into the night.

I followed Rudolf around the rear of our block, where he crouched down in the shadows. I joined him, squatting right next to the building. It was a dark night, and since our block was in the back, the only person who could see us would be the SS on perimeter patrol, if he had a flashlight.

"They are gathering up some of the prisoners tonight," Rudolf said. "They know that the Americans are very close, and they plan to evacuate the camp. Every night, they will take a group of prisoners into the forest. I don't think they have any plans beyond that, which means that everyone will probably be shot."

"Rudolf, I want to survive. What can we do?"

"We are going to stick together, you and I," he said. "We just have to stay hidden until the Americans get here. Then I will run, and you will be safe."

"Just go with one of the groups now," I told him. "You don't have to stay because of me. Just go with a group and run when you get to the forest."

"No, I need to stay," he said. "I need to get you through this. And I have a better chance of running on my own when the Americans are here. The SS will just shoot me if I go with them into the woods."

"How long will we have to hide?" I asked.

"I don't know," he responded. "We need to stay hidden until the Americans are in charge of the camp. We can't risk getting marched out into the woods. You have to trust me, Jens."

Of course I trusted him and also began to agree with him; we sat in silence for what seemed like an eternity. A few hours later, we heard some noise coming through the rows of blocks. Rudolf crawled along the side of our block and saw a contingent of SS officers gathering up prisoners from some of the other blocks.

"As soon as they're gone," he said, "we have to find a place to hide. The SS will be relentless from now on and will kill fast. We can't be found by them."

"Rudolf," I said quickly and quietly, "what about the toilet? We could hide in there. It will be bad, but there is at least water."

"We will have to make sure that nobody else sees us," he said. "We can't even trust any of the other prisoners."

"I remember how it is," I told him. "We should be able to crawl inside the toilet and hide against the back wall. It is too dark to see in there without a flashlight."

"No," Rudolf replied after a moment of consideration, "it's too risky. There are just too many people who go in that building. I also think it is too obvious a place, and others may try to hide there. I think that the storeroom might be a better place."

"That seems even more obvious than the toilet," I said, a bit perturbed.

"Not if we hide in the larger bins," he insisted.

Rudolf was not going to argue with me and was surely not about to take my advice. Remember, he thought of me as a wife who needed her husband to protect her. He looked around the side of the block once more and noticed that the SS officers and their large group of prisoners were walking toward the parade grounds. Every once in a while, a shot rang out in the night, probably warning shots to keep the prisoners in line as they left the iron gates.

"All right, follow me and stay low," Rudolf told me. "Keep your eye on the watchtower, and when the searchlight sweeps, get flat on the ground."

We snuck around the side of the block and crawled our way from block to block, keeping our eyes on the watchtower. I hoped that the watchtower officers were more focused on the group departing the camp than on their normal sweeps and perimeter checks.

Rudolf led me to the side of the parade grounds where it was darker. However, the watchtower SS always directed their searchlights at the fence to keep prisoners away from it. Rudolf and I crawled a fine line between being in the open and being too near the perimeter fence. Finally, we approached the commissary. Rudolf knew exactly how to get in through a side window that was broken. We continued to crawl, as we didn't know who else might be in the dark building. The two of us made our way through the kitchen and into the back hallway where the storage rooms were located.

Rudolf stood near an open door and grabbed a set of keys from behind the door. "Good, the keys are here. This means that no other capo has been in here."

Rudolf explained that the keys were used to give capos access to their offices. The SS were fully aware of the keys, and of course they had their own. But with Rudolf now in control of the keys, no other capo would have access to the storerooms.

We crawled a bit farther, and Rudolf stood again to unlock a door that I had never been through. He pushed me inside and closed the door behind himself. Then he used a key to lock us into the room.

This room was smaller than Rudolf's office, probably half the size. Also, an unusual scent permeated the air. It wasn't unpleasant, but it wasn't entirely pleasant, either. "This is a good place to hide," Rudolf said softly, "because there is no food in here. I'm afraid that any place with food is going to be ransacked by the remaining officers. This room is for storage of chemicals used to spray down the arriving prisoners. I don't know what other supplies are in here, but there's no food."

That explained the chemical smell. Rudolf pulled out a large wooden bin that sat on the floor under the first shelf. It was full of boxes of some type of powdered disinfectant. He began to take the boxes out and line them neatly on one of the shelves, as if they had always been stored that way.

When the bin was empty, he pointed for me to get into it. Then he grabbed a large number of used rags from another shelf and joined me in the bin. Rudolf spread the rags on top of us. The air through the chemical-soaked rags made me nauseated, but I was used to dealing with that by now.

"We can't leave here now, Jens, until we know that the Americans are really inside the camp. The SS are in a state of panic, and there is no telling what they will do."

At first, I was in awe that I had lived so long in such tight quarters and still not seen every room in Buchenwald. If I had known all this stuff was in there, I would have asked Rudolf for some chemicals to clean the block after the forced typhus epidemic.

When the novelty wore off, these became the longest days of my life. I later learned that we hid in that bin for six days. Rudolf left twice to get water; he was not able to find food. We went to the bathroom right there in the bin, but since there was so little food, that wasn't a huge problem.

Several times we heard noises in the hall. We never knew if it was the SS searching for food, or a prisoner looking to hide. Perhaps it was even some capos looking for the keys and cursing when they couldn't find them.

Only once did someone come into the actual storeroom where we hid. We'd heard noise in the hall, and then we heard the door open. Someone came in. Since he had his own key, it must have been an officer, perhaps even the commandant himself. Rudolf and I were very still as they searched among the shelves. We couldn't tell what they were looking for, but they must have found it. They left quickly. Rudolf later checked to make sure that the door was once again locked.

We heard the war getting closer. The airplanes had definitely increased, and we could hear explosions every once in a while. I lived in absolute terror under those rags. There was nothing to do except contemplate that any moment you could be discovered and shot instantly by the SS. Or worse, that at any moment the whole building could explode without warning.

This was also the first time in a long while that I thought about my parents. Despite

all the physical pain and emotional trauma
of being in the camp, I think the worst
part is how much of yourself you lose. I
hardly ever thought of myself as Jens from
Konigswinter who had parents and a house.
I had become someone else, not necessarily
something worse or better, but just someone different. But now, I began to worry
whether my parents had survived. I knew
that Konigswinter was on the very western
edge of Germany and would be one of the first
places the Allies hit after leaving France.
The Allies must have gone through there in
order to be at Buchenwald. I wondered what
was left of the town on the Rhine.

And then, on April 11, 1945, two days
before my twentieth birthday, we heard the
rumbling sound of loud trucks right outside the commissary. Rudolf told me to be
very still. He crawled out of the bin and
unlocked the door. Through the rags, I could
see that the room was lighter, so I knew it
was daylight. Rudolf was gone only a few
minutes. Then he returned and loudly began
to pull the rags off me.

"It's them!" he shouted. "It's the
Americans!"

I jumped out of the bin, and we ran
through the kitchen and out onto the parade
grounds. Four large trucks of the Allies
had entered the camp. Off to the side, I

saw three prisoners waving an American flag; I didn't know where they'd got it, and I didn't care.

Prisoners started coming out of nowhere. From the blocks, the toilet, the brothel, the front building, even from beneath the platform itself. Every hole and cranny in the whole place must have had one or more prisoners stuffed into it.

It was an amazing sight, and none of us could help but smile. Soldiers started coming out of the trucks and onto the parade grounds. They jumped out of the trucks smiling, but soon they became very somber. I didn't know it at the time, but Buchenwald was the first camp that the Americans liberated. They had heard a bit about what was going on in there, but nothing could have prepared them for the actual sight.

Prisoners who were basically just bones walked up to them. Even I had begun to shrink away after the last few weeks of starvation. I could see all of my own ribs, and my legs were white and saggy. I saw two prisoners who were so weak they couldn't walk. They crawled by dragging themselves toward the trucks. An American soldier walked over to them, but when he got close, he stopped. I think he was in complete shock that these were even people.

The Iron Words

Many of us were covered in our own shit, or even someone else's shit. I certainly was. The soldiers looked like they were sick themselves. They were at a loss what to do.

I felt Rudolf grab my hand, squeeze it, and then let go. I stood completely still and silent among the chaos and watched him just simply walk past the trucks, past the front building, and finally through the iron gate. He didn't turn to look at me. I just stood there. It's hard to feel any emotion when there are so many emotions to be felt.

The Americans were yelling something in English. By their gestures, I assumed they were trying to get us all just to sit down and wait for something that must be coming.

I walked over to the nearest truck and sat on the ground. How bizarre it felt to sit on the ground in that place! I had been on those grounds countless times, but always standing for hours and waiting to yell my name, number, and that I was a warm brother. Through the freezing winters and the steaming summers, I had stood there. Now I sat in the spring sun and just observed the frenzy.

Others started to come over and join me on the ground. Either they didn't notice my pink triangle, or they just didn't care, but prisoners of all colors came to sit. Then, a prisoner came and sat right in front of me. He had not looked at me when he sat, but I had seen a glimpse of his face. I could not believe what I saw at that moment! Right in front of me, in a prisoner's uniform, was the commandant!

I sat there, behind him, for a while and contemplated what I should do. I don't think the others would have recognized him. They hadn't seen him up close as much as I had. Remember, he and I had been intimate together, and I would have known him any-where. So I wondered, should I say something to an American soldier?

The commandant sat quietly and put his head in his lap with his hands on top of it. He tried to become as small as he possibly could. I really wanted to say something to him. But would it have made any difference? I started to think that it would be a waste of my energy. But through all this time, Buchenwald had taken my energy. Now I had control myself. It was finally my energy to waste; why shouldn't I have my say?

I reached forward and pulled his left shoulder back, just enough to see a red triangle sewn on his uniform. I chuckled a bit that he chose the red triangle, the one color most likely to get accolades from the Allies. I wondered how long he'd had that uniform hidden in his office.

The Iron Words

As I pulled back, he looked up, saw my face and froze. Our eyes locked for just a few moments. Then, I slowly leaned forward to whisper in his ear. He didn't protest and sat very still; he must have been terrified of discovery.

"The iron words on the gates say, 'To each what he deserves,' and that is finally true," I whispered to him. "After all this time, it's finally true. Bertel told me about your sick wife and her tattoo collection. She is going to get what she deserves, too. You can go ahead and remember me sucking your dick. I don't care about that. But you will also remember the man you killed for not knowing the words to *Stille Nacht*. And the women you raped and murdered in the brothel."

He didn't respond; I didn't think that he would. I let go of his shoulder and stood up.

"He's here!" I shouted, in German, of course. "The commandant is here! He is in disguise as a prisoner, but he is here!"

It did not take long at all for the others to comprehend what I was saying. They began screaming and standing. I don't know how all the energy was able to come out of these emaciated bodies, but it surely poured out. Those of us sitting near him were forced to crawl out of the way to make room for the others who wanted to grab at him. It was such a frenzy that an American had to fight his way through the pile of bodies to get the commandant.

The American looked confused, but a Jewish prisoner who spoke English was able to explain to him who the man in the red triangle was. The soldier called for what I assumed was his superior. They threw the commandant into one of the trucks and stationed another soldier with a machine gun to guard him.

In a few hours, the large relief trucks with their red crosses entered the camp. Those of us on the ground shouted and clapped. Clean women and men jumped from the trucks and immediately got busy giving out food and water. I have no idea what the food was. After only eating stale bread, watery soup, and bad cheese for three years, I would have loved anything they threw at me.

As the sun began to set, the prisoner who knew English spoke to us in German. He explained that a division of the US Army would arrive the next morning to take control of the camp. He said that they would help us to figure out what to do next. In the meantime, we should stay in the camp and eat from the relief trucks; they were also working on getting us new clothing. He concluded by announcing that we could sleep wherever we wanted that night but to stay inside the fence. There were many armed men, on both sides of the war, stalking in the forest.

Out of habit, I had a strange desire to go to the block, but I just couldn't go back to the stench and hardness of the bunks. So, a few of us pinks got together and returned to the block to gather as many blankets as we could. We took the blankets outside and built soft beds for ourselves under the stars. It was a cool night, but we didn't care. All of us slept under the sky, and our hands were under the blankets.

"I can't stop thinking about the commandant and that you discovered him," said Riley.

"It was shocking. I felt like I was in the exact place where I was meant to be. In a way, maybe that was the only time at Buchenwald I got what I deserved."

"More than any of the other prisoners, you probably deserved to be the one to find him. He abused you a lot."

"Well, I'm not sure that's true," said Jens. "I mean, yes, he did abuse me. But there were others who deserved to get revenge more than me. The dead, for one. Actually, my companion maybe deserved revenge the most for being the first victim of the horse."

"Do you think he would have gotten away if you hadn't seen him?" asked Riley.

"It's hard to say. There is a good chance he would have been able to leave the camp. Perhaps he would have even been able to get out of Germany and move to Argentina. But many of these Nazis did eventually get caught."

"You said that when you first discovered him you wondered if you should say anything. Did you really consider just letting him go?"

"Yes, my first thought was to question if his capture would make any difference. You have to remember that in that moment I was broken. After everything I'd been through, I was convinced that the world was a terrible place. I thought all humanity was gone. My first instinct was to question the difference I could make."

Riley became quiet and questioned his own humanity. He thought about the commandant's capture and was glad that the horrible man got what he deserved. Then, his mind turned toward his past. He wondered how he could be glad of the commandant's capture yet still know that he had never been caught for the crime he committed against Jake.

FIFTY ONE

The next morning was the first morning I woke naturally and comfortably. There was no buzzing bell and no uncomfortable wood planks under me. Most of the former prisoners from other blocks had also taken blankets and built outdoor beds; many were now stirring and sitting up on the ground as the sun began to rise.

When I sat up, I saw that the contingent of American soldiers had grown a lot over the night. The division that they spoke about the day before must have arrived very early in the morning. The Red Cross trucks were still there, and when I saw them, I wondered what would be available for breakfast.

Slowly, the former prisoners got up and made their way to the trucks. Many needed to use the bathroom, and they just walked along the fence and did their business; I don't think any of us could ever go into that horrible toilet building again. The

sicker among us had already been identified and were lying on cots placed between
two of the Red Cross trucks. I saw the
relief workers tending to them with food
and water.

When my fellow pinks and I approached
one of the trucks, we were given some bread
with a slice of cheese and meat on it.
It was fresh and wonderful! We spent the
rest of the morning sitting on the parade
grounds and waiting for instructions about
what to do next.

Honestly, I didn't have the slightest
clue about what I should do or where I should
go. My first thought was to make my way back
to Konigswinter, but I was quite frightened
of what I might find there. I wasn't sure how
much damage the war, or my imprisonment,
had done to my parents. So, like all the
others, I sat and waited for the Americans
to figure things out. However, I did not
know then that the Americans indeed already
had my future figured out.

Sometime right after a lunch of canned
meat, a group of three American soldiers
began walking among us and looking at our
badges. When I noticed this, I remember
wondering why none of us had ripped them
off yet. Honestly, I think we had been
wearing the badges so long that none of us
even noticed them anymore. If someone had,

surely we would have all celebrated our liberation by creating a bonfire of badges.

I was sitting with a group of six other pinks when the soldiers came up to us and started asking questions in English. None of us spoke the language, and we tried to interpret through gestures, but that wasn't working. The American soldiers seemed a bit frustrated with us.

During the morning, the Americans had discovered several other prisoners who could speak English. They were using these men as translators to bring some organization to the camp. The soldiers in front of us called for a translator, and before long, a purple badge presented himself.

The translator had a discussion with one of the Americans that lasted quite a long time. We all sat patiently and waited for the information to be relayed. I wondered if everyone else was as anxious for news as I was.

"So," the translator said in German as he turned to us, "the soldiers are requesting that all men with the green and pink triangles be contained in that truck right there."

He pointed to an empty military truck with green canvas covering over the back. For the first few moments, none of us questioned the request because we simply had not yet lost the instinct to bury our curiosity. But after a moment, one of the pinks next to me asked the translator why we should go there.

"The Americans want to be sure that nobody who was supposed to be in prison escapes," replied the translator. "Therefore, all greens and pinks must go in the truck. You have all broken laws that existed before the Third Reich."

I was beginning to understand and anger rose within me. "Where are we supposed to go? What is happening to us?"

The translator turned and had another lengthy conversation with the soldiers. I listened intently, but of course, I could not understand any of the discussion. I remember punishing myself on the inside for ever allowing hope into my heart.

"You are being taken to a military judge appointed by the Americans," the translator said. "These soldiers don't know where that will be, yet. It is all being figured out by the American leaders."

The seven of us were now quite agitated, and we started speaking in German to the translator all at one time. One of the American soldiers stepped between the purple badge and us in an attempt to quiet us; he motioned to his pistol. The translator and the soldiers again had a lengthy

conference. We had no choice but to stand
and wait.

"Listen," said the translator in a much
harsher tone, "you faggots broke the law
in Germany, and the Americans are going to
restore order to our country by upholding
the laws of the Weimar Republic. There is
no choice. This is the end of the discussion. And if you ask me, they are doing the
correct thing!"

The translator turned and left suddenly.
I was sick to my stomach and a few of
the other pinks started crying. One of the
other Americans had a machine gun, and he
gestured with it, indicating that we should
get up and walk to the truck.

We slowly trudged toward the vehicle.
It was a very sad moment for me, made sad-
der when I realized that some of the other
prisoners were pointing and laughing at
us. I couldn't believe that after all this
time, there was still such hatred for us
pinks. We had all suffered in Buchenwald.
How could they possibly point and laugh?

When we got to the truck, a soldier
dropped the end of it, and we all climbed
in. The American with the machine gun stayed
and guarded us for the rest of the afternoon. At certain times, I also cried with
the others. I had been used to hiding all
my emotions so that not even I could feel

them. But the hope that we were free had ignited my heart, and now it was impossible to go back to the apathetic state I had been living in. I was simply heartbroken.

At some point in the afternoon, a small group of other pinks was brought and put in the back with us. When they climbed in, one of the Americans yelled something to the soldier with the machine gun. It must have been something homophobic, because the machine gun soldier yelled back, checked to see who was watching, then unzipped his pants with one hand and dangled his penis for us to see. The first soldier laughed hysterically, and the armed soldier shouted something in English at us before zipping up.

When the truck finally started, there were eleven pinks in the back, an armed American soldier, and no greens. I wasn't surprised that no greens had been discovered; they were all running somewhere through the forest by now, including Rudolf. There should have been more pinks and none of us knew where they were. Perhaps they had just run in the forest. Maybe they were smarter than us. Much later I learned that it would have made no difference if we'd removed our pink triangles. The Americans were vigilant with making sure no criminals left the camp. Since we were technically criminals, we would have eventually been discovered.

The Iron Words

The truck slowly rolled out of Buchenwald. As devastated as I was to still be in captivity, I took a last moment to look at the depressing place. The platform had been torn down by some rowdy prisoners during the night. I noticed pieces of wood lying on the ground that surely were once the horse. The blocks loomed in the back of the camp with their silent stench. The front building where I'd worked was empty and still. The watchtower and fence were now unguarded, and the SS were no more. Finally, we passed through the iron gate. I read the words and wept loudly; I was too distraught to notice what the others were doing.

You see, the words were a reminder of the injustice of life. Yes, the commandant would now get what he deserved, as would the rest of the Nazis. But what about me? Nobody could ever give me back those years, and now, I was still captive for doing nothing more than one kiss. I knew that I would never get what I deserved.

While the truck moved out, I forced myself to think of Rudolf and my companion. I hoped they were both in better places than I was at that moment. I was sick with despair. The eleven of us often looked at each other and shook our heads. I believe the level of frustration actually became physical in that truck, and if we'd had energy, we would have tackled the frustration and beaten it until we dropped.

It grew dark, and at some point we pulled up next to a building and parked. The engine stopped; the soldier riding with us got out and talked to the driver. None of the pinks spoke English, and none of the Americans spoke German, but somehow we got the message that we were supposed to stay in the truck for the night. I hate to say it, but it was less comfortable than the platform in the block because there were no blankets or toilets. The armed soldier sat outside on the ground as we slept.

When the sun came up, I peered around the green canvas and could finally see that we were at some type of prison. This place was too old to be a concentration camp; I guessed it was a prison that must have existed well before the Third Reich. I was not sure where in Germany we were.

I noticed that the soldier guarding us had been replaced by another during the night. Three more soldiers came out of the massive stone building and approached the truck. They dropped the back, and we climbed out and followed them into the building. We walked down a couple of cold hallways and were put into a large holding cell. The door of the cell had bars. When the door was closed and locked, I cried loudly.

The Iron Words

One by one, during the morning, they pulled us out of the holding cell. I just sat on a chair and waited with my head at my knees. I had finally stopped crying, perhaps because I was exhausted and hungry.

Then it was my turn. I followed an armed American soldier down the hall and entered a sparse questioning room. The room contained a small table with two chairs on either side; a uniformed American man sat in one of the chairs. The armed soldier stepped into the room as well and waited by the door.

"Hello," said the American man in German, "my name is…"

His German was very good, and I could understand everything he was saying. However, I don't remember his name. "What is your name?" he asked me.

I told him, and he wrote it down on some paper he had on the table. Even though I could see he was American, he must have had an extensive German background. I watched him write my name, and he spelled it perfectly without asking for direction.

Next, he asked for my birthdate, hometown, and other things of that sort. He did not comment when he discovered that my birthday was that very day, even though he surely must have noticed. Then, he looked straight at me in the eyes and said, "You were in prison for violating Paragraph 175 of the Weimar Republic. How much time have you served?"

I wanted badly to tell him that I'd not had a proper trial, but I was still thinking as if he was part of the SS.

"I was in Buchenwald just short of three years," I told him.

"All right," he said. "So you entered there during the war?"

"Yes."

"You did not serve time anywhere else before that?"

"No, sir."

"The sentence for violating Paragraph 175 is two years," he stated coldly.

I was instantly relieved because I had been at Buchenwald at least that long. I took a couple of deep breaths.

But without a pause, he continued bluntly, "Your time in the camp does not count as time in the republic's prison. You are sentenced to serve two years in this facility."

"What?" I shouted loudly in German.

He must have been used to that reaction from the other pinks who were in there before me. Calmly, he motioned for the armed soldier to take me out of the room. But I did not go docilely. The frustration within me finally began to surface.

The Iron Words

"I did nothing wrong!" I shouted and pleaded with him. "All I did was kiss a boy my own age. That's it. And for that I have been starved and worked hard. I've been raped and forced to do all manner of horrible things. The commandant forced me to give him oral sex many times! My friend was killed. I saw death and rot every single day! You can't do this! I've never had a proper trial; I've never been convicted of anything. You are as bad as the Nazis!"

By this time the soldier had dragged me out in the hall, but I was still yelling. I never saw the uniformed American man again, but I often wonder if my cries softened him at all. I suppose not. It was still 1945, and homosexuals were hated just as much in America as they were in Europe. Simply put, I was just unlucky to have been born way too early.

I continued to yell until the soldier tossed me in the place where I was to wait for my cell assignment. Then, finally, I tore the pink triangle from my breast in one motion and threw it at him.

FIFTY TWO

66 **I**'m a little tired. I'm just going to take a nap for a bit," said Jens. Riley nodded and continued driving. For some reason the Mayo Clinic was running late and it was past dinnertime when Jens and Riley left the parking ramp. They stopped for a quick supper at a fast food restaurant and drove with the setting sun back to the Twin Cities.

Even though he was glad that Jens was getting some needed rest, Riley was impatient to hear more of the man's story. He could hardly believe that after all the time and torture of Buchenwald, Jens had been sent to another prison. *How did he survive? I would have gone crazy from the frustration of injustice.*

Then, intense fear filled Riley. He thought about his future and what he knew he had to do to make amends with Jake. He wondered what prison was like. He wondered if he would go crazy. Riley had seen *The Shawshank Redemption* for a class in high school. He pictured himself in a small cell…the dirty bathroom…the bars everywhere…the large prisoners around every corner wanting to hurt him. His imagination ran wild. He felt his heart beat seemingly out of control.

"Riley, are you okay?" said Jens. He was awake and shaking Riley's shoulder with his hand. "I woke up from your breathing. You're sweating. Is anything wrong?"

Riley, due to years of managing constant stress on the ice, was able to calm down quickly. He forced his mind to focus on driving. Soon, his breathing was normal.

"Sorry about that," Riley said. "I'm just—there's just a lot going on right now. Sorry."

"Anything I can do to help?"

"No—I'll be fine."

"You've spent a lot of time listening to my story this summer. It's been good for me. Let me do the same for you."

Riley wanted to tell him about Jake. He also wanted to talk about college and whether he should dropout. But he couldn't. He was ashamed and afraid of his future.

"It will be better for me if you tell me about your time in the prison after Buchenwald," said Riley. "I'm more interested in your story."

Jens knew there was something bothering Riley. He had developed great admiration for Riley and all the time he had given that summer. Jens was eighty-eight, but he was not dead and still very human. He wasn't afraid to admit to himself that he had an infatuation for Riley. He was glad to know that his infatuation was not just built on appearance. Jens was attracted to Riley's character and caring attitude.

Jens would not pry into Riley's life. Instead, he began to think of a way he could help Riley, even with his failing health.

I spent every night for the next two years in a small cell with another inmate. In some ways, it was much better than Buchenwald, but in other ways, it was worse. In the standard prison, at least, we didn't wear badges, so nobody knew our crimes except

for the American guards. I liked the ano-
nymity of the place, and we had a much more
diverse food menu. Also, our clothes were
cleaned regularly and there were adequate
facilities to use the bathroom. We had mat-
tresses as well.

It was in that prison that I discovered my
irrational fear of using the shower. I would
stand there but just couldn't turn it on; my
mind was full of an intense fear that there
was not water in the pipes. So, I bathed
myself with water from the sink, which was
still way more than I had in the camp.

However, while some of these things were
good, it was still a depressing place to
be. The whole country was strained under the
enormous work of rebuilding and reshaping
a government. This meant that things were
unorganized at times. We always had food,
but there was no attention given to any
sort of education, like most modern prisons
had. The attention of the prison went to
the necessities, but things like activities
and maintenance suffered. Consequently, we
spent a lot of time in our cells, probably a
good twenty-two hours each day. There were
no books; it was hard to pass the time.

And some of the nights were quite bad.

The American soldiers were still soldiers. They were men who had been pulled
away from wives and girlfriends who were

thousands of miles across an ocean. While nothing could rival the drunkards of the SS, the Americans still seemed to have plenty of alcohol. And they knew which of us in the prison used to wear the pink triangle. They fully realized why I was behind bars.

Not often, but several times over the two years, one of them would wake me from my sleep and pull me into a vacant cell. They weren't as gentle as Rudolf, but they smelled much better than the commandant. My cellmate, whom I got to know quite well, hated that they did this. He begged me to report them. However, I just wanted to get out with as little fuss as possible.

I guess it's maybe a bit sad that I didn't think being raped multiple times in two years was very bad. I was just so accustomed to the horror of the camp. My cellmate kept track of each of these forced encounters in his journal; he wrote the date and name of the American perpetrator. When I was being released, and he told me it had been sixteen times, I was shocked. Because it only occurred once every month or so, I truly didn't think it had been that often. Abuse had become so common to me that I had lost all sense of what was considered decent in the world.

But there was one very bright spot to this place, my cellmate, Urban. He had been a teacher at a university in Augsburg and was over sixty years old when I met him. I wasn't always sure what he had done to get into prison, but during the end of the war he was convicted of stealing something from the university. It must have been substantial because his sentence was ten years. He had been in the camp at Sachsenhausen for a few months before being liberated to the prison where I was also held.

Urban was highly educated and understood things about life and homosexuality. We had lengthy discussions. You see, I was in my early twenties and my education had been ripped from me when I was barely seventeen. In many ways, Urban filled in the gap that I was missing. But above all, he spoke excellent English.

Since there was nothing for either of us to do, he spent long hours teaching me. I was eager to learn. My education became the focus of our existence in the prison and a way to pass the time. If fact, some of the happiest times in my whole life were spent learning English in that cell with Urban. By the time I was released in 1947, I had learned enough from Urban to get accepted to a university.

FIFTY THREE

It's usually late by the rest of the country's standards, but when the true summer hits Minnesota in August, it can be unbearably hot and humid. Riley had just finished a run along the Mississippi and was walking back to his dorm through campus. He was wearing his standard running attire of shorts and tank top; he was anxious to get back to exchange socks and running shoes for flip-flops. Most of the women on campus, and some of the men, paused to look at him as he walked past.

As he passed in front of the student union and started up the grassy mall, a small group of professors came walking toward him. Dr. Weber was one of them. He didn't want to bother her while she was with colleagues, but he did intend to call her later. However, as the group passed Riley, Dr. Weber recognized him.

"Riley, how are you?" She motioned for the other professors to keep walking.

Riley stopped and hoped he didn't smell too bad; he was extremely sweaty from the run in the hot sun.

"How is your summer?" she added without waiting for him to answer the first question.

"Good," he replied, "everything is good."

"Are you ready for the fall term?" she asked.

"Yes, looking forward to it," he said, knowing that it was a lie.

"I don't have much time because we are late for a meeting, but I haven't seen Mr. Jaenisch outside much lately. I see your car there, though. How is he doing?"

"He is getting very slow," replied Riley. "I worry about him, but he says that he's doing what he wants and needs to do in order to get better. I don't know. His mind is sharp, but it's taking him more effort all the time to move."

"Well," she said, "will you keep me informed? I worry about him, too. I really have to go, but I will call you next week."

"Okay," he said. "See you later."

She hurried to catch up to the other professors, and Riley continued the hot walk up the mall. When he got to the auditorium, he passed under a new banner welcoming students to freshmen orientation 2013. Seeing the banner reminded him that he needed to check to see which courses the Athletic Department had registered him for that fall.

Riley knew that he had many decisions to make rather quickly. He wanted to take a more active role in his education, and he even looked online and saw some classes he'd like to take. Mostly, he wondered if he should stop playing hockey altogether. He couldn't believe that he was contemplating this, because hockey had given him so much. However, his heart was simply not in it anymore. He wondered if the best thing for his future meant quitting hockey to focus on learning.

And for that matter, he also thought about quitting college. Riley had been thinking about all of these things over the past weeks. He entertained the idea of attending a vocational school to learn a trade. Then, as he was earning money with that, he could figure out what he really wanted to do. He knew that quitting hockey and college meant he would have no revenue stream.

And there was Jake. Through Jens's life story, Riley finally understood that if there was any chance for a happy future, he needed to deal with Jake. There wasn't anyway to avoid it any longer. Even if it meant he'd be unhappy for a while, he had to take action with Jake to be able to move forward. He needed to get what he deserved.

As Riley, still sweating, approached his dorm, he heard his name being called from a distance. He squinted underneath his baseball cap and cursed aloud when he saw his mother walking around the side of the building.

Aside from spending time with Jens and running, the only other activity he'd been doing lately was avoiding his parents. His phone was full of voice mails, texts and e-mails. Now she was here. He quickly contemplated running away from her, but if he faced her, at least he wouldn't have to think about it anymore.

He walked in her direction, and they met at the corner of the building. Riley, without greeting her, slumped against the brick side of the dormitory. He was hoping his body language would make clear how much he didn't want to talk to her.

"Riley, what's going on?" she began harshly without even a hello. "Your coach is furious and calling all the time. Your father and I can't reach you. What's going on?"

"Mom," he answered, "there is some stuff going on, but I don't want to talk about it."

"You have to!" she said. "Do you realize how much trouble you are in? The coach can take away your scholarships any second, plus your chances of playing for the NHL."

"Mom," he said calmly and decisively, "I'm not going to play hockey anymore."

Her eyes bored into his, and all she could manage to say was, "What?"

"I'm not going to play hockey anymore," he said. "I've thought a lot about it, and it's ruining my life. It's not what I want to do anymore; I don't want to be a professional athlete. And I'm especially through hanging out with people like the coach."

"You are throwing away everything your father and I worked for," she said as she began to weep. "I have never been more hurt."

Riley couldn't think of anything to say back. They stood in silence for a long while.

His mother, in an attempt to appeal to his past, pleaded through tears, "What about your dream of seeing your name on an NHL jersey? Your dream of signing autographs and being in *Sports Illustrated*? What about all that?"

"Mom," he said, "none of those things matter to anyone. Well, anyone except you and Dad. Those aren't my dreams, and I'm not sure they ever were. You may care about that stuff, but when you look at the bigger world, none of it matters."

"That hurt, Riley," she quickly replied. "I care about things."

"Do you, Mom?" he asked. "I get it, Mom, I really do. You grew up in Hastings and want nothing more than to be queen of that town; you know my fame is your ticket. I get why you crave that, but it's not fair to put your dream on me. My eyes have been opened to a bigger world, and I'm not going to ignore it. I really don't think I have anything else to say."

"You won't have any money, you know." She had stopped crying and became very serious. "We're not going to give you anything if you do this. Without scholarships, what will you do?"

"I'm going to make it, Mom," Riley said. "A lot of other people have made it through way worse than this. It will take a while, but I'm going to be okay."

"But you deserve so much more than this."

"Deserve? No, you're wrong; I don't deserve anything. Do you know how hard some people have to struggle every day? No, you don't, because you've never thought about it, and you've never left Hastings long enough to see. Look at the other students walking around us right now. They take on a huge amount of debt in order to study their asses off. Nobody deserves to coast through school just because they can play a sport. I know that the way I look gets me a lot of attention, but that doesn't mean I deserve it. I just won the genetic lottery. I did nothing to deserve anything. I was born with my body and parents who knew how to use it."

He was silent for a moment as he contemplated the weight of what his mother said about deserving a life. His mother continued to stare at him. She wondered what was wrong with him and desperately tried to think of a way to get her life as a hockey mom back again.

Before she could speak, Riley said, "You know what, Mom? On second thought, there is something that I deserve, and that's exactly what I'm going after."

FIFTY FOUR

U rban and I created a plan for me to follow after my release. He was a bit ill, and I think it helped him quite a lot to have a purpose that would extend beyond the walls of the prison. Everyone needs a focus; in the camp, my focus was survival. In the prison, my future became the focus for both of us.

When the day of my release finally arrived it was anti-climatic. The Americans in change of the prison system simply let me walk away. Honestly, if I hadn't had some money from Urban I would have been living on the street. But after all that time being locked up, I was free. I had finally paid the price of that one kiss.

There were no halfway houses or special programs in those days, so I walked into the nearby town and rented a room at a small hotel. The first thing I did was to take a long bath. It was hard to sleep because it was so quiet. I can't imagine what happened to others who were released with no support. It must have been even worse for those that were incarcerated in East Germany.

It took a few days to acclimate myself. Everything was difficult. Every time I went anywhere, I believed that people were looking at me as if I still wore the pink triangle. I thought that the entire country knew the secret of my imprisonment. When I bought food from a small market, I looked at the floor while I paid. I did not want to make eye contact with anyone during those days.

After a while, the newness of freedom subsided and I started to make plans for my future. Despite what the American soldiers did to me in the vacant cells, Urban and I continued to believe that living in the United States would offer the best chance for me to escape my past. I always had an interest in literature, but I'm not sure I would have chosen it as a passion to follow. However, Urban had a lot of academic experience with colleges in both countries. He felt that earning a degree in German literature would give me the best chance at being needed by a college in the United States.

I never would have made it out of Germany without him. Urban's connections helped to get me into a university in what was, at the time, West Germany. However, I am most grateful for what he did to finance my education. Remember, I had no money and no resources, not even a home to go to when I was released. Urban was never married and had savings; his lack of children and passion for my future was the greatest gift anyone has ever given me. He paid for my lodging and tuition. I got a job at a bookstore and was quite frugal so as not to waste anything he gave me.

We were both worried that I would have a difficult time getting a visa to work in the United States. Indeed, it was difficult because after all, I had been convicted of a crime and spent time in prison. Fortunately, Urban had a Jewish colleague who had escaped before the war and taught at the University of Iowa. I was able to use that connection to my advantage.

I remained in contact with Urban and visited him often, bringing him new books and other things he wanted. It was a sad day when I learned that he had passed away from a heart attack just a month after his sixty-eighth birthday. He was within a year of his release from prison.

Urban left his money to me; without that money and his support, I would probably still be in Germany. It's amazing how much of my survival had to do with just plain luck of whom I met.

The Iron Words

When I was in my second year at the university, I felt it was time to go back to Konigswinter and find out what happened to my parents. At this point, I looked healthy enough not to scare them, and I was emotionally able to control my frustration about life. So, I boarded a train bound in that direction.

It was 1948, and Germany was in a state of rebuilding. Well, at least West Germany was; I'm not sure what exactly was going on in the East. This was the first time I'd taken a train since I was brought out of Konigswinter to Buchenwald. Of course, it was remarkably different. I'm not talking about the difference inside the train, being able to have a seat and all. No, what I mean is the difference in the country.

Going through Germany this way, I saw for the first time the destruction that occurred during the war. As we got closer to Bonn, the villages and towns that I'd known as a teenager were in various states of disrepair. I began to see what the German citizens had to go through while I was a prisoner. It was sad and complicated, because it was so hard to place blame. In the end, I guess we were all a little guilty about what we let happen there. I think a lot of us from that time realized that blame doesn't rebuild cities and revenge doesn't feed the hungry.

After a transfer, the train pulled into the small station at Konigswinter. As I had seen in all the towns along the way, some things were quite different, and some were the same. I walked through the square and down the street where our house was located.

I had no plan for a reunion, because I was too worried about what I'd find. I remember thinking that I wanted to avoid scaring anyone who might have thought I was dead. Still, as I walked down the street, I didn't think I had much of a choice but to just knock on the door.

I looked at the faces of those I passed; I didn't recognize anyone. I probably knew these people and may even have gone to school with some of them. But it had been over seven years, and the people of Konigswinter had been through a lot. I had been through a lot, too, and probably looked just as different to them.

Finally, I saw the little house where I had lived. The sight of it filled me with mixed emotions of excitement and dread. I was relieved that the bombs had spared my old street. Had I not been as emotionally strong, I would have wept and probably turned around, but deep inside, I knew that

I had a right to know about that house and its occupants.

I walked up to the door and rang the bell. My heart was pounding wildly as I waited to see who would open the door. I was ready to see the face of my mother or father, but the door squeaked open to reveal a woman I did not know.

"Oh, excuse me," I said, "I'm looking for a family who lived here before the war. Do you live here now?"

"Yes, we bought the house from a woman named Jaenisch," replied the woman.

"Do you know what happened to her and her husband?" I asked nervously.

"The man died in the war; somewhere in France, I think," she said. "I bought the house from the woman after that."

I was devastated to know that my father had not survived the Third Reich. I wanted to ask the woman at the door more questions, but no words came to mind as I thought about my dead father.

"If you want to know more," the woman then added, "I think Josephine downstairs would know. She may even still be in contact with Mrs. Jaenisch."

I was very happy and astonished to hear that news and asked, "Josephine is still alive?"

The woman chuckled. "Yes, she will probably outlive us all." The woman at the door invited me in. She descended the steps and knocked on Josephine's door.

While she was down there, I took a moment to look around the main living quarters and kitchen. Even though the furniture had changed, memories came streaming back of my parents and me doing various things. I saw the place where the Christmas tree stood every year and where she baked cakes for my birthday. I saw where my father helped me with my arithmetic every night. I saw the woodstove where Karl and I kissed.

"Go on down," said the woman when she climbed back up the steps, "Josephine is right down there."

"I know the way," I said and descended the stairs.

The door was open; I knocked twice for courtesy and entered the small apartment. I had been in there many times to deliver things as a child. Nothing had changed down there. Even Josephine looked the same; she was old when I left and old when I returned.

Josephine was sitting on a chair next to a small table where she kept her knitting supplies. She was wearing a housedress that looked so old it may have been the very one she was wearing the last time I saw her. She placed some yarn on the table and folded her hands in her lap when I entered.

"Hello, Josephine," I said. "Do you know who I am?"

She looked at me for a few moments and then said, "I'm sorry, I don't."

"I'm Jens Jaenisch," I said softly. "I used to live above here. My mother and I used to look after you."

"Oh yes." I could see on her face that she began to recognize me. However, when the full realization of who I was had set in, her faced turned to stone. There was an immediate change in her demeanor, and it made me very anxious.

"You should get out of here," she said harshly. "I have nothing to say to you."

I didn't know what was going on and asked, "Do you know where my mother is?"

"No," she said loudly. "She went faraway to get away from what you did to her."

I was starting to discover what was happening here; Josephine must have known about the pink triangle. Perhaps the whole town knew.

"Josephine," I said, "I just want to know where to find her. That's all. She is my mother, and I have a right to know."

"You are a filthy faggot," she shouted. "Go back to Berlin!"

I didn't know what she meant by that, and I dismissed it. Now, I wish I had questioned her more. But at the time, it was just so shocking to hear her call me by that horrible name.

"In fact," she said continued, "you should leave the country now before you make things worse again. Your poor mother and father lived in shame; the whole town knew about you. In order to get away, your father enlisted and was killed. That's your fault, faggot! Your mother is gone now, too. That's also your fault. What do you want from me? They should have killed you in that camp. You will burn in hell, and that's no less than what you deserve."

I was prepared for something bad to happen in Konigswinter, but I did not think someone I used to help would say it in such a heinous way. Tears started streaming down my face. I didn't say anything to her; I just turned and ran as fast as I could up the stairs. The woman who owned the home looked weirdly at me as I ran past her and out of the house. I left the front door open and continued running down the street.

I didn't stop until I reached the train station, but the next train going my direction was over an hour wait. I couldn't stand the thought of being in that town for even one more minute. I thought that everyone who glanced my direction was seeing me with a pink triangle nailed to my chest. So I got on the very next train, even though it was going the wrong direction. By the time I got back to the university, it was very late because of all the rerouting I had to do.

I knew now that Urban was right about one thing and very wrong about the other. He was right that I should move to America, but he was wrong that I should find a man to be with. Urban often talked about how being homosexual was natural. He told me every day that I deserved to be happy and to know the love of a partner in life. He was so wrong. Josephine represented the world I knew I would face if I lived as a homo-sexual. The Nazis were wasting their time dealing with us pinks; they should have just let the world have at us. The world was cruel enough.

FIFTY FIVE

I believe there were five people who ever loved me, and they were all dead by the time I was twenty-nine years old in 1954.

Urban loved me; I really don't believe he was gay, but he loved me like the son he wished he had. Urban was dead. My own father loved me, I have no doubt of this, and he was dead. I believe that my companion from Buchenwald was in love with me; he was also dead.

My mother loved me very much, and I don't remember a time when I didn't know that. However, for all intents and purposes, she was completely dead to me; she may have actually been dead by 1954, but I had no way of knowing that. Last, Karl loved me. But I know for certain that the Karl who loved me died when we were seventeen, when he was castrated.

I used to spend time wondering whether or not Rudolf loved me. In the end, I think he loved loving me as a surrogate wife, but he never actually loved me as the man I was. He was the kind of man who had an intense need to mate with a woman and protect her. I can't hold his nature against him, even though I don't think he ever understood my natural desires.

So, there I was in 1954, almost thirty years old, with a master's degree in literature. There was no reason for me to stay in Germany, and I wanted to honor Urban by following our plan. For over a year, I had been in correspondence with Urban's friend who taught at the University of Iowa. He sympathized with my story and arranged for me to take a teaching assistantship with a former colleague of his in Minnesota.

It took a lot of dedication to get a work visa for the United States. Because of my status as a convicted criminal, I had to rely on the testimony of Urban's Iowan friend to sponsor me. Fortunately, I still had a fair amount of money from Urban. When I received permission to work in the United States, I bought my one-way plane ticket that day and left the next. I did not have many possessions, and most of the things I did have, I didn't want to take with me.

I remember my last night in Germany. I stayed in a small hotel in Cologne near the train station. The next day I would take a train to Paris and fly to Minneapolis through

New York. That last night was bittersweet for me. I spent a great deal of time sitting by the window and looking out at the street. People looked so normal as they went about their lives, shopping at the market, coming home from work and school. I knew that each of them had a story about how they survived the war, but it was 1954, and people kept those stories hid deeply within their shame, regret, and frustration.

When I look back on the flight now, I wonder why I wasn't more nervous. Not only was this the first time I'd left Germany, but it was also the first time I had been on an airplane. I had only ever seen the North Sea, and flying over the vast ocean should have scared me to the core. However, on the contrary, I remember being quite relaxed and excited during the flight. Perhaps I knew that after I'd been through Buchenwald and prison, nothing in Minnesota could scare me.

It was a cool summer day when I landed in Minneapolis. I have to admit that I was a bit disappointed at how similar it looked to Europe. I guess, after years of hearing about America, I was expecting to land in Yellowstone National Park or the Grand Canyon. Now that I've been to a few other places, I realize that airport tarmacs look pretty much the same no matter where you land.

I stayed at a hotel near the campus for the first couple of weeks until I found an apartment with a small view of the Mississippi River. I don't know if it was my upbringing on the Rhine or the years spent in Buchenwald being constantly thirsty, but I've always loved the river as it flows through Minneapolis.

So, I started as an assistant instructor at the University of Minnesota and worked my way up through the academic hierarchy.

"Did you like what you did for your career?" interrupted Riley. "I mean teaching at the University?"

"Yes," Jens answered, "I did like most of it. Of course, there were some things that I hated. I've seen my share of politics and policies that cost students thousands of dollars; I hate what the system does to young people by putting you in so much debt. But for the most part, I had a good career, and it provided me a long and comfortable retirement. I'm not sure I would choose to teach German literature, if I could go back, but it is the career that led me to Minnesota. There are many things in this state that I love."

"You have a good setup in St. Paul," said Riley. "I like your house on the river."

"I like it, too," replied Jens, "and I've had good neighbors who didn't bother me."

Riley drove silently for a moment and considered the amount of time that Jens lived fairly reclusively, bereft of intimate human relationships. Of course, Riley understood that there had been colleagues and students in Jens's life, but he found it depressing that Jens had spent sixty years living on the outside of society.

Riley thought about his own relationships and how superficial they had been. Even the relationship he had with his parents was based on his skills with a hockey stick. In fact, he now realized that the most intimate and time-consuming relationship of his life had been with hockey. He was not about to allow that relationship to control his life any longer.

"You said that only those five people loved you," Riley said hesitantly. "I understand that the timing was all wrong, and society wouldn't let you live openly. But why not find some other gay guy in Minnesota and have a secret relationship? I mean, who knows, you maybe even could have been married, now that things are so different."

Jens needed a few moments to consider his answer. He knew what he wanted to say, but felt the need to be careful in his choice of words. Even though he had been extremely honest and blunt with Riley, he still understood that Riley was young and had a lot of development ahead of him.

"Riley, let me ask you something very personal," said Jens. "Now, I'm going to make an assumption here, but I was around student athletes long enough to know what happens. I'm sure you've had sex, right?"

"Yeah," answered Riley without hesitation, "lots of times. It's pretty easy to find a girl to sleep with when you're an athlete in high school and college."

"I thought so," responded Jens with a chuckle. "And if you don't mind my asking, what do you think about while you are having sex?"

Suddenly, Jens felt more like a professor conducting an academic study and less like the old man who had been confiding in Riley. If anyone else had asked this, Riley would have thought he was perverted. But he had grown to know Jens so well during these drives that he trusted him completely.

"Well," Riley answered, "I don't know. I guess I think about how awesome it feels."

Jens paused another moment to figure out how to push Riley into the correct direction of thought. "How do you know it's going to feel awesome when you first start?" Jens asked.

"Uh, well, because I've done it before," replied Riley. "I think about the times before, especially the really hot times, things the girls did to me, stuff like that."

"All right," said Jens getting quite serious. "Now put yourself in my shoes. What do you think goes through my mind when I'm feeling sexual?"

They sat in silence as the car continued down the highway. Jens was very interested in hearing Riley's response, because it would be a test of the young man's empathy. Riley's mind flashed back through the black-and white-images of Jens at Buchenwald. The images were not pretty or erotic in any way. "When you start to feel sexual, you can't stop thinking about the pain and suffering you saw at Buchenwald," Riley finally said. "You think about sex as a horrible act. All your sexual experiences were bad, weren't they?"

"Most of them, yes. Even the few good memories with Karl are overshadowed by the camp."

"It messed you up, right?" asked Riley. "You can't really enjoy sex, can you?"

"I am messed up. I mean, yes, it did mess me up," replied Jens attempting to use Riley's words. "It was all just too much to deal with; it became a lot easier to just avoid it. When I feel sexual, the images that flash through my mind are repulsive and make me retch: the tortures on the horse while I serviced the commandant, the Jewish women of the brothel, Rudolf in his office, the American soldiers at the prison. I can't stop them."

"Are you angry?" Riley asked. "I mean, that you weren't able to have a normal life?"

"Yes," answered Jens, "much of the time I am angry when I think about Germany and what they did to us pink triangles. I think it's the reason I've lived so long. Anger is powerful, and I can feel it push me forward, as if my living is some kind of revenge on the SS."

Riley hesitated and then asked, "Did you ever forgive any of them?"

"No!" stated Jens louder than Riley expected. "I know, I know all about forgiving and forgetting. I've read all that stuff and seen the movies. In my opinion, forgiveness is overrated. I don't care what Oprah says. Forgiveness doesn't make me feel any better. In fact, it just makes me angrier. I can sit around and try to rationalize their behavior, why they did it. Perhaps it was the bad economy coming out of World War One, or they were corrupted by a charismatic leader, or they needed to be part of a special club to make them feel good. I can rationalize what it was like to be in that kill-or-be-killed environment. But none of that helps me; it just makes me angry that nobody stood up to them. I don't care what reason you have, you should never masturbate while someone is being tortured right in front of you. That is reprehensible, and it cannot be forgiven.

"No, I will never forgive them. What helps me is to think about them as being irrelevant. They are all gone now, and the mayor of Berlin is an openly gay man. They were completely irrelevant to the future of Berlin. They thought they would control all of Europe for one thousand years, but the French flag flies again over the Louvre and the Union Jack has never left Big Ben. After all the pain and death, they are irrelevant to this planet and do not deserve my forgiveness."

FIFTY SIX

"**W**ell," Jens said with weak excitement, "this is quite a treat!"

"It's the end of summer," replied Riley. "Why not live it up a little?"

Riley had stopped at Byerly's grocery store in St. Paul to pick up food from their famous selection of hot entrees. He arrived at Jens's home with two bags that contained a complete turkey dinner with all the sides, and pumpkin pie.

"Feels like Thanksgiving," said Riley as he placed a tray next to Jens on the couch.

Jens had become accustomed to eating in the living room, since it was difficult to get enough energy to move to the kitchen. He didn't know what he would have done without Riley's help this summer.

"Even though I became an American in 1978," Jens responded, "I still never got the Thanksgiving spirit."

"It helps if you have a family around. Oh, sorry about that. I wasn't thinking, and it just came out."

"Don't worry," Jens said. "I guess I have never had a traditional Thanksgiving meal around the table with family; that's probably why I don't understand it."

Riley took some plastic containers out of the bags and placed them on the coffee table in front of them. He had grabbed two plates and the required utensils from the kitchen. Now he dished the dinner onto the plates and gave one to Jens.

"I want to ask you a question, but we don't have to talk about it if you don't want to," Riley said as they settled down to eat. "Since you moved to Minnesota, did you ever go back to Germany?"

"No," answered Jens, "and it was difficult. As a professor of German literature I had many opportunities to travel there and do some research. I was tempted a few times, but I was always scared to face it all. Instead I took opportunities to study at other universities around the world with strong German programs. But I never again stepped on German soil."

"What about your mother?" asked Riley. "Did you ever find out what happened?"

"No," replied Jens. "You see, Riley, you have to understand that things were so different back then. It was not 2013, not like today at all. There was no Internet or gay clubs for me to learn from supportive people. There was only the information I received from Josephine; the information that I was hated. I could never put my mother through that. I hope she thought I was killed in the camp during one of my first days there. Yes, it's sometimes sad to think about, but I suppose at some point, she died."

"And what about your father?" asked Riley. "You don't really believe that you are responsible for his death, do you?"

"I used to," Jens answered. "For the first few years I thought I was directly responsible because I pushed him into the army, but now I think that there were a whole lot of people responsible. The Third Reich, for one. But the people of Konigswinter, who were hateful toward homosexuals, were also to blame. The Nazis would not have been able to turn my parents against their son, but I think an entire community of their friends probably did."

Riley nodded his head to indicate that he understood; he also got a feeling from Jens that it was okay to keep talking about Germany. Riley had a number of questions he wasn't able to ask during the drives, and he took the opportunity to listen to Jens.

"What about Karl?" Riley asked. "I know you never saw him again, but you must have wondered what happened to him."

"I thought about Karl so many times in the camp," Jens answered. "In fact, thinking of Karl and fantasizing about a life with him got me through many long and cold nights. However, by the time I was in college, I was mature enough to know that my idea of Karl was not at all based on reality. He had been castrated, and who knows where he had ended up in life. My life with Karl was truly a fantasy, and it was healthy for me to understand that."

"But what if he hadn't changed his feelings and still loved you?"

"The times were different. We didn't think that way."

"How about any of the others from the camp?" said Riley as his curiosity continued to prompt questions. "What about Rudolf? Did you ever see or hear from any of them again?"

"No, it just was not possible," responded Jens. "You see, we were all ashamed. None of us dared even think of contacting another pink triangle. We wanted desperately to avoid all association with one another. We had no community to go back to. There were no newsletters or support groups, no Web sites. There was no survivors' network back then. It's hard to keep in contact with members of a club that nobody wants to be in.

"It's also the same reason why I was never able to locate Bertel; there just was no way for people like her to connect with each other. If I'd known her last name, perhaps I would have had a better chance of finding her. I wanted to know that she survived the destruction of Berlin and at least found some kind of happiness. There were thousands of children in Germany whose births were tied to the Nazis. Maybe someday they will tell their story, and we can know what life was like for them.

"And as for Rudolf, well, I've thought a lot about him. I guess the main question I wanted to answer for myself was whether I wished him well or not. Do I hope that he and his family had a happy life, or do I hope he suffered? I've never been able to answer that. In reality, he probably went through a lot of both, as we all do. Although, in the end, I have to admit that he was my biggest reason for surviving. I do owe him something for that, even if he did it in exchange for sex. And I can't begrudge him for wanting to protect me like his wife. Yes, I will admit that I love him, or rather, I have love for him."

They continued their dinner. Jens ate a tiny portion of each item and sat back to relax. Riley ate well, but he was distracted. He was trying to decide whether to tell Jens about Jake. Riley knew that he could use some advice, but he admired Jens immensely. Riley didn't think he could handle it if Jens thought poorly of him because of what he'd done. So, Riley didn't say anything about what he'd done to Jake and continued with his curiosity about Buchenwald.

"What about the commandant?" Riley asked. "I hope you don't mind that I'm bringing him up. Did you ever find out what happened to him?"

"Well, yes," answered Jens, "those Nazis facing their crimes were always big news in Germany. Pretty much every newspaper during the entire time I went to college was full of the trial accounts of former Nazis. The commandant did not last long. Because he was apprehended right at the camp, thanks to me, it was easy for the prosecution to gain evidence against him. He was one of the first tried and was executed quite quickly. Personally, I think he got off a bit easy. It would have been nice if he'd had his time on the horse. Although, I could never do what he did while someone was on the horse, even if it was someone I hated as much as I hated him.

"His wife was caught, too. She was tried a couple of times, but there was never sufficient evidence against her. Sometime in the sixties, she hanged herself."

"And the other SS?" asked Riley. "You must have known a lot of SS guys. The young SS officer and the one with the hose? What happened to them?"

"I used to go through periods where I'd become obsessed with the SS," Jens said. "Sometimes, I'd spend every day for weeks in the library going through old German newspapers on microfiche; I was looking for any information about those who tormented us. When the Internet came about in the late nineties, I started using that to find information. Then I'd go for long periods of time, even years, when I couldn't have cared less about them.

"So to answer your question, I was able to get information about a few of the SS officers who were at Buchenwald. In all cases, they were found guilty and sentenced to prison; I'm not sure who among them is still alive or not. It was always chilling when I'd see a photograph of one of the SS I knew from the camp. The photos showed older versions of the men, but I could see their younger selves by looking in their eyes. Throughout the years, every once in a while, I'd be at the grocery store or someplace, and I'd see someone who reminded me of one of the SS. It always made my heart stop.

"I know that the young SS officer was apprehended in Argentina in the mideighties. I think he is still in prison in Germany.

I never was able to locate information about the SS officer who raped us with the hose on my first night in Buchenwald. Perhaps he escaped somewhere. Regardless, he was quite a bit older than me and must surely be dead by now."

"So, they are no more, then?" Riley stated and asked at the same time.

"I was one of the youngest people to be persecuted for homosexuality during that time," said Jens. "Which means, now that I'm almost ninety, I'm one of the very few left."

"Jens, can I tell people about you? I think people could learn from your story. I know that I have."

Jens was silent for a moment. He turned to look out his side window and saw the 2013 version of St. Paul; it was quite different from the 1994 version he had moved to. More important, the 2013 version of the planet was completely different from the 1925 version he was born into.

"I guess I don't mind now," Jens said softly. "Is eighty-eight too late to come out of the closet?"

They both tried to laugh, but only Riley succeeded; Jens wasn't able to get enough air.

"Seriously," Jens continued after a few moments, "I have goofed some things up in my life. In Germany, I never really had the chance to be in the closet. Now here, I spend over sixty years living in the closet so that nobody finds out. Most people do it the other way around. In many ways, I escaped from Germany to become a prisoner of myself."

"You didn't have a choice," Riley said.

"I didn't have a choice when I was in Germany," Jens replied, "and I guess I didn't have a choice for a long time in America. But there comes a time when you have to do the hard work required to be free."

FIFTY SEVEN

That night, Riley couldn't stop thinking about Jens. He replayed Jens's words about hard work and freedom many times in his mind. He wanted to be free from Jake; so, finally, he began to make preparations for the hard work required of him.

FIFTY EIGHT

The humidity dropped as the second summer session came to a close. This also meant the end of Riley's special access to the athletic dorm. He was surprised at how easy it was to sever his connections with the University of Minnesota. The coach never called, and nobody contacted him to find out why he had canceled his courses. Because of his scholarships, he did not owe the university any money and could simply walk away.

As he was carrying a box of stuff from the building to his car, he wondered if it had been a mistake to attend college at all. With the exception of meeting Dr. Weber and Jens, pretty much everything else connected with the experience had been a complete disaster. But there was nothing he could do about that now.

He crossed a sidewalk and a group of freshmen girls came walking past in their very tight shorts and Welcome Week T-shirts. Riley was wearing flip-flops, shorts, and a tank top. The girls stared, smiled, and giggled when they passed. Riley turned his head to get a better look; he wondered if he would ever enjoy sex again. He knew he probably wouldn't have the opportunity for a very long time.

Riley approached his car, and suddenly, his phone started ringing. He set the box he was carrying on the roof of the car. The caller was Dr. Weber.

"Hello, this is Riley."

"Riley, it's Jade Weber. First, how are you?"

"I'm as good as can be," Riley answered; he quickly felt a strong need to explain his immediate future. "I'm leaving the U for a while to figure out what I want to do. I'm not playing hockey anymore."

Even though she had noticed a change in him over of the summer, Jade was still quite surprised to discover how much he was willing to give up. She had called with important news for him, but she also needed to support him during this time.

"Have you talked to anyone about this?" she asked. "These kinds of decisions can be difficult, and there are people on campus who have experience guiding students through it."

"I don't need to talk to anyone," he said. "I'm not changing my mind."

Jade had worked with enough students to know when to drop the topic with the hopes of picking it up again later. "Riley," she said, "we'll talk later about all that. Right now, I need you to know that Jens was just taken to United Hospital in St. Paul."

"What happened?"

"My husband was worried because Jens hadn't collected his mail for a few days," she explained. "I decided to check on him. When I got over there, he was very weak. He told me that he was having a hard time getting air. It didn't sound like he was filling with fluid, so I think it must be a muscular problem, but what do I know? I thought it was best to call an ambulance. He was adamant that I not go with him to the hospital. He was very clear that he wanted to be alone, but he did ask me to call you."

"Do you think I should go there?" Riley asked. "If he wants to be alone, I—"

"Riley, he wouldn't have told me to call you if he didn't want a friend. I don't think he has anyone else here. Seriously, Riley, I could tell by the way he talked about you that he would like to see you."

"I know he doesn't have anyone else," Riley said. "I'll go and see what's happening."

"Okay," she replied, "thank you."

He had started to hang up when he heard her voice once again.

"And Riley," she continued bluntly, "I'm not the kind of person who thinks college is the only way to succeed in life. It costs a lot of money and may not provide much benefit. Why don't you come over my house and have dinner sometime? I know some tools that can help you figure out what you want to do to support yourself. Are you moving back to Hastings?"

"Yes, just for a few days, then I'm not sure where I'll be," he said.

"Take care. Call me," she said and ended the call.

Riley was worried about Jens. He worked as quickly as he could to load the rest of his stuff into the car. Other groups of new students crossed his path, but Riley ignored them and practically ran to get the boxes and plastic bins from his room. He was glad he was able to do this before the rest of the hockey team arrived for the term. The Gopher football team had already been in practice and had even played a few games, but since Riley did not party, he was able to avoid them.

The timing was good, and he was able to avoid the horrible rush-hour traffic that clogged the quickest way between the two cities; it did not take long for him to get to United Hospital in St. Paul, which was adjacent to the downtown area. The hospital was quite large, and it took some time for him to navigate to the correct parking ramp.

Riley made his way through a maze of stairs and tunnels and finally reached one of the entrances. He stopped at an information desk and was both surprised and saddened to learn the Jens was in the intensive care unit. Riley wondered how quickly Jens had taken a turn for the worse. When he'd had dinner with Jens a few days before, he thought Jens was weak, but Riley didn't think he was bad enough for the ICU.

Riley used a map provided by the woman at the information desk, and after a few wrong turns, found his way to the unit. He began walking around the circular shape of the ICU when a nurse caught his attention from the nursing station.

"Can I help you find someone?" she asked.

"Yes," he replied, "Jens Jaenisch."

"Oh yes," she said, "he was brought in this morning. He's in that second room, right there."

She pointed in the correct direction, but Riley wanted more information before disturbing Jens. He took a few steps toward the nursing station.

"How is he?" Riley asked.

"Are you related?" she replied. "What is your name?"

"Riley Hunter," he said.

The nurse walked over to a computer and took a few minutes to check Jens's record.

"Yes, your name is on here," she responded. "He gave permission for you to get information about him."

Riley could almost feel his spirit float as he realized how honored he felt that Jens had remembered him. Until now, Riley hadn't been sure that Jens thought of him as a friend; it was very nice to know.

"So," she continued, "Dr. Nathan Tescher was just here on rounds, and we talked about Jens. He has been in contact with the Mayo Clinic. I'm afraid it's not very good news."

"It's okay," Riley said calmly. "You can tell me."

"His condition is deteriorating," she began. "Under normal circumstances he would have been able to beat this thing. But his age is against him. I'm sorry to tell you that we are not optimistic. Sometimes we just don't know why some people respond to a treatment while others don't. There are a lot of variables when we're talking about a patient who is in his late eighties. Everyone has a different history."

"So," asked Riley hesitantly, "you don't think he's going to survive, right? You think he's going to die?"

"I'm sorry," she replied, "but yes, he is going to die. Dr. Tescher and I spoke about it; the paralysis is making it very difficult for him to open his lungs to allow air in. However, he is still conscious and knows what's happening to him; at least he did throughout the morning. He signed an advance directive and is adamant that we not use artificial life support."

"Do you know how long?" Riley asked.

"Once the breathing has become as shallow as his has," she responded, "it will go quickly. Probably tonight or tomorrow. Since he was admitted to the ICU, we'll leave him in that room tonight. Tomorrow, there won't be any reason for him to be in this unit, so we will move him to a different floor."

"I understand, thank you," said Riley.

"I can see if Dr. Tescher is still around," added the nurse. "Or you can leave a message for him; he is pretty good about getting back quickly. I know he was concerned that Jens didn't have any family listed to contact. We've all been concerned about that."

"No," answered Riley, "I think you've given me enough information. Can I go in?"

"Certainly, and let me know if you need anything," she said.

As he was turning toward the direction of Jens's room, he stopped and asked her, "Are there hours here? I mean, visiting hours? I might want to stay awhile if he is that bad."

"Well," she answered, "normally, we only allow immediate family to spend the night. But since you are his only contact, I will make sure you have some bedding so you can sleep on the couch in his room." The nurse turned back to the computer.

"Thanks." Riley crossed the hall and entered the room. He was careful to be quiet and had to walk stiffly to keep his flip-flops from making their customary slapping sound. The blue privacy curtain was pulled halfway, just as it was when he visited Jake at Gillette Hospital that spring.

Riley peered around the curtain and found Jens fast asleep in his hospital bed. The expected equipment was attached to him, and he slept on his back. Riley stepped up and looked at his hands, which were clasped together over his stomach. Riley immediately noticed that his hands were very still, they were not shaking as usual. He also looked to see that Jens was breathing, but it was quite shallow and slow.

Riley did not want to wake him, so he sat on a chair next to him and waited.

FIFTY NINE

Someone brought a tray of food for Jens around dinnertime, but nobody woke him, and the full tray was collected later. The nurse continued to take vital signs at the appropriate intervals; Jens slept through that, too. In the room, under the window, there was a hard institutional couch. Riley was spread out on the couch; he used the provided bedding to make himself as comfortable as he could. He had eaten dinner from the hospital cafeteria and now fell asleep. Riley was determined that Jens would not wake up alone.

Two hours later, around eleven, he heard a voice say, "Riley."

He sat up instantly and was very glad to see that Jens was now facing him, still in bed, and saying his name. Riley sprang up from the couch.

"Hey, man! How do you feel?"

"I've been better," replied Jens in a bit stronger voice. "But as you know, I've been worse, too."

They both actually managed to laugh. Riley grabbed a plastic-covered cup and straw from Jens's tray and handed it to him. Jens drank just a little of the water and then dropped the cup. Riley caught the cup from Jens's lap and offered it to him again. Jens refused.

"Is there anything I can get you?" Riley asked. Like all people his age, Riley felt a need to act as normal as possible in this situation. In fact, Riley had an urge to act with lots of energy; he wasn't sure why. Perhaps he thought that his youth could distract Jens from the truth.

"No," said Jens, "I'm fine. Really."

"You know"—Riley pointed to Jens's hands—"you can sleep with your hands inside the blanket here."

Riley didn't know if it was appropriate to make that joke, but Jens smiled and put him at ease with a small gesture of raising his hands. Jens continued to smile and looked directly into Riley's eyes.

"I'm glad to have known you," said Jens sincerely.

"I'm glad to know you, too," Riley replied.

Jens sighed. "I'm very tired. I think I will go back to sleep. Go on home, and I'll see you later."

"I'm not going anywhere," Riley said. "I'll just be over here on the couch if you need anything."

Jens was too tired to argue with Riley, and he also very much wanted the young man to stay with him. He was fully aware of the situation.

Riley began to walk to the couch, but he stopped and turned back to look at Jens. Jens did not look as peaceful as Riley had seen people look in the movies when they were quite ill. Riley continued to the couch and sat down. As Riley once again studied Jens, he began to feel unbearable sadness for him. Because of what other people did to him, Jens had lived his entire life without knowing love. Jens had no choice, no control in the matter; other people, for their own malicious reasons, had changed his life.

Riley was about to cry, but he saw Jens open his eyes. He did not want to startle or scare Jens by letting him see tears. Riley desperately tried to find a way to ease his own pain along with the pain of Jens. Suddenly, he knew what he wanted to do—not what he had to do, but what he really wanted to do.

Riley stood from the couch and walked over to the bed; Jens continued to watch him. Riley grabbed the edge of the privacy curtain and pulled it completely across the room. Then, he took off his tank top in a one quick move and threw it on the couch. He kicked off his flip-flops and stood there, looking like Michelangelo's *David* in running shorts.

"What are you doing?" Jens asked quietly.

"Go back to sleep," Riley answered.

"What are you doing?" Jens asked again.

"Be quiet," said Riley softly.

Riley pulled back the blankets that were over Jens and climbed into the bed next to him. He pulled the covers back over them and scooted next to Jens. It was a standard-size hospital bed, so the two were very close. Riley turned on his side and put his arms around Jens; he pulled him into his body.

"You once told me that your biggest regret was not being able to sleep with Karl," Riley whispered in Jens's ear. "Just think of me as Karl."

Jens relaxed at those words and surrendered to the situation. However, he did not want to think of the man holding him as being Karl. Karl was not real anymore. But Riley was real, and he was here. Jens fell into the hard, warm body all around him; he felt each of Riley's breaths and descended more with every exhale.

"Thank you," Jens said softly.

Riley didn't respond, he just hugged tighter, not even worrying at this point if his grip was too much for Jens. He kissed the back of Jens's neck twice. Jens felt each sensation followed by Riley's warm breath. There were no tears from either one of them. Jens was happy and felt safer than he'd ever felt in his whole life. He finally surrendered completely and allowed himself to sink into Riley's embrace.

Riley knew there were two people in that bed whose lives would end that night; he was happy for both of them.

SIXTY

The next morning, on his way to Hastings from the hospital, Riley crossed the Mississippi River. He looked down at the gray water and thought of the view of blue water from Jens's house in St. Paul. He wondered if the river was cleaner in St. Paul, or had the water turned gray overnight to signal Jens's departure from the planet.

Riley was in one of those places where young people go when they are incapable of processing all the emotions swirling around in their bodies. He looked at the clock in his car and saw that he would be ten minutes late; he had called Jake's home that morning to arrange a meeting.

He drove through the small river town and out to the subdivisions that formed the southeastern edge of the Twin Cities metropolitan area. From there, there was nothing but prairie to Rochester and the Mayo Clinic.

Riley drove into the driveway and parked his car. He was nervous but pushed that feeling way down in the hope he could remain calm; he would do that a lot in the coming years. Riley got out of the car, still dressed in shorts, tank top, and flip-flops; he approached the front door and rang the bell.

"Riley!" said Mrs. Fred when she opened the door, "it's good to see you."

368

"Did Jake tell you that I wanted to talk to you?" asked Riley as he stepped through.

"Yes," she replied, "and our attorney, Mari Bender, is here, as you asked. We're a little nervous, but we're hoping you have good news."

Riley kicked off his flip-flops and followed Mrs. Fred into the living room. He was surprised to see that Mrs. Fred was wearing a Hastings hockey T-shirt, since it might remind Jake of better days. But perhaps it was her way of accepting and moving forward.

When they entered the living room, Jake, Mr. Fred, and a woman Riley assumed was the attorney were already assembled. Jake reclined in his special chair near the window; he was wearing cargo shorts, a Minnesota Twins T-shirt, and no shoes.

"Hey, man!" said Jake excitedly when he saw Riley. "How are you?"

Even though Jake made a gesture with his head inviting Riley to come over to him, Riley declined and quickly sat in an unoccupied armchair.

"Hey, Riley," said Mr. Fred. "This is Jake's attorney, Mari Bender."

Riley and Ms. Bender exchanged a quick greeting. More than any of the others, Mr. Fred must have realized that something bizarre was to occur, because he already sat stiffly and was less than welcoming to Riley.

"I guess you have some information about Jake's case," said Mrs. Fred when she sat next to her husband on the couch. "Did you discover something in the Athletic Department?"

When Riley sat down without acknowledging him, Jake knew there was something horribly wrong. He now began to get nervous as well.

"I have something I need to say," said Riley, avoiding their eyes and looking straight at the carpet. "It's not going to be easy."

"Go ahead, Riley, it's okay," said Mr. Fred as he was anxious to end the moment.

But Riley knew it wasn't going to be okay; he continued to stare at the floor. So far, Ms. Bender sat and observed, not entirely understanding why she was asked to be there.

Riley began, "Jake, do you remember the night of your accident? I mean, do you remember being at the dorm and everything that happened?"

Jake was relieved that Riley had finally acknowledged him. He looked back at his friend. "Sure," he answered. "I remember all of it up until the accident."

"You were up a couple of floors in Tyler's room, right?"

"Yeah, we were hanging around and watching TV. It's where we started drinking the beer I brought from my room."

"Right, and then you came downstairs to see me," Riley said.

"Yep," Jake agreed. "Tyler had some girl stop by, and I knew he wanted to be alone with her. So, I decided to stop in and see how things were going with you."

"You had a can of beer with you," said Riley.

"Did I? I guess I don't remember if I was drinking in your room or just Tyler's."

"You did," clarified Riley. "You told me that it was your second beer, but you were quitting after that and going to bed, because we had early practice the next morning. It was a Friday night, so I think we were going to skate at five or something."

"Yes," said Jake, "that's right. I remember having that conversation with you in your dorm. You were watching TV and talked about going to bed."

"Then, Mrs. Fred called," Riley said. "You looked at your phone, said it was your mom, and you answered it. You went out in the hall to talk."

"Right," Jake responded, "I remember now. You were watching *The Avengers,* and it was loud."

"Yes, so you set your beer on the counter by my closet and went out into the hall."

"I guess," said Jake. "I still don't remember having a beer in your room, but you could be right. Anyway, I do remember going out in the hall to talk to my mom."

"Okay," Riley replied, "this is the part that's hard to say. I was under a lot of stress from my parents, and I knew that the next morning there were going to be drills. It was the first day of drills, and I really wanted to be noticed by the coaching staff. Jake, you were always just as good as, if not better than, me. All of high school we worked together. But now, I knew that I had to get into the NHL, because I'm not smart enough for anything else. My mom kept drilling me about taking advantage of every moment to impress. My dad just kept telling me all the time how much more money I'd make in the NHL if I was a star, and not just a player. Everyone was telling me why it was so important that I be the best player on the team."

"Riley," Mr. Fred interrupted in a very serious voice, "what exactly are you saying here? Did you do something to Jake?"

"I just didn't think," Riley continued. "I don't know what I was thinking. I grabbed three Klonopin from a bottle in my closet. I put them on the counter and used my trophy to smash them. I put them into the beer can."

There was silence in the room. Now Ms. Bender knew why Riley wanted her there: he was confessing.

"I didn't think anything like this was going happen," Riley broke the silence in a pleading voice. "You have to believe me! I just thought you'd go to bed and be very sleepy the next morning. I wasn't even hoping you'd oversleep, I just wanted you to be slow. You had just told me that you were going to sleep. I didn't know you were going to drive somewhere. You were supposed to just sleep and be in a haze the next morning. I just needed one off morning for you and I could get ahead with the coach."

Again, silence in the room.

"I had a flat tire," said Mrs. Fred in a stunned voice after a few moments. "Dad was in St. Cloud for work and I called to ask Jake to help me. I always thought it was my fault that he drove drunk!"

With that, Mrs. Fred broke into sobs, left the room, and slammed a door somewhere in the house. Up to this point, all his guilt had been focused on Jake. Now, for the first time, Riley truly saw how his actions had hurt other people he knew and loved.

"Jake, I'm so sorry," Riley said to his former friend; he turned to look at him. "You came back into my dorm room and said you had to go. You slammed the rest of the beer so fast and left. I didn't know what to do. I really thought you would just fall asleep."

Jake didn't say anything; he just turned his own head away from Riley and looked out the window. Mr. Fred's head dropped into his hands. The truth was now out, but it was way too soon for Riley to feel anything. He didn't think he had anything left to say and desperately wanted to find a way to get out of that house and away from those he hurt.

Riley looked at the attorney and said sincerely, "You can tell me what to do next. I'm ready for whatever happens. I want to pay for what I did. I ruined Jake's life, and I deserve whatever is supposed to happen to me. I don't know what to do next. Can you help me?"

Ms. Bender now spoke for the first time, with an authoritative voice. "I think nobody else in this room needs to say anything further. We need to do this correctly. This is a difficult situation, and we will need to follow procedures and laws. I'm going to take Mr. Hunter with me right now. I'll be back this afternoon to talk to the rest of you."

She stood, squeezed Mr. Fred's shoulder as she passed him, and gestured for Riley to follow her. Riley stood and began crying for the second time that sad day.

"Jake, I'm really sorry," sobbed Riley. He left the room, without looking at his friend, and slid into his flip-flops.

Riley followed the attorney out of the front door. He was not able to look back or say anything else to the distraught family. He avoided looking at the front window, in case Jake was still sitting near it. "What's going to happen to me?" he asked Ms. Bender through his tears.

"I'm going to take you to be deposed," she answered. "The system will take over from there. It's more than likely that you will be charged with a federal crime, because it involves a controlled substance."

They approached her car, and she opened the door.

"How long will it take?" he asked.

"To be deposed?"

"No, until it's all over. How many years."

"That's really something you need to discuss with your own attorney," she said. "You should probably call someone in the car. But this is serious. You've ruined a life; I think I can say that there will be some incarceration involved. If you don't have an attorney, you need to get one. You should call your parents immediately. The media will likely get involved."

"I don't want to go to prison!" he sobbed loudly. "But it's the only way. I just want it all to be done."

As the car pulled out of the driveway, Riley continued to cry. He cried for Jake, hockey, college, and Jens. But mostly, he cried for the relief he hoped to feel someday.

Epilogue

"So, before I go," Dr. Jade Weber said in the visiting room of the Rochester Federal Medical Center, "what should I tell the renters?"

"You should tell them that I want to move into the house when their lease is up next month," Riley responded.

The Federal Medical Center serves as a hospital for the federal prison system. When prisoners become seriously ill at any of the regular federal prisons in the United States, they are sent to a medical center, one of which is in Rochester, Minnesota. This facility also holds a number of healthy inmates who provide the non-medical services needed to maintain the buildings and grounds. Because he was from Minnesota, and the judge requested it, Riley had been placed in this medical prison.

"You sure you want to do that?" she asked. "Does this mean you're staying in Minnesota? I can definitely tell the renters to find another place to live, but I want to know that you plan to move into the house before I do that."

"Yes, I'm definitely staying here," Riley answered without any hesitation. "You know, Dr. Weber, when Jens left the house to me, I initially thought I'd want to sell it and use the money to get far away from here. When I entered prison, the last thing I ever wanted was to run into my past. But now that I've had a lot of time to think, I don't want to make the same mistake that Jens made."

"What do you mean? What kind of mistake?"

Riley replied, "When Jens got out of prison and got his degree back in Germany, he immediately escaped so that he wouldn't have to face his problem. Now, don't get me wrong, I completely understand that our situations are different…"

"Right," Jade interrupted immediately, "Jens was unjustly incarcerated, while you—"

"While I did something very wrong and deserve to be in here. Believe me, not a day goes by that I don't think about that. I know there is a very crucial difference between Jens and me. I'm not talking about imprisonment, justified or not, I'm talking about what happens after prison. What I meant about Jens is that he didn't stay and fight for his life, for his parents, or for Karl. He left before he could discover the truth about any of that."

"But you must be fair," Jade added. "Jens was living in the forties; there was no way he could have been openly gay back then. It simply would not have been possible. You might be too judgmental of him."

"I get that, too," Riley responded, "but he lived in the United States for a very long time and saw a lot of changes. I don't think I'm being too judgmental because Jens would be the first person to admit that he gave up on being himself. I guess what I'm saying is that I don't want to run away so that I never have to see Jake, his parents, my parents, or anyone else who knows what I did."

During the six years of his incarceration, Riley's parents never visited him once. He heard at one point that they'd moved out of Minnesota, and Riley didn't even know where they were. Riley had many mixed emotions about his parents, and the time in prison helped him to understand that they didn't have to be entirely good or entirely bad; it was all right for them to exist somewhere between.

Professor Weber had been an annual visitor over the years. She agreed to manage Jens's home and look after the renters. Jade fully realized the impact of Riley's horrible act on the Fredrichs family, but she still admired Riley for confessing and paying for his crime.

However, if there was a bright spot in the situation for Jade, it was the opportunity to get to know the real story of her former neighbor. Over the years, the main topic of conversation between her and Riley had been the account of Jens's life during the Holocaust. Jade was honored that she was able to hear the story. Despite the fact that she still felt she had meddled with their lives, Jade was finally at peace that she put the two of them together. Jens's cathartic story and Riley's ultimate confession both came about as a product of their relationship; Jade was proud she'd had a small part in making that happen.

"Okay," she said, "I'm starting to understand your comparison of yourself and Jens. I think I get it, and I think you get it, too. But how will you feel when you run into Jake? You surely will at some point."

"No doubt it will be awkward," Riley replied, "but I'll just greet him and see what happens. I don't need or want anything from him, so I think I need to find out what he needs from me."

"And what if he needs to hate you forever?" Jade asked.

"Then," he answered, "he will absolutely have the right to hate me forever. I can't change that any more than I can take back the horrible thing that I did."

"Riley, I have to say that you have not wasted your time in here," she said as she sat back on the hard institutional chair.

"You're so much more articulate than you were six years ago. And you still look good, too."

"Thanks," he said. "I came in here knowing that I did not want to squander the few opportunities that I had in here."

Indeed, he had not. Riley took advantage of the various academic programs offered to him. Even though he studied English and computer science, he found that he was most interested in modern world history. Riley also capitalized on the time he had to physically exercise and stay fit. He did not have his boyish, heart-throb face anymore; it had been replaced by a handsome, chiseled profile. His body remained lean and strong.

However, Riley was quite self-conscious about painting federal prison in too positive a light. For all the opportunities, it was still prison, and he was being punished. Sleeping in a barrack with twenty other men snoring away was not easy. The food was processed—bland and as repetitive as a public-school lunch menu. Contrary to popular belief, there were only two televisions in his whole building, and one was permanently tuned to the Spanish station.

The nights at the Federal Medical Center were long, especially in the winter. He had no iPhone or computer of his own, no video games. And sometimes he was violated the way Jens had been at Buchenwald. Prison was not a good place to be.

So many times during those six years he compared himself to Jens. Each time, he thought about the words written in iron on the gate at Buchenwald. Riley knew he was exactly where he deserved to be, and it broke his heart to think of Jens having to endure these things without deserving them. Many nights, Riley would cry himself to sleep thinking of Jake and Jens.

"What will you do to make a living?" Jade asked.

"Well," he replied, "I have the money that Jens left me; one good thing about prison is that you don't spend anything. I want to get a master's degree in social work. I think that could make a good life for me."

Dr. Weber paused for a moment and then asked, "Will you be able to get a license to practice social work with your record? I don't mean to be negative or dissuade you, but it's something you should know before you put time and money into it."

"Don't worry about being negative; I appreciate your help," he replied. "I've been checking into that very matter. I can appeal to the licensing board about my past; people who have made mistakes and spent time in the system often work well in the field. It's not a guarantee, but there is a good chance that I can get a license. Anyway, it will be a long time from now, since I'll have to get both a bachelor's and a master's degree."

"It's just something to think about," she said. "You don't want to put all your time and money into getting degrees if you aren't qualified to actually work in the field."

"I understand. And thank you for thinking about that."

"If it all works out," Jade said, "I think that you would make an excellent social worker. You certainly have experienced some hard times and have worked to fix them. But a career isn't the only thing in life. What about any personal aspirations?"

"As I said before, I'd like to make things right with Jake," he said, "but I realize that I have no control over that. Aside from that, I would really like to have a wife and kids someday. I would tell them the truth about me, so they learn from my mistakes. Most important, I will let each kid do what they want to do and be who they want to be."

"You should write that down, Riley," Jade said sincerely. "It's easy to forget those things when you do have kids."

"I don't think I will forget," Riley said. "Every time they ask about their grandparents I will remember what happened to me."

"And what about hockey?" she asked. "It was the biggest part of your life before prison. Do you think you will still play or even watch the sport?"

"When I first got in here," he said, "I was happy that I didn't have to think about hockey for the first time in my life. But as the months went on, I have to admit that I missed it. Maybe I didn't miss the competition, but I missed skating and the challenge of getting the puck into the net. I'm able to exercise in here, but of course there is no ice. I haven't skated for a long time. I would very much like to skate again when I get out. I've even thought about working with kids and teaching them. I'd like to be the coach I wish I'd had."

"If you do that," Jade said, "you'll have to get used to working with parents who might remind you of your own."

"Good point. I'd have to think about how to handle that."

"Hopefully, you will gain some tools on working with parents in your social work classes," she said.

They sat in silence for a few moments; Jade wanted to say something to him and didn't know how best to express herself. She wanted him to know that she was glad for the person he had become, but she didn't want him to think she'd forgotten about the crime he'd committed. It was an odd paradox that she explored inside herself; she admired Riley's success in dealing with confession and punishment for a terrible crime. She wondered if it was okay to be happy for Riley's growth when Jacob still could not walk, while at the same time realizing that Riley paid his due and deserved to move forward.

"Riley," she said finally, "I'm very proud of you. I'm proud for what you did for Jens and for yourself. And I'm glad you have decided to give Minnesota another try; it won't be easy, but you've experienced worse."

"I don't necessarily like it that you are proud of me," he said as he shook his head. "I don't think anyone should be proud of me; I did a terrible thing. Really, I don't like hearing those words at all. I'm not someone to be proud of."

"No, Riley," she said sternly, "you're wrong! You are definitely someone to be proud of, and I look forward to having you as a neighbor so that my grandkids can know you. Yes, you did a terrible thing. But you have served your time, even when you could have walked away from that responsibility. I know it's harsh to say, but ruining your life will not make Jake walk again. I'm proud that you love yourself enough to move on."

Riley did not respond. He understood what she said, but he wasn't quite ready to acknowledge his right to a happy life. He smiled at her and nodded. Jade smiled back and recognized that there was still a difficult path ahead for the young man. She got up from the table in the visiting room and pushed in the metal chair.

"Thank you again for coming," Riley said sincerely to her. "I'm looking forward to living next to you, too."

The prison system allowed each visitor one hug. Riley grabbed Jade and embraced deeply. She loved that she could be there for him. When he let go, she turned to leave. "Oh, Riley," she glanced back and said, "I almost forgot. I have the picture of Jens that you wanted. The guard said I can just hand it to you."

"Oh, thanks," Riley replied. He took the photograph from Jade and looked at it. He recognized Jens's eyes looking back at him. "He's younger in this picture than when I knew him."

"Yes, I asked a librarian friend of mine to find a photo of Jens in the archives. She found a couple and this is the one I like best. I made a copy so you can keep it. It was taken when he retired."

"His eyes are the same," Riley said as he looked at his good friend. "Thank you for the photograph." Jade smiled at him but he was too occupied with the photo to notice. She left the room feeling quite happy.

Later that night, Riley Hunter sat on his bed among the other beds and prisoners getting ready for lights out. He looked again at the picture of Jens and smiled. He reached to his right and grabbed a shoebox from a ledge under a barred window. Riley opened the shoebox and took out a stack of photographs. He had first seen these photos as a freshman when they were pinned to the back of a brown shower curtain. He took the picture of Jens and placed it on top of the stack.

"Hey," said another inmate and a friend of Riley, "you still have another month in here. Are you packing already?"

"Don't worry," laughed Riley, "I won't leave without saying goodbye."

"What do you have there anyway?"

"Just a box of pictures."

"Your family?"

"Nope," said Riley, "pictures of—well—pictures of survivors."

"Survivors, huh? Well, when you get out of here throw your own picture in there with 'em. You deserve it."

THE END

Author's Note

J ens Jaenisch is a fictional character, but unfortunately, Buchenwald did really exist. As hard as it is to believe, everything Jens experienced actually happened to real people who lived through that terrible time. Paragraph 175 remained law until it was removed from the German Criminal Code in 1994.

For more information, please read the following excellent books:

The Men With the Pink Triangle by Heinz Heger, published by Alyson Books.

The Pink Triangle by Richard Plant, published by Holt Paperbacks.

In addition to the books above, the United States Holocaust Memorial Museum contains a wealth of information about the victims of the Third Reich, including those who wore the colored triangle badges. The Web site and the physical museum in Washington, DC, are excellent resources.

Queen Elizabeth II granted a full pardon to Alan Turing on December 24, 2013.

Even though there is an ongoing national discussion about student athletes and their relationship to academics, all characters and situations connected with the University of Minnesota are fictional in this work. More information about collegiate athletic privilege is widely available online.

Made in the USA
Charleston, SC
26 July 2014